SECOND LIVES

By Carrie Mack

ISBN: 978-1-965541-32-6

Dedication

To my Children: Maddy, Mac, Lily, and Will. I would be nothing without you.

Acknowledgment

This novel would not have been possible without the support and feedback from my family and friends. Chris, thank you for being a constant sounding board and not being afraid to tell me if I was on the wrong track. I appreciate you. Mom, thank you for the encouragement and countless books you bought for me throughout my childhood. My love for reading turned into a passion for writing that I will never tire of. To the readers of my earlier work who provided feedback and support, I couldn’t have done it without you.

Content Warning

This book contains scenes that reference domestic violence, physical abuse, violence, and sexually related content. If you or anyone you know is experiencing a domestic abuse situation, please reach out to the Domestic Violence Hotline at: 800-799-SAFE (7233).

If you would like to help women who have experienced abuse or become a volunteer, please contact the center at www.thehotline.org.

Contents

Page Blank Intentionally

Look around your room, you find the paint is peelin'

Your reflective skin is fallin' off your bones

Well, I must admit I know just how you're feelin'

Must grab each other's collar, must rise out of the water

'Cause you know as well as I do that it's no fun to die alone

-- *Widespread Panic, Climb to Safety*

Chapter One

It was routine as usual until the moment the world went black. Shelby walked down the stairs to make herself a cup of coffee before heading toward the door for work like she had done thousands of times before. Maja was already at the bus stop; she could see the bus pulling up as the last few drips from the Nespresso fell into her favorite travel mug. This one had a scene from *Twilight* on it. Shelby was a total book and movie nerd, collecting mugs featuring her favorite quotes or pictures. When it was washed, her Bella and Edward mug always got first pick. She grabbed her mug full of her favorite Nespresso maple walnut coffee, twisted the lid closed, and then fell face-first onto the hardwood floor. Shelby felt nothing; she saw nothing and felt no pain.

"Babe?" Steve yelled from upstairs, hearing a loud thud from below. "Shelby?" in a much louder voice. He made it halfway down the stairs when he saw her dark hair on the floor. He lunged off the third stair from the bottom and ran to the kitchen. At first, he was frozen; he couldn't see her face. It looked as if she had laid down face-first on the floor but wasn't moving. It took him only a second to realize she wasn't breathing, either. There was no noise; he just stood there, cemented in place.

"Oh, God, oh shit… oh God," he repeated to the empty room. Steve knelt beside his wife of twelve years and cried, never touching her or even checking for a pulse. She was dead, and he knew it; his wife and the mother of his only child was dead. His thirty-four-year-old brilliant and beautiful wife was dead on a sunny September morning like any other. Minutes passed, what seemed much longer, as he trudged up the stairs to find his cell phone and make the inevitable call. The discussion with 9-1-1 was a blur, just as most of the morning. The paramedics came and went so quickly, and all he could do was stand there and watch. An officer asked him questions, but his eyes wouldn't leave the kitchen floor. Shelby will be so mad; her mug is broken, he thought. The lid was chipped in three pieces, and coffee had poured out on the hardwoods they had just replaced last year. How many times had they seen that stupid, sparkly vampire movie together?

"Mr. Wise, do you understand what I'm asking you?" The officer said. He sounded distant.

"Yes, I'm here. I understand." Steve tells him.

"Okay, your wife is being taken to Collin County Hospital. Are you okay to drive?"

"Yeah, I can drive. I just need my keys."

"Do you need me to call anyone for you?" He was searching for Steve's eyes; he had yet to give him any sort of recognition.

"No, I'm fine; I'll make some calls when I get there, I guess."

The officer felt sorry for him; it was in his voice and all over his face. He had probably seen this type of thing a dozen times. Steve felt numb and offhandedly looked up at the clock on the microwave; it was 8:45 AM. His life had changed more than he could ever imagine in one hour. His wife was irrevocably gone.

As Steve drove to the hospital, it dawned on him that he would have to talk to Maja. Just let me get through this first part, he thought. This was something he hadn't even considered at thirty-five years old, especially not having his thirty-something wife drop dead right in the middle of the kitchen. A car accident or something like that is always in the back of your mind, but not this. He looked around the car; everything in his world had her stamp on it. Shelby insisted on the heated seats because she hated being cold; he got the Audi with a black interior because she claimed it was "cooler." How in the hell was he going to deal with this and Maja? He pushed the thought out of his mind as quickly as it appeared. Not Maja, not now; he just needs to get to the hospital.

Once he pulled into the lot, he wasn't even sure where to park; where do you go when your wife is already dead? Would the doctors try to work on her more here, or would they take her to the morgue? Emergency will have to do, Steve thinks. Once inside, he realizes that the stupid COVID protocols are still in place. That was four years ago! Weren't we all done with that by now? He didn't have a mask on or even consider bringing one. A woman in scrubs motioned to him to take a mask from the desk across the lobby. Yes, yes, okay… he grabbed one and put it on. Now, where is my wife?

Steve hadn't attended a funeral in at least five years, and that was back home in Illinois. His grandparents had passed away just three months apart, and he and Shelby went back for both funerals. They died in their late eighties, just like people should. He had no idea where to begin looking for a funeral home here.

"I guess I'll Google it like I do everything else," he said aloud.

He had been constantly looking at the clock since he left the hospital; time was winding down until Maja would be home, and he would have to face the inevitable. Time was no longer on his side; he had just about ninety minutes until the bus would drop her off. Steve wanted to plan, at least, where his wife was going after the autopsy. The doctor at the hospital told him that the funeral home would pick her up; all he had to do was choose one and call them. Why did funeral homes all have family names when most are corporately owned now? Shelby explained to him how it worked. Big corporations bought out these mom-and-pop funeral homes or threatened to put them out of business.

Maxwell Family, Homer and Marquise, and Bishop Family Funeral Homes were the top three in Google rankings, all with five stars. He clicked on the Bishop Family website, where a picture of a man far into his seventies stood next to the building in the cover photo. The outside of the facility seemed nice enough. He picked up the phone to make the call when suddenly it dawned on him that he hadn't even called her work this morning to tell them what happened. He didn't even call either one of their parents or her best friend a few houses down. The overwhelming weight of responsibility and endless tasks that awaited him poured on top of his grief. Steve was a good man, but just like any other, he had counted on his wife to make most of the difficult decisions over the last decade. Not just the daily decisions but most of the complex "stuff," too. He could not escape this quickly; all he wanted to do was go upstairs, sit in his office chair, and watch some mindless TikTok videos on his iPad.

Realizing the phone was still halfway up to his ear, he looked at the keypad again and faintly heard a voice coming from the phone.

"Yes, sorry, hello. My name is Steve Wise. My wife died this morning in our kitchen, and I am not exactly sure what I need to do."

"Mr. Wise, of course, I am sorry for your loss. You called the right place. My name is Ansel Bishop. I will ask you a few questions, and then I can take care of the rest from here until we meet face-to-face tomorrow or the next day. How does that sound?"

The voice on the other end was compassionate yet professional. It was the voice of a man who had handled hundreds of calls from shell-shocked relatives. Steve immediately trusted that voice and felt slightly calmer.

"Yes… that works," Steve stammered.

They decided on the day after tomorrow due to the scheduled autopsy. Once the meeting was scheduled, he looked at the clock again…forty minutes. He began to wonder what kind of father would wait all day to tell his nine-year-old daughter that her mother was dead. Isn't that the kind of thing good fathers take their kids out of school for? Jesus, this was all on him from now on. Shelby was the one who always took care of their daughter's emotional well-being. Neither was the perfect parent, but they loved their daughter fiercely. Maja only had the two of them; both grandparents were back home in Illinois. When Maja was five, they moved to Texas for Shelby's work; with no other family around, Maja's entire world was her mother and father. Evenings at the dinner table talking about their days, weekends at the zoo, museums, parks, or just hanging out watching movies.

He must have been wool gathering for a while because the next thing he heard was the front door slamming shut. Steve was usually home by 3 pm daily and worked another hour from home to make sure someone was there when Maja came home. She was used to being quiet until after 4:30 pm, when he was officially done with his day. He knew he would find her scavenging for a snack in the pantry or fridge.

"Hey, Dad!" She barely glanced his way as she was rummaging through the bottom drawer of the refrigerator for an apple sauce, and he figured a cheese stick, too.

"Maja, can we sit down at the table?" Steve finally managed to say.

She looked at him with curiosity but with absolutely no fear. You learn the fear later, he thought. Afterlife beats the shit out of you with these kinds of surprises out of nowhere, you certainly do learn the fear. This was the time he got the news about his aunt's motorcycle accident in the middle of the night. One day, you're out learning how to ride your new Honda Gold Wing and then BAM, just like that, it's all over.

Maja took her applesauce to the table and was already halfway done with it before he managed to pull out a chair and sit down in front of her.

"I need to tell you something, and this will not be easy." For the first time, there was a crinkle on her forehead, the beginning of what would become a worry line, years down the road. She looked like Shelby, with long very dark brown hair and green eyes. She was already tall for her age and looked at least a few years older than nine. It would be the two of them in the future, and for the moment, it was hard knowing that she would grow up to look just like her mother.

"Maja, something happened this morning. Something happened… and your mom passed away. She is dead. I'm so sorry, baby." It came out much faster than he intended, but he didn't know what else to do or how else to say it.

Maja just sat there with no tears and no discernible expression. Steve could understand that perfectly; he knew what shock looked like.

Ansel placed the receiver down gently, subconsciously searching for any special feeling from his exchange with Steve Wise. It had been almost twelve years since he had felt it; just a few decades ago, it was more like once every few years. His duties had become mundane and routine; he hadn't been able to accomplish what he was called to do in twelve long years. Ansel didn't mind caring for the dead, although far more of his work was caring for the living. That was what all of this was for as he looked around the lobby and selection room. The living needed to know that their loved one was cared for and to be guided through the necessary process of remembrance. He hoped he would be able to fulfill his purpose at least one more time before he died. While he looked like a man in his seventies, a fit man at that, he was far into his nineties. With gifts like his, he knew he was no ordinary man, although he had no idea how long he may live. People saw a tall man with stark white hair that was a little too long to be in fashion for older men but a style that still conveyed professionalism and dignity. They saw his wrinkles and automatically assumed experience. If they only knew.

The Bishop Family funeral home had been in business for seventy years, although he was the only one who had ever run it, with little assistance from anyone else. He outsourced the pickup of the deceased and had two part-time workers to assist with visitations and church funeral services, but he personally saw to everything else. He needed to meet with the family himself; if he didn't, there was a chance that he would miss the signals required to perform his purpose. Being with the body would ultimately tell him what he needed to know, although the family provided context. In the past, he would always get that feeling when speaking to the family first before the preparation of the deceased.

Mr. Wise would be here the day after tomorrow, and for some reason, he still held out some hope. He did with almost everyone, but the situation with his wife was somewhat unique. She was so young and died without any physical trauma, making her an ideal candidate. Until then, he would be busy preparing for this evening's visitation. Flowers had been arriving all day, and it was time to begin setting them out and placing Mr. Ambros in his casket.

He had three hours, but as he began to work, his thoughts trailed back to Mrs. Shelby Wise.

Visitation was well attended, and Mr. Ambros's children were all present and adequately bereft. This was their last parents' death, after all. The funeral and burial will be at the church tomorrow at 3:00 PM. There is plenty of time to meet with Mr. Wise at 11:00 AM and be at the church by 2:00 PM for set up. He reminded himself to call the coroner's office to determine a potential release date for Mrs. Wise. Most people think that autopsies are a routine part of the death process, but that couldn't be further from the truth. Most people who died were old; the cause of death was determined by illnesses or diseases they had before, and the death certificate was written up due to those causes. Only in the event of accidents or sudden death without illness was an autopsy performed, and then again, most people have watched movies where the coroner carefully stitches up the body and perfectly cleans up afterward. Stitching did take place, but the cleaning was up to him, along with plugging holes and ensuring the eyes and lips didn't come apart during the service. Shelby would take more extensive preparation, so he would want services to be held at least a few days after he received her. He would keep the gruesome but necessary details from Mr. Wise, although he would still share his views on the timeframe of the service.

Younger people generally opt for cremation nowadays.

Older people still prefer to be buried. Over the last seventy years, he had seen a complete shift from 90% burial to almost 70% cremation. Ansel preferred the traditional burial method but understood the more modern trend of cremation; it was more cost-effective, and families could take the urn home with them.

He was gathering wool at this point and didn't quite understand why his thoughts kept drifting. He needed to stay focused on cleaning up the visitation room. He had to admit he was tired; he had lost some of the vigor he once had when he was younger. The energy that allowed him to meet with three or four families a day and even stand two or more visitations or funeral services. His limit these days was two family meetings and one service, getting him home and in bed by 9:00 PM.

It was 8:45 PM when he shut off the lights and locked the back door. He had no fancy electronic security system or coded entry, just a simple but effective deadbolt and key. He walked into the parking lot and straight through the grass behind the lot to his small but adequate two-bedroom home. He had lived there for over sixty-five years once the business had done well enough for him to upgrade from the little apartment to a move private home. Considering his calling, privacy was necessary. Forty-seven paces from door to door wasn't too bad for an old man. Within twenty minutes, he was asleep.

Chapter Two

The house was impossibly crowded, and it wasn't even 9:00 AM. Both sets of parents, Shelby's best friend Morgan and her husband Brandon, had arrived early this morning. Maja and Steve sat at the kitchen table, watching everyone bustle around the kitchen making breakfast while others seemed to find the need to clean. He had made all the calls yesterday evening from Shelby's parents to his and finally to Morgan. Somehow, the parents coordinated and got on the same flight that arrived in Dallas this morning before 6:00 AM. Distantly, he wondered if they had even slept; somehow, he doubted it, but he also wondered how people in their sixties could have so much energy.

After the initial hugs and directions to the two rooms they would occupy, the parents immediately surveyed what was in the fridge. He had yet to tell them exactly where Shelby was when she collapsed and died; right now, her mother, Audrey, was standing in the exact spot where Shelby's coffee mug had landed. She had made coffee in the same place his wife had made her final cup just twenty-four hours earlier. Shelby loved coffee; it was a bitch that she didn't even get to drink her last cup.

"Steve, where do you keep the napkins?" His mother called from inside the pantry.

"On the counter out here, Mom."

She rushed out of the pantry a little too quickly and collided with Morgan, who was attempting to set the table.

"Oh, shit, sorry!" Morgan exclaimed.

His mother looked dazed, not saying a word, but continued her search for the napkins.

A few minutes later, everyone was seated at the table, which coincidently had just enough chairs for all of them. He and Shelby had considered whether a table for eight was too big, although they both agreed they would need the space when the family was over. He wondered if anyone noticed that if Shelby was here, they wouldn't have enough chairs.

He had to admit it was nice to have them there, especially for Maja, but it was even better when everyone was quietly eating or at least picking at their breakfast. They had made what was in the house, discovering an unopened box of pancake mix in the back of the pantry and some eggs and bacon in the fridge. The hard part would come when they finally had to discuss what happened. Once it was clear that everyone was done eating, the busyness of the morning hustle and bustle seemed distant, and all eyes at the table suddenly became tired and strained.

"Steve, what time is the appointment?" Bill, Shelby's father, asked.

"11:00 AM."

"Ah… Okay… Are you sure that you don't need any help with that?"

Steve hadn't considered that her parents would want to have some say in the arrangements. He hadn't invited them. Bill was trying to covey this respectfully.

"Oh, sure. If you want to come with me, you are welcome."

Bill and Audrey's eyes locked, and Steve could see Audrey's almost indiscernible head nod.

"I think Audrey and I will go with you if that's okay with you, Steve," Bill said slowly and clearly.

Steve began to consider something else after witnessing that head nod from Shelby's mother. Did they think something suspicious about Shelby's death? Thirty-four-year-olds rarely drop dead for no reason; he had a hard time believing it himself, and he was here when it happened. They were all shocked, and he hadn't considered that they would be suspicious of him.

"Maybe we should call the coroner's office before we go? They may have some preliminary information on the cause of death and when she will be released." Steve suggested calmly. It wouldn't take long for anyone to see that he was not at fault here, and he wanted to be clear that he had no fear of what the doctors may find.

His eyes caught Maja's, and she looked both terrified and stunned. Shit! I am such an asshole, Steve thought, this was going to take some getting used to.

"Maja, I'm so sorry, I'm not thinking clearly, and I'm just so damn sorry," Steve murmured into her hair as he held her. For the first time, from what he witnessed, she began to cry. His words made it real for her as she sat there listening to them. Steve wasn't sure if this was a good or bad thing.

It was finally after 10:00 AM, and he still had to gather some papers for the funeral home. Oh, and call the coroner's office before his in-laws accused him of murdering their daughter. He looked desperately at his mother, who seemed to understand what was needed of her.

"Maja, can you come and sit with Grandma for a while? We can talk about anything you want or just sit here, up to you."

Maja's eyes reluctantly opened, and she lifted her chin from its resting place on her father's shoulder. It took him almost a full minute to unleash from her grip. When she finally let go, she didn't look at him, just shuffled to the end of the table where her favorite grandmother sat.

"Why don't we go to your room? It's more comfortable there." Maja took her hand, and they began walking up the stairs.

Steve headed straight for his and Shelby's home office. They had two desks in the room, side by side. The closest to the door was hers, but he steered clear of that as he sat at his desk and opened the bottom right-hand drawer. The last file folder in the back contained birth certificates for all three of them. He pulled Shelby's from the middle and put it on the desk, then took out his cell phone and googled the Parker County Coroner's Office number.

It took longer than he anticipated for an answer, but they gave him all the information he needed once he got one. Shelby died of a brain aneurysm, mostly likely congenital weakness, and she could be released today. Steve had considered the possibilities for the last twenty-four hours, with a heart attack being at the top of the list, but he hadn't thought about an aneurysm. It made sense, although it didn't make it any easier. Bill's face appeared around the corner seconds after getting off the phone. Had he been listening?

Probably, Steve thinks.

"Did they give you any information?"

Warily, Steve relayed what he had been told.

"They are one hundred percent sure?" he asked in a slightly firmer tone than Steve cared for.

"Yes, Bill, they are sure. That is what will be listed on the death certificate, and she can be picked up today. Do you still want to go with me to the funeral home, or would you rather stay with Maja?"

"I think we should go; there could be some things that ask that you don't know."

He had always been close with Shelby's parents. He had been in Shelby's life for the last fourteen years. He would bet money he knew more about Shelby than they ever would. Did they know that her favorite thing to do at night after sex was to sneak into the kitchen and grab the Oreos and milk? She would sneak back in, jump on the bed, and they would sit across from each other, legs crossed, eating their prize. She liked to call it "dessert after dessert." How often had they eaten those cookies naked, with just the soft light of the moon casting shadows on the bedroom walls? Did he know that she was up for a promotion? She had her interview and swore him to secrecy, only wanting to tell people if she got the job. She would have been the director of sales and marketing.

Right now, she was making a ton of cash as a sales manager and loved managing people, but she wanted to continue to climb that corporate ladder. With this new job, she would have the opportunity to impact everyone within the department. God, he loved her.

"Okay, no problem. I have everything Mr. Bishop requested, so we should be set."

Steve glanced at Shelby's desk as he walked by, seeing

another half-empty mug, already creating a dark ring around the inside. This one was another one of her favorites, Game of Thrones. “I Drink Coffee, and I Know Things,” the mug proclaimed. She was so silly in her collection of things that spoke to her. Movies, shows, and music were part of the quirks he loved about her. He grabbed the mug, knowing that he would have to wash it before they left. He couldn’t leave it that way.

Audrey and Bill stood there looking at him as he furiously scrubbed the inside of the mug in the kitchen sink. Once it was dry and back in the cabinet where it belonged, he grabbed the keys and his folder of papers, heading for the garage.

Ansel’s hands were still trembling as he hung up the phone. He had called his third-party removal service to pick up Shelby and bring her here as quickly as possible. He then called both of his part-time associates about the 3:00 PM church service for Mr. Ambros. He told them he would be unable to make it today. Ted needed to come here and drive Mr. Ambros to the service with all the flower arrangements, and Phil needed to meet Ted to help with the service. They both were seasoned veterans and had no issues with being able to handle these last-minute duties.

It would take all the patience he could muster to wait for her arrival. He began to shake the moment he met Steve and Shelby’s parents in person but forced his hand steady as they shook. He hadn't felt that jolt in twelve years; she rubbed off on him over the years, and he could smell her energy like heavy, musty cologne. He could feel a little something coming from her parents, but not nearly as much as what he felt from her husband. Steve loved his wife, but he had no idea how exceptional she was and one of the youngest he had the privilege to care for. The possibilities were almost endless with her; he was practically giddy. He had waited for Shelby for so long; she would be the twenty-third in seventy years. He had to be here when she arrived; technically, it didn't matter how long she was dead; she had been refrigerated, but he was convinced that it was easier for both if he was able to work on her as soon as possible. Steve and her parents had decided on cremation, so that was another issue he would have to contend with, but first, he would be with her.

In the last twelve years, he often wondered how many families had chosen another funeral home instead of his. Had he missed out on many other notable people who he could have cared for? He couldn't even guess. This was a big city, but it was probably at least a dozen.

The tremble finally subsided until he heard the back door open, and his heart skipped a few beats.

"Mr. Bishop?" Ted called.

It was just Ted coming to get the hearse and flowers loaded.

"Yes, Ted. Mr. Ambros is in the hallway by the garage, ready to be loaded. I'll help you."

They both walked to the west side of the building toward the garage; the casket was closed and ready for transport, sitting atop the church truck. Ansel pushed it quickly from behind as Ted held the door open and pressed the garage door button. The church truck was set to the exact height of the back of the hearse, and with no trouble, they pushed the casket into the back, and the rollers inside took care of the rest. Ted secured the rear of the casket with a locking mechanism that held it in place. Finally, they gathered the arrangements from the flower room two at a time and loaded them into the back of the hearse. Just as the last few were loaded, the delivery van Ansel had been waiting for started backing up toward the second bay of the garage.

Within minutes, Ted had driven away, and Shelby was on the embalming table. The delivery service was fast and efficient; once delivery was made, they left as quickly as they had come. He unzipped the bag around her carefully and, when he was ready, flipped the top section over quickly, exposing her fully naked body. The jagged incisions and thick black thread made him cringe immediately, although her beauty was still evident-- even after a day and a half of death taking hold of her body. He didn't want to touch her quite yet; he wanted to examine her first. Her dark brown hair, almost black, was still shiny and fell just below her shoulders. He dared not open her eyes; he didn't want to risk anything happening to them. She would need those in good condition. Almost perfect skin despite a few small scars and imperfections. She had no hair either under her arms or between her legs. She was the most perfect of the twenty-three. When he was finally ready, he placed both hands on her naked body, one on her face and one on her neck. She responded instantly.

"Oh God, my head hurts so bad!" Shelby cried out.

"That will go away. It will take a little time. In the meantime, you need to rest and warm up." Ansel counseled.

He pulled the warming blanket to her chin. It was always best to bring them up to at least ninety before reanimation. He clothed her in leggings and a sweatshirt he kept, just in case, from his storage room. She hadn't opened her eyes yet; no doubt the headache was horrendous considering her cause of death. Repairs would take time, and she had woken up quickly. She would sleep in here for the next few weeks while her body healed, although her mind would be the most difficult, for reasons she would find out over the next few days. For now, let her think she had some accident and is recovering. He had no beds here; all he could do was line the embalming table with blankets as soon as the healing process was complete; for now, she may still be leaking.

"Jesus!" She screamed.

He hadn't realized she would come back so fast. He needed to give her something for the pain and to knock her back out. He kept morphine and midazolam on hand, his suppliers delivering a fresh batch yearly for over the last decade. Before that, he paid highly on the black market, but now, with the internet, there was almost nothing you couldn't accomplish online. She didn't seem to notice when he gave her the morphine injection first, followed by midazolam. In combination, they would allow her to fall asleep as soon as her pain subsided with little to no hangover after she woke. It took a while before her body seemed to relax, finally finding sleep. Now that he had brought her back, it was his duty to care for her. She could be even better than before. Eventually, her scars would heal to the point where they were only visible to her. She would want to know how all of this was possible and how quickly she could return to her family. Ansel had no doubt how much Steve was in love with his wife and how happy he would be to have her back. He assumed Shelby would feel the same. He would hold off that conversation as long as he could, letting her body heal first.

He checked the setting on the heated blanket, ensuring it was set on high, taking the time to tuck the covers around her. He would have to change her like a child for at least a few days, especially her clothing, as her chest wound seeped. In the meantime, he sat in the chair in the corner and stared at her. He had done this many times before, but this time seemed unique for some reason. Maybe it was because it had been so long, he considered. She, of course, was unique, but it was more than that. Finally, he tried to get in a comfortable position to nap, leaning his elbow against the desk and laying his head down. As he attempted to doze, he wondered how he would tell her that seeing her family again was impossible. It was never easy, but he knew that for her, it would be the hardest of them all.

Chapter Three

In a way, Ansel was lucky; if the family had chosen burial, he would've had to wait until after services to bring her back. Since they preferred cremation and no one in the family wanted to go against her wishes to be viewed after death, he was able to bring her back at around forty hours from the exact time of death. He would need to balance her and her family carefully over the next week. They would both be in the same building together, blissfully unaware of each other 's presence, and he had to keep it that way.

Everyone agreed that the service should be held in the chapel, as Shelby and Steve had no religious affiliation. Another stroke of luck that could sometimes be a complication. She had died on a Tuesday morning, was brought back on Thursday afternoon, and her funeral would be on Saturday. Steve mentioned that some additional family members were coming in from out of state. It would be easier once the funeral was over, although the family had yet to decide on final disposition. They may take the urn with them, but they also might intern it. He would need to call Steve today to clarify their wishes. Shelby would also want to know what they decided, but he would wait until everything was said and done to tell her.

She would wake up today wanting answers, and he had some pre-scripted ones to give her but would save any specifics for later. He had hardly left her side since yesterday afternoon except to go to the bathroom and grab some leftovers from the refrigerator at his house. She would not be hungry for at least a few days. However, when that happened, he was prepared for that as well.

Ansel thought about the very first time he did this…Catherine. He was woefully under-prepared, and it took her a month before she was ready. She was a devoted Catholic in her first life, which took special consideration during her recovery. Just because he could bring people back to life didn't mean God didn't exist, but it also didn't mean that he did. No one knew more than he did that the line he walked was a tightrope between heaven and hell. The only thing he was sure of was that he was not God. He also didn't quite understand his power or purpose. When she came back to life, it was just as much a shock to him as it was to her. He immediately understood the consequences of his gift, good and bad, and then made up the rules as he went along.

His first rule was healing. They had to be fully healed before they could leave, healed in every sense of the word. That was the first and most immediate need. Catherine's first life had ended in 1953 at the age of fifty-one, unfortunately at the hands of her husband. Long marriages back then didn't necessarily mean happy ones. She had been strangled and left on the side of the road, her husband feigning ignorance. At the time, Bishop Family Funeral Home was one of only two funeral homes in the area and was selected often. He was young, but the community trusted him after he was able to take on some problematic restoration cases that impressed a few of the more prominent families. He had been called into service from an early age after his short stint in WWII.

By the time he was old enough to go, the war was almost over. He spent less than five months in the Soviet Union helping America's soon-to-be enemies defeat the current ones. After the two years of required military service, he went straight to school, earning his degree in mortuary science in 1949, thanks to the GI Bill. After witnessing so much death at the hands of the Germans in the Soviet Union, he was drawn to making it better somehow. Maybe that was his way of atoning for helping to shove all those bodies into mass graves toward the end of the war. He never ended up killing a soul, but he did help bury them. It had been over seventy years, but he still remembered the smell. Ansel managed to block out the images most of his life, but not the smell.

All the while in school or his early profession, he had no idea what he could do. He was ninety-seven years old, and this was only the twenty-third time he had done it. How many more would he have the chance to care for? None, if he was honest with himself. For a while, he had begun to think he would never have another chance. These twenty-three were his children, and only nine were still around to enjoy their second lives. Catherine had died again in 1974 of heart disease, so he knew pretty quickly he was not granting immortality. He was giving them a second chance at real life. Catherine got to live another twenty-one years free from her abusive husband and ended up creating a life she loved. She wrote him one letter in early 1970 stating that the last, almost twenty years, had been the happiest of her life. He never wrote back to her, not knowing where a letter like that would end up, but he finally understood the grand scale of his purpose. A few of the twenty-three had lived less than ten years, but many had lived much longer. His fourth, Virgil, was still alive at 92, although he was frail and wasn't expected to live much longer. He had died at forty in a car accident in 1964, thrown from a vehicle at a time when most Americans refused to wear seatbelts. Virgil had walked away from a wife and three children, deciding to live his second life as a bachelor in Minnesota for the last sixty years. He ice-fished and drank beer, becoming a fishing guide for local travelers. Ansel would never be able to forget number five either -- James. James was the only suicide, and he thought his efforts may be a futile endeavor. James proved him wrong in such spectacular fashion. Ansel beamed with pride for a moment longer, lingering on thoughts of his grown "children."

Ansel's second rule was distance. Since he was a bachelor, paid off his home quickly, had few expenses, and ran a successful business for many years, he provided each of the twenty-three with some money to get them started, the only requirement being at least a five-hundred-mile distance with the promise never to return. Catherine had moved to New York City and never left once she got there. She worked at Gimbal's in the women's clothing section until she earned enough commission to open her bookstore. She was a business owner for thirteen years, loving every moment. Was all of that justification for him bringing her back? In his mind, every single moment was worth it. He had ended up devoting his life to this and missed out on any real life of his own. His entire family had been dead for years; he had never married and never even seriously dated. Except for a few flings during his military and college days, he also remained celibate. Ansel had only been in love once but had been far too young to act on it. If he tried hard enough, he could still remember Lois' face. But it was too late for all of that; he had made his choices long ago.

His third rule was communication, or lack thereof, to be exact. Everything he had done and was doing would be in jeopardy if their families were to find out they were alive. There is no way to keep that a secret once the family is involved. It could be exploited or stopped if the wrong people discovered what he could do. The previously dead would be captured and studied like science experiments. For a few of the twenty-three, this rule was the easiest. The freedom of leaving their family behind was a welcome one.

Sometimes, starting over was an unexpected gift. For others, it was the hardest part. In Shelby's case, he knew that this would be difficult. He would have to keep her secluded until she understood the importance of his rules, not just for his benefit but primarily for hers. She also needed to realize that others would be put in jeopardy as well. After meeting Steve, Ansel felt their daughter would be in good hands. Shelby would eventually come to this conclusion herself.

He looked her over again, appreciating that inside her skull, her brain was internally healing itself. He lifted the blanket just enough to check her clothing; he could see some pink stains forming at the top of her chest. There were probably more toward the stomach area as well. When he bent down, he didn't smell urine, but it didn't mean there wasn't any. The body doesn't always empty itself after death, but in the case when an autopsy is performed, most of the time, a catheter is used before the start of the procedure to collect any remaining urine. Just because she hadn't drunk anything since didn't mean that her body hadn't started its natural functions of elimination anyway, she would need water soon, in any case. He did know how to start an IV if necessary but wanted to avoid that if he could. He didn't want this to seem like a hospital. Shelby's clothes needed to be changed and washed no matter what, and he needed a look at her wounds. Unfortunately, he had her mostly stripped down before she came around.

“Who are you?” She asked, without opening her eyes.

“Mr. Bishop, Ansel Bishop, Shelby. I am here to take care of you.” He spoke carefully.

“Okay, I guess I’m hurt pretty badly. Am I?” Her striking green eyes opened and looked directly into his for the first time. She wasn’t afraid, nor did she ask the typical questions he had anticipated.

“Yes, you have been hurt but will be better soon. How is your head?”

“Better, I remember a terrible headache; it's still there but not as bad now.”

He helped her as she attempted to lift herself into a sitting position, either not noticing or not caring that she was completely naked. He had fresh clothes for her beside the table, but he wanted to clean her up before she put new clothes on. He took the warm washcloth at the end of the table and began wiping away the fluids that had escaped her incisions. Not even then did she seem to mind.

During this process, he knew he didn’t have to worry about infection. For some reason, the reanimation process eliminated the need for that precaution. He had also found that bandages only seemed to slow the process. If he left everything just how it was to heal on its own, he could cut the black sutures and take them out in just a few days. Her pants had been a little damp when he removed them, so he knew he needed to clean between her legs. He had to consider the best way to do this without scaring her.

"Shelby, we need to clean you up and put clothes back on. Would you like me to hand you the washcloth so you can clean yourself up before we put some fresh clothes on?"

"Yes, thank you. I think I can do that on my own. Maybe."

"Okay, please don't try to stand quite yet. I will hand you the washcloth and turn around; when you are done, I will help you up, and we will put some clothes on you, too."

He handed her the wet cloth and immediately did as he promised, turning around and waiting until she was done. He hoped that she also understood where she needed to clean.

"I'm done, and I'm cold." She stammered.

He turned around to find her shivering, another predictable side effect.

"Yes, let's get you in some clothes and back under the blanket."

Once she was in her new clothes and the warming blanket was pulled up over her chest, the shivers died down to just a tremble. Her eyes remained open and curious throughout the entire procedure. Ansel wondered what she could be thinking.

"Why am I on an embalming table?" She asked, swiveling her head to lock eyes with him again.

"Was I dead?"

Ansel had never had anyone ask him that directly. Most concluded slowly over time. Also, this was the first time anyone had realized they were on an embalming table. With this one, he realized he must be direct and honest.

"Yes, Shelby, you were dead for almost two full days."

This information didn't seem to shock her. It simply confirmed her suspicions.

"How did you know?" Ansel asked. He had to know.

"I used to manage a team of family service counselors at Homer and Marquise. I know a prep room when I see one. I have also seen enough bodies to know what these marks on my chest are. The hospital doesn't cut you open like this if you're alive. These incisions are only made after you are dead."

Ansel was astounded. She was extraordinary. She didn't cry or appear scared; Shelby had accepted her fate without understanding what it all meant.

"I am colder than I have ever been before, even under this heated blanket. I also recognize you. I stood a few burials at the cemetery when you were the funeral director. We only moved here about four years ago. I left the funeral business over three years ago, but I still remember you." She pulled the blanket up even further, covering her lower lip, clearly freezing.

"I didn't realize you knew me. I would have been more prepared."

"It's okay. It's nice to have a little bit of the upper hand in this situation, if you know what I mean." With that, she gave him a smirk.

Without realizing it, he let out a laugh. How amazing! He had waited twelve long years for his prize, for the best of them.

"Shelby, I still need to tell you what happened, how you ended up here, and what to expect next. Are you feeling well enough now, or would you like to wait?"

"I guess I better hear it now, no matter how I feel, ending with when and how I get back home."

He could feel her determination halfway across the room and understood that none of this would be what she wanted to hear. He imagined great difficulty getting her to comprehend what would happen next.

Shelby's best friend Morgan had not yet taken a moment for herself to grieve. She had not cried or considered life without

Shelby; she only thought about Shelby's family and what needed to be done. Steve had not spoken a single word to her since the initial call, but she stayed around the house regardless. Morgan figured that Steve had not called Shelby's office, so she took it upon herself to take care of anything that he would have been too overwhelmed to consider. Men were not equipped to handle tragedy, and she knew that all too well. Her father had crumbled when her mother died. Crumbled was too kind of a word; he had ceased to exist for the subsequent two years, leaving it up to her, at sixteen years old, to take care of her little brother and to graduate high school on time. By the time she was nineteen, he had finally sobered up and found another job. They had almost lost the house and any respect of the neighbors along the way.

She didn't think Steve was as pathetic as her father, but she also didn't have faith that he would rise to the occasion as well as he should. Her suspicions were confirmed when she got off the phone with Shelby's boss. She promised to call back with information about services and remembered to ask for the phone number of the insurance company they used to underwrite their life insurance. Shelby was no fool. She would have planned ahead by ensuring she left some money behind.

The next task was food; they had at least six mouths to feed for the next four-plus days, probably longer. Not to mention food for after the service; there was no way that Steve would even begin to think of that. After Steve and Shelby's parents left to meet with the funeral home, she let her husband return home. He was grateful to be off the hook. Besides, this is where Morgan shined. She was a hero in any crisis, and Shelby had been her best friend. With her cell still in her hand, she immediately began calling the various neighbors. With little thought, she had devised a schedule for meal delivery for the next six days, taking care of at least two meals per day. Dishes would be hand-delivered with condolences on each neighbor's scheduled day, and everyone committed to at least one separate dish for the remembrance gathering after the service.

At first, Morgan thought Shelby was a bitch. When she first moved in a few houses down, Shelby kept to herself and rarely ever came outside. She never came by to introduce herself as new neighbors do, which she felt was rude. When Morgan delivered cookies the week they moved in, she handed them directly to Steve, and Shelby didn't even bother coming to the door. She even mailed a thank you card two weeks later instead of dropping it by and meeting her new neighbors. It was over a year until they formally met, but once they did, they seemed to hit it off. It wasn't until then that Moran began to understand Shelby's hectic life. They didn't go out for "girl's nights," but they did hang out and have a glass of wine or play cards. They listened to each other's rants about their bosses or co-workers when they needed to release some steam. The women had become close in the last four or so years, and she would miss her friend.

She sat down at the table with her notebook and pen, jotting down her food schedule and the contact at the office she needed to call back. She had already written down the information for the insurance company. What else? Had Steve considered the obituary, or was that part of the funeral home process? Then, it dawned on her that Maja would need clothes for the funeral! There is no way that Steve would think of that until the morning of the service, and by then, it would be too late. She headed up the stairs to discuss this with Steve's mom, Donna.

Chapter Four

Almost two hundred people attended Shelby's service. Several of her high school and college friends dropped everything and hopped on a last-minute flight to make it. Shelby's office closed for the day to allow all sixty employees to attend, and none of them skipped it. Two of her college professors made the trip while almost everyone was present from Steve's office and the neighborhood too. Shelby may have been a busy woman, but she made time to impact the lives of those she liked and cared for. Ansel had always seen a significant number of people attend when the decedent was young, but he hadn't witnessed this many attend a service in his chapel.

The urn her parents picked out, and Steve nodded his approval to, was in the traditional urn design, although this one was inlaid with scalloped pearl. It shone and reflected against the 8x10 picture her friend Morgan had brought in with a multi-dimensional silver frame. It was elegant but simple, and it was everything he had witnessed from Shelby over the last day he had spent with her. He hated to lock her away alone this early, although she knew exactly what was happening right now; he had to be completely honest with her; the temptation would be too great. The family had decided to take the urn with them for now and make decisions later on what to do with it; he had expected that. It was too easy to fill it with actual ashes. He had to ensure it was as authentic as possible. There were always people throughout the years who refused to pick up their loved one's remains once the cremation was complete. He had a locked cabinet in the back with over a dozen heavy black plastic boxes that had been left behind over the years, and he was legally required to keep them all. He had to be careful because the process for cremation had changed over the years; he couldn't select the oldest because of the large pieces of tooth and bone left behind that wouldn't occur today using a machine that refines the coarse remains into consistently the same sized pebbles. He also had to be careful to consider height and weight. Each person would produce a different amount of remains based on their size, anywhere from four to eight pounds. Based on the information attached to each box, he selected one from 1994. The woman had been well into her eighties, although she was 5'5 and 140 lbs. A little shorter but slightly heavier than Shelby, which is perfect. He opened the box and sifted the remains through a mesh kitchen strainer and only found a few bone fragments that were to be expected in any cremation. He transferred the remains into a plastic bag and slowly lowered it into the urn. They would never know that a metal ID tag was supposed to be attached to the bag. It would have been a tight turnaround for the service if he had to have her cremated in just two days, but realistically, it could have been done. He considered sealing the lid shut but knew he would have to ask the family first. Curiosity usually got the best of people; they always wanted to peek inside to see what it looked like. Ansel was careful to locate the book from 1994, where he kept a state-required log where he signed out any cremated remains for burial or release to the family. He signed the remains for the family and placed the book back in its place.

Steve insisted on three songs to be played at the service: one at the beginning, one in the middle, and one as everyone was dismissed. He didn't know if Shelby would be embarrassed or delighted at his choices, but he knew they were some of Shelby's favorites. She seemed to go from task to task with different theme songs as she went. When she was in school, she would listen to music as she was doing her homework to help her concentrate, and as an adult, there wasn't a moment that she was without it as she cleaned the house, cooked, drove, or took care of Maja. She had instilled that same passion into Maja; they loved to sing and dance in the car anytime they went together. This was a part of their life where he was an outsider. Steve enjoyed music, but their passion was something he didn't understand. He knew his wife enough to know her favorites and what meant the most to her.

Her friends and family passed by the table at the front of the chapel where the urn and picture were placed, along with other sentimental items that her family had brought. Ansel noticed a few additional objects as they passed, primarily notes and cards, but he also noted a purple tassel, a heart-shaped pin, and a few different friendship bracelets. He moved to the front of the Chapel. It was just a few minutes past 2:00 PM, but people were still shuffling in, trying to find a place to stand against a wall, as every seat had been occupied over ten minutes ago. He reached the podium and turned on the microphone.

"If I could ask for everyone's attention. We will start the service now; please do your best to find a location to sit or stand. Thank you." Ansel then motioned to Ted to start the first song.

The distinct noises of people began over an hour ago, but she knew the service wasn't due to start until 2:00 PM. It was agonizing for Shelby to know that Steve and Maja were just outside that door. She sat rigid in the chair that Ansel was in just two days ago when he explained why she died and why she could never see her family again. Once she gained her composure and her senses, she finally asked him to kill her. That was the only thing Shelby could control out of this situation. She understood she could not jeopardize the others, she understood the rules for the most part, and she understood her situation without asking him to repeat any of it. He left a syringe full of God only knows what on the table that first day. Shelby contemplated her situation for over an hour before deciding to wait. While she couldn't think about her life without Steve and Maja, she couldn't slap life in the face either. What had happened to her was a miracle, and from someone who didn't believe in God, that was saying something.

She rationalized that she could kill herself at any time, but for now, she wanted to know more about what was going on before she did anything. Fuck me, she thought. Why in the hell did she have to listen to her own funeral? Ansel had explained that the family chose to have the service here rather than at a church, which made sense considering her less-than-enthusiastic religious affiliation. Still, it didn't make it any easier. She could hear people walking around and talking, but she couldn't make out even a word. All at once, the voices ceased, and everything was quiet for a full minute before the music drifted down to her from the small speaker in the ceiling.

She knew it before the first word was spoken, her hands flying to her mouth, knowing she would be unable to control her crying as the tears already streamed down her face. He knew her so well. How would she ever let him go?

"I've heard there was a secret chord that David played, and it pleased the Lord... it goes like this, the fourth, the fifth, the minor fall, the major lift, the baffled king composing Hallelujah..." From the time she was young, she had listened to that song whenever she

was sad. For the most part, Shelby understood she had lived a somewhat charmed life, but she still had moments of sadness and loss throughout her life. For all those moments, this song was what she reached for before anything else. Music had always spoken to her soul, and somehow, this bittersweet "Hallelujah" did that better than anything else could. When the music stopped, she was able to pull herself together. There was nothing but silence as she waited in anticipation for the next discernable sound. She waited with her head down and eyes closed.

Shelby's exact words to Ansel were, "There is no way you can keep me from my family, so don't even try." She had blurted it out before he had a chance to provide any real explanations. From his position, he felt justified by the rules he had set, and he wasn't wrong. It didn't make it any easier for any of them to accept. He had more rules, which he said he would share with her once she had finally decided whether she wanted to live or die. "I guess there is no sense in wasting your breath, right?" She snidely remarked to him, but the hurt expression on his face was enough to tell her that she was misjudging his intentions. Again, it didn't make it any easier. For now, she was locked away for who knew how long with oozing wounds and a headache that wouldn't go away. It terrified her when she was alert enough to realize what having an autopsy meant. Didn't they just put all your organs in a bag and sew you back up? How in the hell was she breathing and talking and thinking? All her gross motor skills were functioning correctly, and she was eating and drinking like nothing had happened. Like she wasn't just dead 48 hours ago. He assured her that he had done this before, and he couldn't explain it, but that her body would function perfectly, just like before her death. Shelby wouldn't have to worry about her original cause of death either; apparently, that healed on its own as well. Isn't that neat? Jesus Christ… who knew that the laws of science could just be thrown out of the window and replaced by completely fantastical magic? It made her think of Bella in *Twilight* when she found out vampires and werewolves really existed. If this could happen, what else was out there?

Shelby hadn't even begun to think about what would happen after this; her entire being was wrapped up in the same grief that she imagined Steve, Maja, and her parents were most likely feeling right now. She was dead no matter what her body was doing; that was all there was to it.

She didn't have a bucket list like most people had; she had accomplished almost everything she had set out to do in her life. She had attended Northwestern and graduated Summa Cum Laude with a degree in psychology, where she just so happened to meet the love of her life that gave her the agreed upon one perfect child. They had moved to a town she adored, bought a four-bedroom home with a pool in the backyard, had a prestigious and lucrative career, and even though she could be a little career-obsessed, she had managed to make friends and even enjoy her life and her family. Their life together was enviable, and worst of all, to anyone hearing about it, it wasn't even boring. Her sex life with Steve had always been exciting; she desired him completely, even after fourteen years. Whenever she caught a glimpse of his shoulders or arms, her heart would race just as it did at the beginning. She often held on to his arms and felt his strength when he was inside of her, looking down at her face so he could witness her pleasure. Shelby had experienced a few men before Steve who had not lived up to half of what Steve could give her, so she had no regrets when choosing him. Never once did she wonder what life would be like if they hadn't gotten married; how many married couples could say that?

Steve had chosen the second song to play at the service before selecting the other two. It was the one he had witnessed her listening to most of all because she played it almost daily when pregnant with Maja. Steve had taken Shelby to Breaking Dawn Part 1 during their first year of marriage, a secret obsession that she demanded he tell no one about. She was very private about her little fandoms, and before they even got home, she had downloaded three songs from the film. One of those songs surfaced again on the repeated playlist just a few years later when they were expecting Maja. Shelby was very protective over what they agreed would be their only child, and he never verbalized it to her, but he knew precisely where that song came from when she played it all the time.

Like Bella protecting her child in Twilight, she did the same with Maja. His tears could not be contained for the first time today as "Requiem on Water" began to play.

"And though your arms and legs are under, love will be the echo in your ears; when all is lost and plundered, my love will be there still." He must have heard those words a thousand times in his house over the years, but he didn't understand them until this moment. The intensity of her love for Maja was so great that she had difficulty conveying it in any other way. When Steve looked around the crowded chapel, he could only see a few dry faces looking back at him; all eyes seemed to be on him. He didn't even care that he was blubbering like a child. If Shelby was looking down at him from somewhere right now, his love for her could never be denied. She would know, without a doubt, how much he loved her.

The service was a blur; no minister spoke, and no scripture was read; it was simply her family and friends reading a poem or two and speaking from the heart. Almost a dozen of Shelby's family and friends took to the podium to celebrate and remember her. Audrey, Bill, and he decided not to speak simply because they knew it would be impossible to hold it together enough to say anything meaningful. When the last person spoke and took their seat, he witnessed the funeral director approaching the front of the room.

"Thank you for spending time with the family today

celebrating the amazing life of Shelby Wise. The family has asked that we remain seated or in our places while the last song is played. Afterward, the family invited everyone to Steve and Shelby's home for food and refreshments." Ansel nodded at Ted one last time, and the final tune began to play within seconds.

More than a few small chuckles and smiles could be seen throughout the chapel by the time the chorus played. Everyone knew Shelby's love for music, but not everyone knew of her love for live music. She was a concertgoer, having her favorite bands to see whenever given a chance and even traveling, when possible, to see some of her favorites. Shelby's absolute favorite, seen thirty-eight times, was Widespread Panic. What better send-off than "Ain't Life Grand" to show the world how incredible his wife was? She lived every moment appreciating everything around her, including all the little things. A few people stood up from their seats and began to move with the music, just a little at first, and by the second time the main chorus played, everyone was on their feet. He couldn't imagine a better way to send her off. If only she could be here to see how many people loved her and how they were willing to remember her on her own terms. He couldn't help but take Maja's hand and twirl her around at the right moment.

Most, but not all, two hundred people showed up at his doorstep over the next hour. Every greeting and condolence was a complete blur. Although, he did finally notice Morgan's hard at work refilling drinks and clearing platters. She was the only one who seemed to realize how many people they needed to feed, and she had taken care of everything herself. She had appetizers, cold and hot casseroles, finger sandwiches, and various desserts available with all the appropriate accouterments of matching plates, napkins, and silverware. No one would say that Shelby didn't go out in style.

As soon as he could escape, he grabbed Maja and lifted her in his arms, taking her upstairs. He placed her on his and Shelby's bed and sat beside her with his arm around her shoulder. He didn't look down, but soon, her little body began to convulse with sobs. Steve knew their love for Maja's mother was overwhelming and all-consuming, but he had to allow Maja to start the healing process. She needed the time and space to grieve for her mother but also to be, once again, a kid who had a lot of life yet to live.

"Babe, I love you so much. Anytime you need to come in here to cry, go right ahead. Just know that, above anything, your mother would want you to be happy. So, eventually, it will be okay not to cry anymore, too. Right now, you have the right to feel any way you need to feel."

Maja stared at him, seeming much smaller now than her nine years.

"I know, Dad. Mom would be mad if we were so sad all the time. Can I go back to school on Monday? Mom wouldn't want me to get behind either."

"Um, sure, babe. Let's see how you feel on Monday morning. I'm not going back to work until the week after next, so if you want to stay home, you can."

"No, I wouldn't want to let her down." With that, she slipped off the side of the bed, opened the bedroom door, and walked out.

Steve sat there wondering how his daughter had such a handle on how Shelby would feel, and she was right. Shelby would have been worried about school after just a single day, let alone another week. For the first time, he allowed himself to think about what life would look like now. Going back to work, that big project he had been working on for Nike had been put on hold when they really couldn't afford it to be. The yard work needed to be done. He should have mowed this week but hadn't even remembered until now that he hadn't done it. He would also have to figure out the finances, life insurance, and all of that. It's incredible how quickly death can turn into a to-do list, he thought.

Chapter Five

All she heard were the songs, but that was enough. She could not have picked out anything more appropriate. She had cried and cried and then laughed so hard her incisions began to ooze, which was so weird because it didn't even hurt. Gratitude for her incredible life and husband was all she felt.

Shelby was still smiling when Ansel walked in. She wondered how old he was to be so agile. She guessed about seventy-five but suspected he was older than that based on some of his earlier comments. Her mood was significantly improved than in the last two days. She was finally able to appreciate how lucky she was. Not to be alive but to have lived so fully. Ansel had called it her "first life," and her "first life" had been pretty damn good.

"How was it?" Shelby asked.

"Standing room only. How much did you hear?"

"Only the music; I couldn't hear anything between the songs."

Good, he thought. That is precisely what he intended. Ansel wanted her to know how much thought was put into her service but not to wallow in it. She had a lot of healing to do; this was not the time for too much sentiment. Shelby would be giving up her life, but she had to realize that to those who loved her, she was already gone.

He leaned against the embalming table as Shelby was sitting in his chair by the door.

"You had some very eloquent friends and family speak on your behalf. You would have been proud. Your attendees stood up and danced during the last song. I have never seen anything like it." Ansel admitted.

"What?" Her eyes widened and began to water again. How freakin cool! Even after death, her husband could still surprise her.

"It's time to talk about what's next. I don't usually do this part yet, but you seem to be ready for some reason, and I am not in the business of holding people back. As I have told you, the priority is healing. First, we must make sure you are physically healing. I can tell by your shirt that we still have some seeping, so I will wait until tomorrow to remove your sutures. After I do, I hope you are open to moving to my house where you can sleep in a real bed. I have to convince myself that you aren't going to try and run, especially back to your family. You are the twenty-third person I have cared for, and there is a procedure to follow to ensure it goes as smoothly as possible." Ansel counseled.

"I am not going to run, Ansel. The biggest reason is Maja; it would traumatize her, and I could never do that to my child. Better for her to understand death and to grieve than for the walking dead to show up at her door."

"Then I am convinced. Tomorrow, it is. In the meantime, I want to review a few more rules with you. Better to start processing these now and think about the future than dwelling on a past that you can't change."

Shelby looked down at her hands, primarily where her engagement ring and wedding ring used to sit, momentarily forbidding herself to think about the future in sort of meaningful way. She couldn't just sit here in an embalming room forever, though. When her resolve improved, she looked up, signaling that he could continue.

"Rule number four… wait, do you remember what we discussed yesterday?"

"Yes, sir. Healing, distance, and communication. How could I forget?"

"Yes, young lady. That will not be the last time we discuss those, so prepare to hear it all again. Rule number four is about technology."

As he began to speak, she curled her fingers underneath the chair, all of the details; how was she supposed to start a new life and avoid the internet?

"Now, I can see your expression. I understand. I don't expect you to forgo technology, mostly social media."

He had not been living under a rock these last twenty years. Two of those he cared for had to abide by this rule, but he admitted that it would be more difficult for Shelby than the others. Facebook had already existed the last time he did this in 2011, but AI and many other platforms had yet to. She would have to be vigilant.

"Before you tell me all of this, explain to me how you are doing this. Is it some drug?" Shelby inquired. She had been consumed with her death and her family but had missed the elephant in the room entirely.

"No, it isn't a drug, but it isn't something I can readily explain either. It isn't something I can do by myself, either. There is some energy coming off you and the others that I can feel -- even through the people who love you. I hypothesize that whatever I give you in combination with what is already there makes reanimation possible," Ansel attempted to explain.

"You are going to have to give me more than that. How in the hell do you combine our energies?" She was starting to get impatient; he was hiding something, and surely, she wasn't the first to ask these questions. Her perfectly manicured black nails were beginning to dig into the chair without her realizing it until her forearms began to hurt. She crossed her arms quickly across her chest, noticing the crustiness of the fabric, but again, no pain. This was just too weird to be real, Shelby thinks.

"Of course, you are right to ask these questions, although I'm afraid there isn't much to it. I place my hands on your chest and neck, and then somehow, my energy is transferred into your body, giving you a second life. It works almost instantly. The first time I did it, it was like I was hypnotized…almost forced to do it. Same with the second time, I have no other explanations." Ansel didn't know why he felt so defensive, but he couldn't explain it fully. She would never understand.

"You John Coffey'd me?" Shelby blurted out.

He couldn't help but laugh. Yes, he supposed he had. Of course, he had seen The Green Mile, although he never thought about his powers in that way. A single man with no children or family seemed to have endless evenings to fill, and books and movies were his indulgences.

"John Coffey is a bit taller than I am, but you could say that, minus the gnats."

"So, you can't just do this to anyone?"

"No, in seventy years, just twenty-three. I have tried many times on others when I could tell they did not have the energy you did. None were successful. I have to wait and hope. It has become my life's work. I have kept up with all of you as I would if you were my children. Which brings me to the fifth and final rule."

"Before you jump into the next rule, I just want to say that if at some point my skin starts to sparkle in the sun or I begin to crave blood, I will be really pissed."

Chapter Six

The Arizona sun beat down on her tanned backside as she turned the page in her book. She was lying on her stomach in an oversized pool float that was slowly circling the water. Music played on her Bluetooth speaker, but not loud enough for the neighbors to hear. This week, she is exposing herself to the exciting world of home composting. Over the last five years, her mission has been to learn new skills or hobbies as often as possible; after all, no one knew how long they had left in this world. Shelby knew better than anyone, shit,… Scarlett, she corrected herself. She still shook her head over that one. She had never known another Scarlet in life, although she imagined she hadn't met one because they were too busy dancing at the club or perhaps participating in Civil War reenactments. For some reason, she thought she would get to choose her new name. Still, when Ansel handed her a thick envelope containing a birth certificate, passport, checkbook, and car keys the week before her departure, she was disappointed when she opened it to discover her new identity was that of Scarlett Marie Winchell. The initials were a coincidence, but the name stunk.

"You mean I don't get to choose my name?" She had asked petulantly.

"No, darling, how do you think I get these documents? I had to buy the identity of someone who recently passed away. It's more difficult than you would think. Nowadays, everything is electronic; there is no easy way to forge these anymore. You will have to pass for two years older than you are, but I think you can manage that." He had given her a wink, indicating his joke at her expense.

"When you get settled, you can take these to get a new driver's license in the state you end up in. Have you given that any more thought?"

Now, her back was beginning to get warm. She closed her book and used her hands to slowly paddle to the side of the pool, jumping in the water, and throwing her book and the float over the side. The water was cool and refreshing, a daily ritual of her new life. She had chosen Arizona without giving it much thought; she had never been here but imagined a new life surrounded by palm trees might be the way to go. Before she left Texas, she had time to reflect quite a bit on her old life, although she also began to realize that there was a certain freedom in never being able to go back. Life had been so whole and fulfilling that she hardly had time to feel the weight of the responsibility that had piled on her shoulders over the years. School, career, husband, child, and all that comes with it… the house cleaning, cooking, bills, and let's not forget keeping up with the Jones. I loved every moment of it, she said to herself. She continued to justify her feelings, even after five years. She felt guilty for every carefree stroke she made in the water.

This life had been carefully crafted with every detail considered, as no everyday life could be. When growing up, you take things as they come to you, and then you add them to your life. Her parents had expected college, so she went. She anticipated meeting the man she would marry while attending, so she did. Layer upon layer gets built up until you realize there is no going back. How often had she considered another career or living in another city? Hundreds! The problem was that once you have kids in school, stable jobs, and a mortgage, there is no changing the play mid-game. Just because she had made money in the sales profession didn't mean that was her calling. Ansel had set her up with enough money that she didn't have to rush to make decisions. During those first few weeks in her little apartment, almost all she had done was write lists of the potential possibilities. She would write, scratch out, and then write some more, always with an overwhelming sense of guilt and anguish, which resulted in the list inevitably being thrown in the trash. Two months after her death, she was finally able to move from her little table in the kitchen, scribbling out her thoughts, to buying a planner that would allow her to map out her goals for the following year. Shelby was a planner, and that would never change; it took her only two days to fill out each and every month with what she wanted to accomplish.

The hour she allowed herself in the pool each day was about to be up, and after today's reading, it seemed like she was finally ready to make the trip to Home Depot for her first composter. It would make the perfect addition to the pasta and sushi makers, herb garden, and wine-making kit, not to mention all her hand-painted and blown dishware. She found the ideal place where the trash can used to be, right underneath a scene she had photographed of Camelback Mountain. Her newest obsession, or so-called "hobby", usually lasted about three months, give or take, but it kept life interesting. Her hobbies were also part of the plan.

"You must keep yourself occupied as much as possible at first, especially away from the computer. With the internet so accessible, it's not hard to track people online. Once you start, you can easily find yourself down the rabbit hole," Ansel had counseled.

Shelby had carefully locked away any possibility of doing that. She had never once typed their names into her MacBook's search engine. Not because she had forgotten them but because she loved them so fiercely. There was no doubt in her mind that Steve would give Maja every opportunity for the life she deserved; if she looked even once, the danger was all on her end. She feared she would be unable to stay away. She hadn't attended a Panic concert, desperately wanting to, but knowing someone would recognize her. Another depression to add to the list.

Her initial bank account balance was just over $100,000 when she arrived in Arizona driving her used 2019 black Toyota

Corolla, a very sensible and fuel-efficient selection. More money than she had in her old checking account, by more than a mile. However, she had no home, education, or experience to draw from to set herself up to make any more money. Ansel had been able to send her off with far more money than any of his past "children" due to the twelve years he had been waiting, but primarily due to inflation, he joked. At first, it had been so surreal that she had woken up for months expecting to return to her old bed, discovering that it had all been a dream. When her planner was finally complete, that was when her second life had truly begun.

Toweling off under the bright red umbrella next to the pool, she recalled how hard it had been to take those first significant steps toward establishing herself in a new reality. The first item on her list was a shopping trip. Three pairs of pants and five shirts were all she brought with her, and she had constantly rotated those items for almost six weeks. Scarlett, she decided, was a casual chick, or woman, or lady…whatever. She was not tied down by responsibility or obligation, nor would she ever be. The rent on her apartment was embarrassingly low, meaning that her first home wasn't in the best part of Phoenix, although she still had the palm trees outside of the window to look at. That first shopping trip had resulted in shorts, t-shirts, and several halter and shift dresses that she could wear with Birkenstocks or tennis shoes. Once that was done, she had to find a way to make money. She had no way of knowing she would become a millionaire in less than four years. Besides the obvious hiccup of her death, she continued to live an absolutely charmed life.

After setting up her new composter, Shelby fixed herself an extra cold martini straight up with three blue cheese olives, smiling at the perfect ice layer that had formed within seconds of pouring it into her glass. Of course, the layer would melt once she settled at the table on the back patio, but it was the initial perfection that counted. MacBook in one hand and martini in the other, she sat down to begin the third chapter of her newest book.

Who knew that the market for erotic fiction was so lucrative? She had intended to make enough money to pay the bills and ended up with a completely paid-off three-bedroom home with a pool and brand-new Genesis G90 in the garage, black on black, of course. She wrote under the pseudonym Sara Winters, keeping with the initials theme. At least she got to choose the name this time, although three names were hard to keep straight. No one, including her publisher or agent, had her real address; everything was sent to a P.O. Box over seven miles away. An AI-generated picture was used for the back of her books, and when the publishing company insisted on using social media, she hired someone to manage it for her. Even though she was tied to her computer for at least five hours a day, she still had never ventured onto Facebook, Instagram, or even TikTok. Reagan must have been doing an excellent job because the money kept pouring in. She never attended a book signing or even a single public appearance, although she did sign batches of books when they were sent to her. Five books have been published so far, with the sixth expected to be released by January of next year, giving her just two more months to finish it so that editing and the rest could be completed. For someone who had zero sex life, she allowed herself to live vicariously through her characters, whose experiences ranged from romantic lovemaking to extreme bondage and even some in the femdom genre. Shelby's research skills in underground fetish communities astounded her; so foreign to anything she would ever be interested in, it was nonetheless fascinating. Working at home, going at her own pace, and dabbling in something so seemingly forbidden gave her the freedom and excitement she never realized had been so lacking in her old life.

Did she miss sex? Yes-- Hell, Yes, actually. Three vibrators, a rabbit, two different-sized dildos, and a butt plug used regularly were proof enough. After all, She had to keep up the practical research for her work, she rationalized. The truth was that she still felt married. Steve and she had sex at least a few times a week for over fourteen years, excluding after her delivery of Maja. She had considered arranging a Tinder date and at least engaging in a one-night stand. But she hadn't been able to go through with it. At thirty-nine, excuse me, forty-one, she had no illusions of being celibate forever. Each day made it slightly easier to think about dipping her toe back into the dating pool, or at least another part of her. This was not about judgment; no one around would even know. It was about the vow she made to her husband. She imagined he was so busy raising their daughter and with his career that he would not have found time to date yet, either. Those thoughts didn't make it any easier. Damn… she missed fucking with a passion. Was that a double entendre? As an author, she should probably know that. Shelby rolled her eyes, dismissing these thoughts that crept into her writing time. Describing the color of her latest heroine's nipples as she removed her blouse was not helping her current mood. Draining the last bit of martini, she soldiered on for another few hours until her stomach demanded attention.

It was time, she decided. A relationship was a little out of her realm for now, but a friends-with-benefits situation would be perfect. She had moved the MacBook to the kitchen table, where she could munch on leftover stir fry while creating her dating profile. With so many options, deciding which one to choose was difficult. Ultimately, she chose Bumble because it gave her the most control, and she didn't need to post a public profile picture.

When the profile was complete less than an hour later, she neither had the energy nor inclination to conduct any preliminary searches—after five years, the daylight hours belonged to her, although the evening still belonged to Maja. The bright orange sun had turned gold, while the horizon, clearly visible through the large kitchen windows, had turned a majestic pink and purple. Shelby stood up, not bothering to turn off the computer, and walked to the back patio again. The colors faded within minutes, but she still revealed that she could witness this beauty a few days a week. Her happiness was the most challenging part of her second life. Just as the colors disappeared from the sky, thoughts of her child appeared without warning. Maja had never seen a sunset like this, or at least up to nine, she hadn't. She would be fourteen now, just a few years away from being a woman. That fact didn't seem real any more than her new name.

As Shelby returned to the house, she was careful to lock up, turn off the computer, and then change into an old, oversized t-shirt-sans underwear. She nestled into the corner of the couch with a blanket over her legs and another book in her lap. This was Stephen King's newest, one she had pre-ordered months ago and finally received a few days ago. If only he could live forever, what was he now, eighty? The thought terrified her. She had read King since she was ten, only skipping the Dark Tower Series but reading every other book he had published. King was the one who deserved a second life, not her. For Maja's tenth birthday, Shelby would have introduced her to The Eyes of the Dragon, a wonderful fairy tale about a prince imprisoned in a tower by his brother, and his only means of escape was crafting a rope made of napkins. Since the day she was born, Shelby had read a story to her every night. Maja had loved reading short books by age four and was advancing to a second-grade reading level by the time she entered kindergarten.

Education was Shelby's first major; she had always thought about becoming an elementary school teacher, even going through student teaching in her third year. She went through the entire background check process, but by the time she was done teaching second grade, she realized the required patience was not something she possessed. She used most of her education courses as electives and moved to psychology without dragging out her graduation date any further. Steve laughed when she told him about her decision. He had seen that coming a mile away, already understanding her true nature. The chaos was too much for her, and the learning was secondary to discipline, which she despised. When they spoke of children, the agreement for one took less than five minutes. It was understood that controlled chaos was all they could collectively handle.

Shelby's mind continued to wander, but eventually, she was able to pull herself out of it long enough to begin the new novel. Two hours later, her eyes were barely open enough to read the words any longer. She went to bed, pulling the covers up as far as possible. Just as they had for the last five years, thoughts of Maja threatened her ability to drift off. Once she finally did, the dreams that inevitably followed were those of her sweet daughter.

Chapter Seven

"Bob, can I get you another beer?" Catherine called out from the kitchen.

"Yes, I can't very well eat my dinner without a drink, can I?" Her husband yelled sarcastically.

Oh joy, he was in another one of his moods. Great. Thirty-one years of marriage to that man had made her docile, but it had also made her bitter. She had been beaten so many times that she lost count by the second year of marriage when he was still "breaking her in," as he called it. Other than walking to the market and carrying all the groceries back herself, she hadn't left the house in years. The two kids that managed to survive moved to Kansas City and never wrote. She knew they had their own families now and didn't blame them for not returning. The boys had been beaten almost as severely as she had, and when they turned seventeen and eighteen, they signed up for the war before the draft could scoop them up. It was a miracle they weren't killed, but she knew it was because they had developed their survival instincts right here in their house.

The girls hadn't lived to adulthood. Stella had been stillborn, and Mary died from the flu when she was three. When Catherine went into labor after a particularly horrific beating, she vowed to take the other kids and run, but in 1938, there was nowhere for women to go. Instead, Stella had died, and she had stayed, even giving him another child. In 1953, things weren't much better for women, but at least she couldn't feel much anymore. He didn't bother getting on top of her nowadays, a blessing she thanked God for every night. Her emotions were carefully controlled, and she had learned over time not to cry when he hit her. When he couldn't see her suffering, it took the fun out of it. Bob stopped almost as soon as he started these days, he lost his breath quickly. Catherine was fifty-one and had gotten fat. In her heart, she hoped she wouldn't have to live much longer.

She sat the beer and plate down in front of her husband without a word and then returned to the kitchen to eat her dinner alone. With each bite, she prayed for death.

"Lord, please take me to heaven. I have lived my life in your service and done my duty. Please take my body and let me come home," Catherine whispered as she wiped away a little mashed potato that clung to her lip.

The following day, after Bob had left for the auto shop, she put on her only remaining dress with sensible heels and walked the mile and a quarter to the market. When she was younger, she only had to come a few times a week. She was strong enough to carry the supplies home with a few bags under each arm. Now, she had a hard time carrying one in each hand all the way home, so she was forced to make the walk at least every other day. It pained her, but not as badly as not having stocked beer in the fridge and hot meatloaf on the table. This was her life, and as people do, she had adapted.

"Mrs. Davis, It sure is good to see you again!" The owner called out as she entered.

"Thank you, Mr. Snyder, you too," Catherine said, barely glancing his way. She walked straight to the back of the store where the beer was kept. While Catherine was a woman who had learned to do what she was told, she was also practical. She astutely correlated Bob's increased alcohol intake with his lack of desire and his inability to stay interested on the occasions when he did get angry and strike her. She preferred to keep it that way. While she used to buy only a twelve-pack of Pearl, now she bought two. It would be hard for her to carry, but the cost was far less severe than the alternative. She took the cases to the counter, like always, and then quickly filled a basket with eggs, corn starch, and mayonnaise, finally heading to the meat counter for bologna and pork chops.

"Is that all you need, Mrs. Davis?"

"Yes, sir. Thank you."

"That will be $8.25. Would you like some help out with these?"

Instead of simply saying no, and for a reason she would

never be able to understand, she told him the truth. Something she had learned long ago could be dangerous.

"That's okay. I will be walking, so I may as well get used to the weight on the way out." Was she asking for pity? Lord help her, was she feeling sorry for herself?

"Mrs. Davis, don't you live over a mile away on Rt. 42? That's too long to walk with all of this. Can I offer you a ride home? It would be no problem at all."

Catherine's eyes widened in surprise, "Oh no, I couldn't. Thank you, but no."

"I won't take no for an answer! It will only take a few minutes, and no one will mind if I close up to take a fine woman home, such as yourself," laying on thick, his southern gentlemanly charm. He had already taken both packs of beer in his hands and threw the brown paper sack filled with the rest of her sundries under his arm.

Panic rose in her chest. How could she get in the car with a man? Catherine also inherently knew better than to argue with one, though. She prayed to God as fast as she could for no one to see them, promising him that she would never again open her mouth. "In the name of the Father, Son, and Holy Spirit, amen." Mr. Snyder had already slung the items in the back of his car parked out front and didn't seem to catch her as she quickly made the sign of the cross before walking over to the passenger seat. He trotted over to open her door and closed it behind her, then jogged to the front door, drew out his keys from his pocket, locked the door, and hurried back to the car.

"No problem at all, Mrs. Davis. I couldn't have you walking all that way in this heat," He offered as if she had just thanked him.

"Thank you." Head down as far as she could, she hoped the ride would end quickly.

Within five minutes, he pulled into the driveway, hopping out of the car to open her door again. She pulled herself out while he went to the other side of his blue Oldsmobile to retrieve her groceries.

"Let me help you inside."

Quickly looking around, Catherine could not see anyone, firmly believing God had given her this gift.

"Okay, thank you."

She opened the unlocked door and directed him to the table in the center of the kitchen nook. He placed the beer and groceries on the table, commented on her lovely home, and, within seconds, was in his car and off to his store.

Once the groceries were put away, she finally noticed her heartbeat beginning to slow and her breath becoming steady again.

That was close, but there was no way Bob would find out, and she had saved her back today, to boot!

Catherine set about sweeping, then sat down in her chair by the side table to repair a few pairs of her husband's pants, the adrenaline of the day leaving her body. After a few minutes, her eyes became heavy, and she began to doze in the middle of the day for the first time since her children were babies.

"Catherine…" She heard a man's voice calling her name from a distance.

"Catherine!" This time, it was closer… and she began to open her eyes, never fully seeing the face of the man who belonged to the voice. A voice she had come to know for over thirty years as her husbands. Just as her eyes began to flutter, a fist connected with her temple. Shock more than pain filled her head before she was knocked to the floor, her pretty sky-blue floral dress coming up over her knees as she slipped down from her chair. Bob climbed on top of her with a knee on each side of her body, wrapping his hands around the neck of his wife and the mother of his four children, two dead. He willed his hands to squeeze harder until he could no longer hear her strained breathing.

"Whore, you dirty fucking whore!" He yelled in her face, dribbling spittle down his chin, landing on her nose. His wife was not going to humiliate him in front of his neighbors, no matter how old, ugly, or fat she had gotten.

Catherine never heard her husband's final words. She had already slipped into blackness. All she could do was thank God repeatedly that he had finally answered her prayers. She was going home. Maybe she would be with her little girls again! Blackness was replaced by images of two little girls with strawberry blonde hair in pigtails wearing frilly little pink matching dresses. All she felt in those final moments was relief.

It took less than three minutes for Bob to murder his wife. The only part he regretted was that she didn't open her eyes to see him do it. He felt stronger than he had in years, powerful. The bitch had deserved it. When he got the call at work from his neighbor, John Boseman, two doors down, that Mr. Snyder was parked in his driveway and had gone into his house… he never doubted what would happen when he got home. He was humiliated, and a man could never be humiliated at the hands of his wife.

Bob sat in his oversized chair with a cold beer, staring proudly at his handiwork, mind distantly wondering what he would eat for dinner. He experienced no guilt. Even in the coming days, when he had to cook his own meals and get a stain out of his work shirt, he told himself it was worth it. Cooking wasn't something he hadn't done since his wife had let their youngest daughter die.

Rummaging through the cooler and cabinet, he found the

bologna and made himself a sandwich with too much meat. He didn't care. Bob planned to drive to the market tomorrow and see Mr. Snyder anyway. After his abbreviated dinner, he watched The Perry Como Show and the local news, waiting for the sky to darken. He already knew his neighbor was keeping an eye on his house, that jackass. After dark, he waited a bit longer until he saw the last light go out from inside his neighbor's windows.

Bob took the two piles of newspaper on the back porch in his hands, opened the front door, and headed to his truck, making it seem that he would finally get rid of those old newspapers tomorrow if anyone should be outside. He placed the newspapers in the passenger's seat and then opened the back gate of his truck. Once he had dragged her to the back of the truck from the living floor, the hardest part was getting her body up and into the bed. Fuck, he thought, this bitch is heavier than she looked, and that was saying something.

He started with her shoulders and tried to pick her up that way, sliding her head and back as far as he could past the open gate. He quickly had to move his hands down to her sides and then finally was able to push her feet forward until her whole body was contained. Walking back inside the house, he found an old blue tarp in the mud room to cover her. Tying it down was a pain in the ass in the middle of the night with no light, he thought. She was always more trouble than she was worth, anyway.

Bob left her body in the back of the truck and went to sleep. Leaving this late would be suspicious, but dumping her in the morning on his way to work would be just fine. He went back inside, removed his boots, jeans, and work shirt, and left them where they lay on the side of the bed, crawling into bed still smelling of the sweat he had worked up from strangling her.

He had no breakfast to eat, he considered bitterly but set out anyway; he had business to attend to this morning. Old Creek Rd wasn't too far; he knew that was the perfect place to dump her. Catherine would be found, but not for a few days, and no one would see him this early in the morning. He had fished out there a few times years back and knew it was a local secret spot. The entrance to the road was no longer marked and difficult to see when driving by. It took twenty minutes to get out there, and he only saw a few cars he didn't recognize on his drive. Finding a spot about half a mile down with tall underbrush, he stopped the truck and hastily ran to the back without turning off the engine. He lifted the tarp just enough to grab her legs and drag her toward the end of the gate, not bothering to try and catch her as her torso and head hit the ground with an audible thud. Catherine's skull had cracked in three places, but she had been dead long enough for no blood to flow. He took his hands under her abdomen and rolled her as hard as he could down the embankment. Momentum took hold, and her body rolled another three times before resting at the bottom, barely visible from his vantage point. Part of her sky-blue floral dress was all that could be seen, and that was if Bob was really looking for it.

Bob jumped back into his truck, quickly executed a three-point turn, and returned to where he had come from, not taking even a moment to look back. Ruth's diner was on the way to the shop. He stopped in and sat at the bar, eating the best-corned beef hash and eggs he had ever tasted before arriving to work five minutes before his scheduled shift.

Chapter Eight

"Thank you for a lovely evening," Shelby said as she smiled kindly at her latest suitor. Kind was all she could say about this one. She had seen worse. At least he resembled his profile picture and chewed with his mouth closed. She would have to start taking her neighbor's advice and meet them for a drink first instead of dinner. Shelby had to admit she was being a bit picky for someone who only desired a fling. This was candidate number three, and nothing on earth would make her go to bed with this man. He was simply too nice. One of the things she had always admired about Steve was his edge. He was never afraid to go after what he wanted. He was unrelenting yet gentle when necessary. Shelby would have to put this one out of his misery. He was practically squirming in anticipation of a kiss that would never come to pass.

Shelby held out her hand and again smiled politely. She wasn't sure if relief or disappointment flashed across his face, although he quickly hid it behind a radiating smile.

"Scarlett, it was a pleasure. I hope to see you again soon."

"Thank you," she said, turning and walking toward her car. She felt a little bit sorry for him. He was friendly, after all. The whole endeavor was turning out to be more difficult than she had imagined. Her next date was scheduled for tomorrow. Maybe that one would be better. She officially marked Thomas off her mental list and resigned to spend another night with one of her vibrators. Hell, maybe even some porn. This is what five years alone does to you, she thinks, reminding herself to block his profile when she got home. There was no sense in dragging these things out. Before she blocked him, she would send him a note thanking him for the nice dinner, but politely declining to see him again. She had not given anyone her phone number and was careful to meet them in a public location. When it came down to someone she was actually interested in, she would either have to be comfortable enough to accompany him alone to his house, or she would have to invite him to hers. She would cross that bridge when she came to it. If it ever did… There is no sense in worrying about the details after these last few disasters.

Reaching for her laptop first thing upon arriving home, she noticed she had a new message. Not giving in to temptation, she was determined to block Thomas before reading whatever awaited her. Once the profile was blocked, she also deleted their message chain. Done and done! Now, to reward herself with a new message--- from Jeremy. Jeremy was tomorrow's date. She hoped he wasn't bailing, although letting her know a day in advance wouldn't be the worst thing that had happened to her. She had yet to be stood up, but she did have one last-minute cancelation, last minute as in twenty minutes before she was expecting to leave the house. She double-checked the app while she was curling her hair and saw the notification. There is no sense in getting dolled up for nothing. She had turned off the curling iron with less than a fourth of it to go and settled in for the night with her book. So far, in the last two weeks, she had messaged five men in total, receiving messages and setting up dates with four. She was getting the hang of this online dating thing. She just needed to meet someone she wanted to rip the clothes off by the time they returned to the parking lot. Was that too much to ask? Pulling her long, dyed, auburn locks away from her face, she read his message:

Scarlett, I am looking forward to meeting you tomorrow. I will be driving a black BMW X7 and wearing a grey polo with jeans, just in case you don't recognize me from my photo. I'll meet you outside the front doors of Nonna's Bistro on Lincoln St. at 7:00 PM.

Best, Jeremy

Wow, was that too over the top or just perfect? She couldn't tell. He was courteous yet professional in his tone and verbiage. Once upon a time, she would have offered him a job after getting an email like that. They had already discussed the details back and forth in a chain of several messages, although he wanted to send her a re-cap so they would both be on the same page. Oddly attractive. She clicked on his profile again and read through it for the fifth or sixth time. His profile picture was not too revealing, which was right on the money. She skipped the shirtless, surfboard, golfing, or strange group photo profiles. He was sitting at a table with his leg over his knee, a polo shirt, and a ball cap with a KC logo on it. There was sand behind him but no water. Not too flashy, not too conservative, his porridge seemed just right, she chuckled to herself. Yum!

His profile read like a resume, which made her believe he hadn't been doing this for long. There was something comforting about that. He worked in the energy sector, whatever that meant. He enjoyed traveling, water sports, watching football and hockey, and his favorite pastime was enjoying live music and wine tastings. If she could have created a man out of thin air, his resume wouldn't be half as good as this guy's. His only drawback, which she had yet to see based on the one picture he had posted, was his hair. His profile said he was blonde, ugh! She had never been attracted to blond men. Maybe he could wear the cap to bed. That might not be so bad. It didn't matter, though. She was intent on meeting him tomorrow, no matter what. The BMW was also a good sign, not that she was considering a relationship or anything close to it, but the fact that he mostly likely had some money in the bank helped with the thoughts of maybe taking him back to her place. It would be clear at that point that she was wealthy, but she wasn't in the market to be taken advantage of. She closed the MacBook, got up, and went to the bathroom to wash her face and pull her hair up. Her mood had lifted these last few weeks since she had decided to meet someone. It felt like progress, and for someone who could never sit still, progress was reassuring.

She recalled Jeremy's face as she slipped under the covers and opened the bottom drawer to her bedside table. She was naked, forgoing her usual oversized t-shirt, determined to enjoy herself tonight. It turned out she didn't even need the porn. Calling up his face was all that was required. Ten minutes later, she was sound asleep. Maja was there, and they were laughing.

She chose a green blouse to accentuate her eyes and a white denim skirt with gold sandals. Simple enough to be casual, although just a step up to match his collared shirt. Maybe she should have written him back telling him what she was wearing… although the message wasn't one that needed confirmation. Everything would be fine! Shelby barely curled the ends of her hair, giving it body, and decided on very little makeup. Her skin was perfectly sun-kissed, and she hardly wore foundation or rouge anymore. Eyeliner, a bit of shadow, and some gloss, then she was ready to go.

She pulled into the parking lot five minutes before seven to find him already waiting by the front door. Punctual, too, wow. The anonymity the lack of reply gave her was perfect. She was able to park without any recognition and was free to take him in for a moment. He was wearing a grey polo shirt, just as he advertised, with blue shorts and white sneakers. But he was most certainly not wearing his hat. His hair was sandy blonde at best, mostly salt and pepper, styled short and spiked just in front. Grey hair, yes, please! So far, so good. She stepped out of the car and confidently walked toward him, realizing how tall he was as she walked toward him, at least 6'3, if not taller. Desire began to bloom in her belly for the first time in years.

"Hello, Scarlett. I had a feeling I would recognize you." His voice was low, a guttural sound, but somehow soothing. He offered his hand, "Jeremy Locke."

"The grey polo was a dead giveaway. I would never have recognized you without the hat." She laughed as she placed her hand in his, not offering her full name quite yet.

"It is very nice to meet you. Let's go inside where it's cooler." There it was again. Demanding in a way, but not forceful.

"Of course, lead the way."

She followed him to a table he had reserved in the bar area of the bistro.

"Have you been here before?" He asked.

"No, I have not. I don't have the chance to get out very often. I have only begun to see different parts of the city in the last few weeks. I haven't lived here that long."

"Oh, where are you from?" he asked, seeming genuinely

curious.

As a writer, she knew how to do her research. “I am from Ohio, born and raised. I wanted to move to a place where snow doesn’t exist, and it looks like I found it. What about you? Are you from Arizona?”

“No, I’m from everyone… almost,” He laughed. “No, seriously, I have lived in five states, but I call Texas home.

Oh, shit, shit, shit…of course he is. What are the odds? It’s not like she was from Texas really. She only lived the last four years of her life there.

“What part of Texas were you in?” She asked coolly.

“I was born in Virginia, but my family moved us to San Antonio for my father's work when I was six. I grew up there and didn’t leave until I was in my thirties. After my divorce, I took an opportunity to travel where my business took me and had short stints in New Orleans, Seattle, and Wichita. I bought my house in Phoenix over ten years ago but didn’t move here full-time until recently.”

Excellent, she thought, coming from the outskirts of the Dallas area, San Antonio and Dallas were practically on opposite sides of the world. She took a deep breath and once again became determined to enjoy the evening.

“Wow, I’m envious. I love traveling to new places and

learning how the other half lives. What was your favorite place where you lived?"

"New Orleans, hands down. The humidity was a little much, but I loved the culture, history, and music."

"You liked the music, you say? What kind of music speaks to you?" Shelby asked.

"The jazz music in New Orleans is different from anywhere else on earth. It's raw and feels real in a way that no other music does. I spent many nights sitting on a park bench under the stars, listening to trumpets, saxophones, and some of the best gospel voices I have ever heard." Jeremy's eyes wondered as he recalled his adventures.

"I'm jealous! That sounds wonderful. I'm a music lover myself. I appreciate it all. I was never able to pick a favorite, exactly. I can find something meaningful in the lyrics or movement of just about any song," Shelby closed her eyes, thinking about the way certain songs made her feel.

"You are already speaking my language, Scarlet." The sound of her new name was a momentary disappointment. She already wanted to know what her real name sounded like from his lips. She quickly decided to change the subject before he could read her expression.

"What exactly is the energy sector? That is what your profile said." She chuckled and learned in.

"Ha, yep, was that ambiguous enough for you?" Jeremy laughed.

"Very, I have all sorts of guesses on what that may mean. Nuclear power plant operations or oil baron were at the top of the list."

Their bodies began to angle toward the other as comfort set in for both of them.

"Nuclear power, not so much. Oil, I have to admit that I do dabble a little bit. I am primarily focused on several different natural gas energy applications, but I still have some oil investments as well. As you can imagine, I try not to advertise that." His look clearly conveys the underlying issue: he had money and seemingly lots of it. This was getting better and better by the moment, not that the money mattered, but as they continued to speak, her anxiety about her personal situation and potentially being taken advantage of dissipated.

"Enough about me, what about you?" He asked eagerly.

"Did we forget to order our drinks?" Shelby dodged for a moment.

"Oh, shoot, we did!" Jeremey said, looking around. "I will

go to the bar. I'm surprised a waiter hasn't come by yet." Jeremy stood up quickly, surveying his surroundings for the best available route to the bar, and headed in that direction. Shelby wondered how long it would take him to realize that he didn't know her drink order before turning around. Just as the thought crossed her mind, he stopped in his tracks and swung around in a perfect 180-degree turn, smiling sheepishly at her from across the restaurant. Oh, wow, he was more adorable than she could have hoped for.

"Um, so what will you be having, my lady?" he asked gallantly, trying to make up for his initial mistake.

"Kettle martini, slightly dirty, three blue cheese olives, extra cold. If you get that right, you'll get a kiss." Her face reddened as soon as the words slipped from her mouth.

"I have my mission, and I will succeed at all costs." His eyes widened, and he was off as quickly as he had returned.

What was she thinking? That was too forward, no doubt about it. She had known him for, like, five minutes. Shelby, you are thinking with what's between your legs! Think with your brain, woman, she scolded herself. Jesus, Is this what it's like to be a man? All she had to do was become a celibate middle-aged woman to find out. She waited an uncomfortably long fifteen minutes, watching three different servers walk by the table without saying a word. He returned with the drinks in his hand, setting them both down on the table. He sat down and then lifted her drink high as if presenting it to her.

"Will you try it and let me know if I have earned my reward?" His dark eyes stared into hers. She took a sip from the ice-cold glass, savoring the vodka as it hit the back of her throat with a hint of saltiness.

"It's perfect." She admitted, with no hesitation. She wanted his lips. There was no denying it, public restaurant or not. She stood up and took the two steps toward his chair as he rose again to his feet. Shelby leaned in, and he met her halfway, their lips touching softly at first, then pressing harder, neither one pulling away. She tasted his lips lightly with her tongue, with his reciprocating timidly until their tongues were fully intertwined and dancing. Shelby became distantly aware of the voices around them becoming silent. There was no noise, just his taste and smell. Her hands wrapped around his forearms, squeezing them until he stopped and pulled away. He opened his eyes, kissed her lightly on the lips, and then sat back down. Dazed, it took her a moment before taking her seat. He reached across the table for her hand, which she gave to him willingly. Neither spoke but squeezed each other's hands reassuringly.

"Are you hungry?" he asked finally.

"No, are you?"

"No."

Shelby lifted her martini toward him. He grabbed his glass, and they drank, both wondering who was going to make the next move. When each glass was over half empty, he spoke first.

"Want to get out of here?"

Shelby couldn't believe she was saying or doing any of this, but she never hesitated.

"Yes."

He held her hand without saying a word, stood up, and led her to the door. Within seconds, they were at the passenger door of his BMW, which he opened and then closed behind her. She had no fear or concern that she had just climbed into a stranger's car.

Less than twenty minutes later, as his bare chest weighed down upon her breasts and he finally entered her, she knew she would never regret this, no matter what happened next. She cried out so loudly he feared that he had hurt her.

"Are you okay?" he whispered in her ear, pulling out slowly.

"No, don't leave me. I am perfect, please, don't stop," She said breathlessly as she squeezed his ass, forcing him further inside of her.

"You are beautiful, Scarlet, in every way." Jeremy crooned, resting his lips on her shoulder as he continued to ride her.

If only he knew my name, she thought distantly, for now, it didn't matter. This moment, this feeling, this closeness, was everything.

"Is this the appropriate time to tell you that you have a lovely home?" She giggled as she turned over to her stomach, watching him intently as he returned naked from the bathroom. His skin was perfectly tan and firm despite his forty-six years. She would have to ask him how he managed that.

"You are silly. I like that." He said as he lifted the covers and climbed in next to her. "Are you hungry?"

"After that? Yes, ravenous."

He grabbed her hand once more and pulled her out of the covers. "Let's go see what we have in the kitchen." Instead of walking toward the door, he went to the closet, pulled out a T-shirt, and handed it to her. While she slipped it over her head, he stepped into a fresh pair of black cotton boxer briefs.

"We are dressed for dinner!" He laughed.

Jeremy rummaged through the kitchen, finding a frozen pizza, popped it into the oven, and poured them both a glass of chardonnay he had chilled in the fridge.

"Digiorno it is," he laughed, "Would you like the dime tour

while we wait?"

She nodded enthusiastically, not bothering to set down her wine as he took her hand and guided her to the living room.

"This is where I sit watching football and drinking beer," he winked. His home was vast. The living room had vaulted ceilings that required three fans and was adorned with crown molding and stark white walls accented with brushed silver fixtures. A gigantic flat screen hung on each side of the gigantic room. Original works of art, she assumed, were the room's centerpieces. Two separate black leather wrap-around sofas and several chairs created the living space. As he continued to walk her around the house, the enormity of his wealth set in. She was surprised that he was so willing to bring her back here after such a brief meeting, although she had to assume he probably did this all the time to impress women. He was certainly making a statement with her now, that's for sure, she thought. And he didn't even have her phone number. If he didn't ask, that would be the sign she needed to bury this evening far away from her heart and mind, never to be spoken of again. She didn't want to be taken in by the guy with two flat screens in his living room! In the distance, they both heard the oven buzzer, signaling their pizza was ready.

He set out plates, brought out the pizza and cutter on a round stone to the center of the table, and then returned to the kitchen for the rest of the bottle of chardonnay. He lifted his glass towards her.

"To an extraordinary and unexpected evening," Jeremy toasted.

She lifted her glass and repeated after him, disappointment and mild regret already creeping into her voice. This was a mistake. How could she have gone home with someone within thirty minutes of meeting them, and why did she like him so much already? She hardly knew anything about him.

"Are you okay, Scarlett?" He asked, taking her hand once again.

"Of course!" She said, a little too brightly.

They ate their pizza in silence. Once she was done, she would dress quickly and bow out gracefully. There is no sense in dragging this out with an awkward goodbye, she thinks. His voice startled her thoughts.

"Scarlett, I would like to ask you to stay. I know that seems strange after just meeting, and I understand completely if you feel uncomfortable. You may not believe it, but this isn't something I'm used to. I am unsure what our next step is, but I know I want to spend more time with you if you're open to it."

Unexpected relief washed over her. She had no intentions of getting involved with someone, so why did his words have such an effect on her?

"I would like that very much."

"Excellent, then I propose we start where we ended off. Tell me about yourself, Scarlet…" His eyes never left hers.

That was how Shelby Wise, aka Scarlett Winchell, fell in love, all at once and without warning.

Chapter Nine

Ansel hung up the phone, shaking his head. He had agreed to pro bono services for a murder victim, Mrs. Catherine Davis, whose husband was unable to afford a funeral, although the community was so distraught over the situation that the mayor had called him personally to ask for the favor. He may be young, but he was respected in the community, and he couldn't say no. They would be bringing her body from the hospital in an ambulance in little less than half an hour, and then Mr. Davis would come by to meet with him later in the afternoon.

He had read about the discovery of her body in this morning's paper, an apparent strangulation. The article stated that the authorities were looking for drifters in the area to detain and question. He had not known Mrs. Davis, although Ansel had met Mr. Davis when he needed his vehicle's hoses replaced a few years back. His impression was less than endearing. Mr. Davis was rough in demeanor and appearance, with a reputation for violence. He wondered if the police were looking for suspects a little closer to home, perhaps.

The ambulance arrived at the front of the building. He ran outside to direct them to the east entrance where they could load the body through the garage, outside of plain view. He thanked the driver and wheeled her sheeted body into the embalming room. She was already starting to decompose, and the smell was strong. His mind immediately returned to the battlefield, dismembered body parts decomposing in the streets along with beaten and raped men and women. Those were the things no one wrote about in the stories of what really happened in the war. The men fighting, holding on to those secrets, even after they returned.

He flipped over the sheet and winced at the sight of her, her grey milky skin sagging and then darkening when the blood settled in her back. The body must have been lying flat among the weeds. She was covered in dead leaves and grasses that clung to her dress and hair. He carefully removed her shoes, which had both survived the tumble down the embankment, and then reached for the sheers to remove her floral dress. She was about the age of his mother, and it broke his heart to have to undress her in this way, never taking his eyes off the angry red streaks and splotches around her neck. He could clearly see two round thumbprints on either side. Strangulation was a very intimate crime, and he couldn't help considering Mr. Davis, who was due to arrive in the next few hours when he stared at those marks.

As he removed her dress, he began to feel a buzzing with an almost audible humming noise accompanying the feeling. His hands were both tingling and burning at the same time. His head began to swim, and again, he thought of his mother. A single tear ran down his cheek. Completely unaware of his actions, he bent down and placed one hand on her neck and one on her face as if embracing her for a kiss. Something rushed from his body he had never felt before, a whoosh of electric energy…and then nothing. The buzzing continued for a few minutes, requiring Ansel to sit down and wait for the dizziness and disorientation to pass. When he had regained his composure, he covered her body with a clean sheet and left the room.

That had never happened before, and he wanted to step away for a while to make sure he was feeling well enough to continue. Ansel walked to his office, sat in his brown leather chair, and began reviewing the calls he needed to make for the upcoming services this weekend. Both families intended to hold services at St. Stephens, so he would need to reach out to the parish to confirm the details again and ensure Father Atkins would be available. As he picked up the receiver, he heard the bell, signaling someone had come through the front door. Ansel stood up and walked briskly to the entrance of the building.

"Mr. Davis, welcome. I'm so sorry for your loss. I didn't expect you so soon, or I would have been waiting at the door for you. My apologies," Ansel offered.

"Okay, should we sit down and go over things? Barney Johnson said you would be helping me. I got no money for the funeral." Bob mumbled without looking up from his brown work boots.

“Of course, Mr. Davis, I am here to assist you with everything to take care of your wife’s final expenses.” Ansel guided Bob to the desk where they could sit down and discuss the options.

“I am going to ask you some questions to get us started and then make some recommendations based on your answers, is that okay?”

Bob nodded again without looking up from his now seated legs.

“Do you or your wife have any religious affiliation?” Ansel asked.

After the question-and-answer session with limited one-word answers from Bob, Ansel recommended a rosary on Monday evening, followed by services and burial on Friday. Considering the circumstances, the county would cover the cost of the burial, and Ansel would provide the rest.

“I do need you to bring in a dress for Mrs. Davis to wear along with her makeup kit so I can prepare her in the way she would have preferred. When do you think you can drop these items by?” Ansel asked.

“I’ll come by tomorrow after work.” Bob walked to the door and jutted his hand out awkwardly toward Ansel, who shook it. He turned quickly toward the entrance and left without another word.

Ansel still did not care for the man. He didn't know if Bob had killed his wife or not, but he knew the type. He had known numerous killers, war or not, it left its stink on the man responsible. Bob carried something unsavory around with him, and Ansel strongly suspected it was the stink of a man who crushed his wife's neck with his bare hands, pressing his thumbs into her flesh until he had no strength left.

After he made his calls to St. Stephens about the now three upcoming services, he was ready to begin attending to Mrs. Davis. Ansel had to start the embalming process now before decomposition accelerated any further. He made his way down the hall to the embalming room, entered, and then closed the door behind him.

"WHAT?!" Ansel called out as he stumbled back, having lifted the sheet, Mrs. Davis's skin had changed colors from a bluish grey with dark blackish splotching to a light pink. The marks around her neck had also begun to fade; he could have sworn he could see the thumbprints made on the side of her neck just a few hours ago, and now they were gone entirely. Bodies simply did not heal themselves.

"What the hell is going on here?" he asked aloud. Had Mr. Davis found his way back here and done something to the body, perhaps? He had been with him the whole time.

"Bob! Stop! Please don't…" Catherine's voice croaked from the table, her hands darting to her throat, expecting to feel his hands around her neck.

Ansel jumped toward the door, catching his left shoe on the chair positioned directly behind him. He fell to the floor, barely catching himself with his hands as his head hit the cabinet with a loud thud. "Dammit!" He crawled the rest of the way, positioning his back against the door and staring up at the embalming table less than 5 steps away from him. He could see her arms flailing and hear the raspy sounds of her trying to catch her breath, but fortunately was unable to see her face. Terror gripped him as he drew his knees up to his chest and wrapped his arms around them. Rocking himself back and forth with eyes squeezed shut, she called out again and again to her supposed attacker. There was no doubt in his mind that she had been dead, he knew what dead looked and smelled like, this should not be happening. Yet, it was. Minutes passed before she became silent. Summoning every ounce of courage, Ansel snapped his eyes open to find her staring down at him. This time, it was his scream that wrung out.

Chapter Ten

Trust proliferated between them in a way that Shelby never expected. He was more attractive than she was typically drawn to. Shelby had always had a difficult time trusting perfect-looking men, but tall ones with a tan and an equally large bank account… nearly impossible. Perfect men tended to believe they were God's gift to women and the world. Lying and cheating were simply part of the package if you wanted to bask in their glory. Shelby did not need to bask in anyone's glory but was quickly able to see through the perfect exterior of a man who had been heartbroken by the ending of his first marriage, spending the next several years throwing himself into his work. He had not anticipated their connection any more than she had. After finishing their pizza, they sat up talking until dawn, getting to know each other by telling stories of the past. While Shelby had to be careful, she was as honest as she could be, showing her true self behind the careful lies about location, marriage, children, and career. Exhausted, they crawled back into his bed, waking up a few hours later to make love and then returning easily to sleep. Day one bled into day two, and only when the weekend was over did she return home to reflect on what had happened.

As the months passed, her writing became even more impassioned. She floated through the days until the evenings when they spent their time together. Shelby hadn't realized how isolated she'd become in the last five years, and it felt good to get out in the world. They had been to two concerts, one comedy show, a murder mystery dinner theater experience, a showing of Wicked, and dinner out almost every night in the last three months. Not to mention as many joint swims as possible at either home. He seemed to lack as many friends in Phoenix as she did, so they spent all their time together. She was able to discover that his fitness routine consisted of a combination of running in the mornings five days a week, swimming daily, and weightlifting in his home gym. He ate well but indulged when he wanted. He seemed to miss sex as much as she did, no matter the day's schedule; they texted to determine what house they would be spending the evening at and fell into each other's arms fervently once they were together again. She struggled to remember a single evening he had not finished inside of her.

Shelby was no fool. Even as a writer, she knew this was the honeymoon phase where lust fueled her feelings far more than love. Did she love him? Maybe… probably, she reasoned. It wasn't simply that she had missed companionship and physical touch-- it was him. Jeremy had brought adventure, anticipation, humor, and comfort back into her life, not to mention lots and lots of orgasms. Not that she would tell him about her feelings at this point. They were just now enjoying each other's company and feeling things out as they went. She told herself not to dwell too much on the details.

It was still early. Although, what is it that they say, hope springs eternal? She was supposed to be writing, and here she was again, daydreaming. The day she had enough courage to tell him about her specific writing specialty, they had decided on a low-key evening on her back deck. She brought out the Greek salads she whipped up along with her first book, casually setting it down beside his plate without saying a word.

"What's this?" he asked, turning it over and reviewing the back flap and the computer-generated picture on the back. "She's not really my type, babe." He laughed as he set the book between them on the table.

"Very funny, although I hope she is becoming your type. She is me."

"What do you mean?" He looked at her quizzically.

"I wrote it. That's what I do. I write erotic fiction under a pseudonym." She braced for a laugh, but he took the book back in his hands and began reading the synopsis, and then turned to the beginning and started reading the first page with nothing but a serious expression.

"Wait, I didn't mean for you to sit here and read it."

"I had been wondering when you would tell me about your writing. I admit I Googled you and tried to find something online, but when I couldn't find it, I knew you would tell me when the time was right. I'm so glad that you have. I would love to read it, do you mind?" His face was genuine and interested.

"Um, no. I thought you might wait, but honestly, I don't mind at all," she admitted.

Shelby watched as he simultaneously dug into his salad and her book. When she finished her dinner, she left him in his chair on the patio. She attempted to busy herself, putting in her earbuds and listening to Taylor Swift, the upbeat music allowing her to complete her kitchen chores quickly. She did manage to find excuses to walk past the back window on no less than four occasions over the next hour to check on his progress. Finally, she decided to settle in on the couch with her own book, this time a thriller about a crime spree in Paris she suspected was perpetrated by the guy's wife instead of the dark and mysterious businessman who the reader was supposed to assume was responsible. In the writing biz, we called that the "red herring." At some point, she heard the back door open. She saw Jeremy over the top of the book, looking around for her, finally locating her on the couch. He moved quickly from the back door to her spot, lifting her gently by the hand and leading her directly to the bedroom.

"You are an unbelievably sexy and talented woman, Scarlet. How did I get so lucky to meet you? Do you mind if I try out what you so deliciously described on page 124?" He slyly smiled down at her while placing the hand he had grasped down the front of his pants, finding him already hard.

"I don't remember what's on page 124. You will have to guide me, babe." She whispered as her grip tightened, moving slowly down the length of him. He pulled down his shorts and briefs while she kept her hand firmly in place until he removed them and walked toward the closet. She stood at the edge of the bed, fully dressed, and watched him as he surveyed the contents intently, suddenly finding something that would suit his purpose. He pulled two of her differently colored scarves from a hanger and brought them to her, placing them in her hands ceremoniously.

"Tie me up." His words hung between them as she searched her mind for what she could possibly have written, wanting the details to be perfect enough to fulfill his fantasy. So, her books didn't just affect women. Fascinating, she thought.

Wordlessly, she placed the scarves on the bed and reached for him, pulling his shirt over his head until he was naked in front of her. Without undressing, she pushed him down on the bed, grabbing his left wrist and pulling it up over his head, securing it to the headboard with her favorite purple scarf, repeating the action with his right wrist. Shelby gazed down from her vantage point and saw him staring at her. She loved the control he was gifting her, bending her neck and tracing his lips with her tongue as desire grew in her abdomen. Knowing that he was helpless only made every movement more intense.

"Fuck, Scarlett." He called out as he began to move uncontrollably underneath her.

"I know," She said, taking her powerful position on top of him, moving further down until the heat through her shorts was right on top of him. She tilted her head forward, nipping, kissing, and licking his chest and stomach as slowly as she could restrain herself until her mouth arrived just below his belly button. She heard Jeremy's panting catch in his throat as she finally took him into her mouth…

"Let me finish you, please," He pleaded after she was done.

"I thought we were sticking to page 124." She quipped, untying his restraints.

"I thought you didn't remember what was on page 124."

She laughed out loud, "You refreshed my memory." He grabbed her waist, pulled her down on the bed, and immediately pulled her shorts around her ankles.

"Let me see how I can show you how appreciative I am, starting with my fingers," his face disappearing from view.

He had finished the book the following day, sharing his

favorite parts and not just what they could try in the bedroom. He seemed fascinated with her storytelling abilities along with her exotic imagination. What he knew was that most of her readers didn't know that her imagination was limitless, while her personal experiences had very defined boundaries. Writing was a way to allow herself to explore life without crossing over. Once he had read her writings, a deeper intimacy grew between them, the kind only honestly can develop. That was three weeks ago, and since then, there seemed to be no holding back in their lovemaking or relationship. While she could never tell him about her past, Shelby did everything possible to be honest with him in any way she could. He was becoming more open about his business dealings, mineral gas rights, and oil field investments, along with additional details about his broken marriage. Jeremy claimed no hard feelings against his ex-wife, although, after fifteen years of marriage and years of failed attempts at conceiving a child, they had become distant from one another. Distance had led to contempt and eventually resentment. Finally, Jenny asked him for a divorce. The heartbreak he suffered was more about what he wished he could have done to console her, blaming himself for the inability to give her a child along with failing to repair their marriage. He then engaged in frivolous "hook-ups," which he sheepishly admitted helped him move past the heartbreak and finally think about what he wanted for a change. When some of his investments began to take off, his energy was refocused on his career and strategic expansion throughout the country. He had dated two women since settling in Phoenix a few years ago, but neither had become serious.

"Is this what you would call serious?" she had asked in response just a week ago.

"You're kidding, right?" Sounding incredulous, "Yes, Scarlet, I consider this serious. I have no intention of seeing anyone else. I love spending time with you. I know you haven't had the time to date anyone else because I've monopolized every possible moment of your time." Smiling and holding her face in his hands, pulling her lips towards his.

Again, he took just the right amount of control, reassuring her. That night they visited the Phoenix Art Museum, returning to his house for a night of what she could only consider "fucking". It was rare, but when they were in the mood, they were able to use each other's bodies however they wished, with little concern about the other's perceptions of their behavior. They communicated their desires and needs effortlessly. Afterward, as she lay in the crook of his arm, breathless, he had asked her a question.

"Do you ever wish you had children?"

"Yes," she said before she even knew the word was coming out of her mouth. How she wished every single day that she had the chance to be a real mother to a child, her child. Tears welled up in her eyes without warning. She turned her head quickly before he saw her face.

"Oh shit, I'm sorry, Scarlet. I'm sorry. I shouldn't have brought that up in such a way, I'm an ass." Jeremy apologized hurriedly.

Sniffling, "No, not your fault, you couldn't have known. I didn't even realize how upset I'd be by the question."

"Listen, I know we haven't been together that long, but you are still young enough to have children. I can't give them to you, but I would step aside if that's what you really wanted. You deserve that chance." She could feel his arm start to tremble under her head.

"Jeremy, no. That time has passed. I want you…" his mouth clamping down on hers before she could finish.

The cell next to her computer buzzed twice in quick succession, signaling a text message.

My place, 6pm? I have a question to ask you.

Smiling, she texted him back:

I wonder what it could be… see you soon. XO

Perhaps tonight, she would take a little extra care in selecting an outfit. She couldn't help but wonder what he was going to ask her. For the first time in over six years, she visited a lingerie store over the weekend, selecting over ten matching sets of bras and panties along with several nighties and even a few corsets with matching garters and stockings. Thirteen hundred dollars later, she left the store with six bags and her imagination full of possibilities. This could be a legitimate tax write-off, she laughed to herself. Reviewing the options, she selected a set of white panties and bra made from pure lace, just transparent enough to show a hint of her nipples. After the shower, she rubbed vanilla-scented lotion all over her body, dressed in her white lace, and finally covered it with a simple peach shift dress with white flowers and the same gold sandals she had worn on their first meeting. Shelby pulled her hair back and pinned it up, leaving a single strand dangling on each side of her face. This is as good as it gets. Looking across the room, she noted 5:45 pm on the bedside table clock. Good thing his house was minutes away.

The garage was open for her as usual, and she let herself in, closing the door behind her. The dining room table had three red candles in the middle that she had never seen before, their place settings were complimented with two glasses of red wine. As she admired the table, he came from behind her, kissing the nape of her neck where her hair would have typically hung.

"You look amazing," He said slowly as he walked in front of her and intentionally gave her a once-over.

"Thank you. This is amazing. What's the special occasion?" Shelby asked, hoping she wouldn't have to wait long to find out what he was going to ask her.

"I am hoping this will be a special occasion. Let's eat." Jeremy smirked as he looked at her and walked to the kitchen, bringing back the first course of a fresh salad with strawberries, blueberries, almonds, and vinaigrette. He was careful not to look directly at her, knowing that she would be dying to know what all of this was about. Hardly keeping a straight face, he picked up the small plates and then returned with dinner consisting of roasted vegetables, marinated tomatoes with burrata drizzled with balsamic glaze, and blue lump crab cakes.

"How did you do all of this?" she asked, astonished at the extravagance and elegance of the dinner.

"Don't worry, I didn't cook, if that's what you're worried about! I ordered out and re-plated." He winked at her as he took the first bite of his crab cake. God, could he be any sexier? His arms flexed under his shirt as he moved the fork to his mouth, making it almost impossible to concentrate, let alone eat. Tearing her eyes off him, she pushed her fork into the crab cake, hitting something hard. Shelby's head jerked up, staring at him, heart pounding. She dragged her fork, and with it came a purple key. A house key.

"A little too cheesy?" he asked nervously.

Speechless, she stood up and crawled into his lap. She had never been happier, ever. Tears were pricking the corner of her eyes. Her heart was close to exploding as she whispered in his ear, "I love you."

"I love you too, Scarlet, and I don't want to spend another day without you in my life. I want us to share our lives together. Please make this your home." It was the first time they had said it aloud, although it had been apparent to each of them for weeks.

"Are you crying because you're happy or because living with me would be a fate worse than death?" He pulled her face toward his, smiling slyly.

"I have firsthand experience with a fate worse than death, and this is nothing close." His eyebrows furrowed, clearly confused by her comment.

Shelby's tears of joy brought her thoughts back to a conversation she had just a week after her second life had begun. It took her over six years to believe him, but Ansel had been right.

"One day, all of this will be behind you, and you will be happy. Once you allow yourself to be free, the possibilities are endless. I don't know why you were chosen, Shelby. I don't know why I was chosen to do this, but I know your second chance is my life's work. There isn't just one life out there for each person. There is a whole other life out there waiting for you if you have the courage to find it," Ansel had explained. She was too consumed in her grief to take his words to heart. Only now did she realize what Ansel had done for her. She had wasted the last five years hanging on to the past, to a life that was no longer hers. While her body had been taking in air, she had not truly been living. It wasn't all about Jeremy. It was the opportunity to do something meaningful with her life. Why was she continuing to hide when no one was looking for her?

"Babe, are you okay?" Jeremy asked with genuine concern shining in his eyes.

"Yes," she smiled at him assuredly, "I am simply grateful to have found you. When in the hell did you have time to get a purple key made?"

"The day after, you sat in that chair in my t-shirt and ate frozen pizza with me. I think I loved you then." Rubbing his cheek against hers. She climbed down from his lap, returning to her seat at the table and wiping the tears from her face. This moment felt like the first day of the rest of her life.

"I think I did, too. I have loved you for a while now. Yes, I will share my life with you. Nothing would make me happier." Shelby beamed.

"I don't want to wait, Scarlet. I'm not getting any younger, and at this point in my life, I know what I want and what kind of life

I want to live. I want to live that life with you. I have no doubt that at some point, I will ask you to marry me, I have never felt this way about anyone," the words tumbled out of him, as if he worried, he wouldn't have the courage to finish if he didn't get them out.

"Jeremy, I love you more than I could ever possibly imagine. Let's do this." She laughed, reaching for his hand. They left dinner on the table as she led him to what would become their bedroom.

"As long as you don't bring that composting thing, we'll be in good shape!" he said from behind her.

Chapter Eleven

Catherine often wondered how Ansel and she endured those first early days. She still didn't understand how it had all happened, but for the first time in over twenty years, she was happy to be alive. Over the last few weeks since she had woken up, they had talked a great deal about how and why this had happened to her. She felt the hand of God. However, Ansel claimed he had no divine powers. Catherine would argue otherwise; God was working through him. She had been resurrected from the grave after three days. In her mind, it doesn't get much more sacred than that. She had slept, she had eaten, and she had truly rested. It had been years since she could say that. The fact that her husband had killed her was the least of her worries. She always knew he would, and she had prayed for it. The Lord answered her prayers and gave her a chance at a new life. They hadn't worked out all the details yet, but Ansel said he would help her move far away to somewhere she could start over again. The question that kept circulating in her mind was the purpose. How did God want her to live out the rest of her life? Just as she contemplated her future for the hundredth time, Ansel knocked on his bedroom door. He had been kind enough to allow her to stay in his little house while she regained her strength, and they decided what to do next.

"Come in!" She called from the chair in the corner of the room.

"Are you okay?" Ansel asked before he could see her face.

"Yes, just thinking, as usual."

"How can I help?" Ansel understood what she was thinking about but still didn't know how to help her get past it.

"I don't think you can. I have to figure this out on my own, pray to God, and then wait for an answer."

Ansel sat on the bed, staring at the floor for several minutes before speaking.

"I want you to consider something for a moment, Catherine. Maybe you were brought back to live your life, nothing more. Not to fulfill some purpose or mission, but to live a happy life on your own terms. You may never get the answers you want, and I fear that your second chance will pass you by while you wait for this grand purpose that never existed in the first place. I brought you back, Catherine, and all I want is for you to find peace and live the best possible way you know how."

Tears were flowing down both sides of his face as he declared his wishes for her future. He felt profoundly responsible for her. He had just as much at stake in this as she did, and he would be damned if he was going to let her waste any more time. After he had to sit across the table from Bob and then stand next to him at the funeral when he knew the truth… it was almost too much for him.

When Bob returned to bring her a dress to wear for the service, it was far too easy to convince him of a closed casket. All he had to do was mention the marks on her neck. His face instantly paled, nodding, not even opening his mouth to consent. The dress he had brought was a nightgown, not even fit for going out of the house, let alone her funeral. Ansel let it pass only because he knew Catherine would never have to wear it. They ended up burying almost two hundred pounds of sandbags he had to purchase from out of town so as not to raise any suspicions. Even though the funeral was well attended, hardly anyone knew the woman who was murdered and left in a ditch on the side of a back country road. Curiosity, rather than grief, brought them out.

"Ansel, I appreciate everything you have and will do for me. I promise to do my very best. That's all I can do." Smiling to reassure him that she would be okay. Her eyes shone with excitement. If she had been standing in front of a mirror at that moment, she wouldn't have recognized herself. Over the last thirty years, she had endured, never really living. For the first time in the last three weeks, she began to allow herself to do something she hadn't done since before her wedding night-- hope.

Both were standing up, and they hugged each other like mother and son. It was almost time to let her go and find her way.

"Have you thought any more about where you want to go?"

He asked.

"Yes, I've decided on New York," Catherine said excitedly.

"Oh, Wow." He was surprised. The big city was very different from the small town she had grown up and lived in her entire life. Ansel doubted if she had ever taken a bus, let alone flagged down a cab in the middle of a busy downtown street.

"Why New York?" Ansel asked as casually as his tone would allow.

"I've seen pictures of the big buildings in magazines and always wondered what it would be like to go there. I will never forgive myself if I waste this opportunity and pick a place to start my life over again because it is small and safe. I want everything to be new, and I want to expose myself to everything I missed out on in my old life. Does that make sense?"

"It does, it does. I want to make sure you are going to be okay. I feel responsible for you, and the last thing I want to worry about is you being out there scared and alone."

"Ansel, I want to be scared, and I want to do all the hard things ahead alone. I have never done that before. In fifty years, I haven't made a single decision by myself, let alone get to decide things like where I would live, how I would dress, who I could talk to, what I want to eat, anything." Catherine's eyes welled up with tears as she considered how much she had missed. "I need to do this one big thing and put myself in the middle of it. The only way to survive is to figure out how to do things on my own."

"At least let me get you started. I will make some calls and get you a hotel reservation somewhere centrally located. That way you have some time to find a place you would like to live. I wish I had more money to give you to get started, but you should be able to live for at least six months without worrying. I will also figure out the best bus routes to get you from here to New York. It will most likely take you a few days to get there."

"Ansel, you have been so kind. The money is more than I have ever seen and should carry me through for longer than that if I stretch it. I would appreciate the help with the bus and hotel. Once I get there, it will be up to me to find the hotel and figure out the rest. I have never been so excited about anything in my life. Glory to God."

"Well, Catherine, when would you like to go?" Ansel asked with a tinge of pride in his voice.

"How about this weekend? Maybe I can make you a meal Friday night and set off on Saturday morning?"

"Ok, that's four days. I think that gives me enough time to get some things figured out. The clothes I bought you will have to do until you get there and can go shopping."

They hugged again, this time for almost a full minute. Each silently wondered what the future would hold, full of worries and excitement. Little did they know then that the real excitement would come just before her bus left for New York.

Shelby lay on her stomach, wrapped up in Jeremy's grey cotton sheets, observing him washing his hands in the sink through the crack in the bathroom door. She never tired of watching him, his cock bounced ever so slightly as he rubbed his hands together. She could hardly peel her eyes away. He was hers, the man himself, but the love and pleasure that came with him also belonged to her entirely. She rolled over just as he walked toward the door and returned to her side in bed.

"Should we rescue dinner from the table or go out?" Jeremy asked as he crawled under the covers.

"I don't see why we need to leave this bed at all," she said as her hand slid down his chest and his stomach. She finally found what she was searching for just a little further down. His surprised groan brought a smile to her face. All of this was hers for the taking. She always felt powerful as she claimed what she wanted, climbing on top of him and sliding down until he was buried deeply inside of her. Shelby continued to push her body down, wanting everything she could get. It wasn't just lust driving her. She wanted him, but she desired to lay her claim to him. After everything that had happened in the last five years, more than anything, she wanted him and their lives together to be authentic. With every thrust, she felt his hunger for her, the realness of it all.

His eyes never left hers, seemingly understanding her need for his undivided attention.

"I love you, Scarlet," he whispered, causing her to move her hips faster, wanting to please him. Jeremy's face tensed. His brows were firmly set in concentration. She knew he was close, trying to hold back until she could finish herself. Her orgasm wasn't what she was after, she wanted his, and she wanted it inside of her. Her pace quickened even more for just a few seconds until he could no longer take it, releasing himself inside of her. She smiled down at him triumphantly. She accomplished what she had worked hard for.

"Fuck, Scarlet. I didn't know that was possible at my age, twice in less than fifteen minutes, what have you done to me?" His smile broadened, matching her own.

"I just want to make sure you understand what you signed up for."

"Is that a threat, darling?" he asked as he grabbed her and wrapped his arms around her waist.

"That is a guarantee, Mr. Locke. I will always want you this way, and I do tend to get what I want."

"I have no doubt, Miss Winchell. I have no doubt you do." He nuzzled his nose and mouth into her neck, taking in her scent as he spoke.

Shelby pulled back, staring at his face, wondering again how she ended up in this bed so blissfully happy. She took her hand, rubbed deeply between her legs until her index and middle fingers were sufficiently wet, and pulled her hands out of the covers, circling his lips with the tips of her fingers. To her surprise, he opened his mouth and took her fingers inside, licking off all the moisture. Every fantasy, everything she had ever desired, was hers. She would never have to worry about him holding back. At that moment, she knew that for the first time in her life, she was experiencing true freedom, true love, and true intimacy. This was the stuff you only read about in novels, just like the ones she wrote.

"Okay, so I admit, I'm hungry." She laughed as she swatted his backside.

"Just say the word babe. What are you hungry for?"

"Sushi!"

"Let's do it! I'm going to hop in the shower really quick. Be ready in ten." He said, jumping out of bed.

"Deal!" She watched again as he walked toward the

bathroom door, beaming.

Dinner was perfect, as usual. They picked a favorite sushi spot early on that they both enjoyed and visited on a rotating basis. Each time they went, they agreed to try a new roll, and their options for something new were diminishing quickly. This time, it would have to be the octopus. They both agreed, but they ordered several of their favorites to go with it, just in case.

"Huh, a bit chewy, but pretty good," he commented after the first bite.

"Exactly, that is what I was just thinking," Shelby laughed through a bite of octopus' tentacle.

"Not that I am going to be adding this to our list, but it's not as bad as I thought it was going to be!" Jeremy exclaimed. They continued to eat and talk, drink Sapporo beer, and enjoy each other's company.

"When do you think you will want to move in?" Jeremy asked between bites.

"I was considering next week if that works for you. I will most likely rent out my place for a year, and then if things work out between us after that long, I can think about selling." She smirked and took another sip of beer.

"You don't think things will work out, my love, even after

that amazing display in "our" bed?" Jeremy asked, winking to let her know he understood her completely.

"Ha, at our ages, babe, we know better. I love you, but I also know how life can kick you in the ass at any time. I trust you and am willing to take this leap with you wholeheartedly, but I have no intention of being stupid, either. You know what I mean?"

"One hundred percent, Scarlet. All I know is that I want us to be together; I can't believe it's taken me forty years to find you, and I have no intention of letting you go. You can move in tomorrow or next week, or you can do whatever you want. I have a real estate agent friend I can call about your house. Just say the word when you're ready, and we can have it rented out in a matter of weeks." He leaned in to kiss her from across the table, and she leaned right back with a mouth full of spicy salmon.

It all seemed just a little too good to be true. Can this man really love me if he doesn't even know my real name, she thought wryly. He knows me, though. He knows the new me. Me, the writer, the swimmer, the adventurer. That is the me I was always meant to be, she thinks. As she finished her last bite, Shelby put the remainder of her doubts to rest. This is my life now. I have to live it. That was her final thought as he took her hand in his and began to kiss each knuckle.

Chapter Twelve

Catherine had finished packing in less than fifteen minutes. She had so few possessions now that everything fit into Ansel's military duffle bag. Now that the day had come, the excitement she felt had turned to anxiety. She had a painful tightening in her chest, and her heart was beating two times faster than it should have. At her age, that was nothing to joke about. Wouldn't it be funny to die of a heart attack just weeks after your husband murdered you? She was glad she could find some humor in it.

The only thing left to do was go to the kitchen and make a few sandwiches for the trip. She had to keep herself busy waiting for Ansel until he was due to take her to the bus stop. It would be the first time she had been out of the house, and that part was truly exciting. As Catherine walked to the kitchen, she didn't initially notice the open window or the truck pulling into the funeral home parking lot across the street. She made three ham and cheese sandwiches, wrapping each one in parchment paper as she went. Ansel would be walking over in just a few minutes.

Just then, anticipating Ansel's expected arrival, she noticed the kitchen window open for the first time since she had been here. Ansel was usually so careful. Maybe today was unique due to her imminent departure. Catherine peered out toward the sun, immediately noticing a familiar truck in the funeral home parking lot. The door had been left ajar, and suddenly, there was a sinking feeling in her gut. Whatever was happening over there couldn't be good, especially if Bob didn't even bother to turn off his truck or close the door.

In a split second, she knew what she had to do. She grabbed one of Ansel's jackets from the coat rack next to the door, and she dashed across the street, covering the best she could.

Bob Davis was visited by the police that morning. They said they wanted to ask him some routine questions about Catherine's death, but he could smell trouble. The police didn't come around unless there was something to come around about. Not a month later, anyway. They were either on to something or suspected something. Either way, it was no good. Bob could tell they were fishing, so he kept his answer short, sticking to his story about being at work the morning Catherine was killed. After twenty minutes, he could tell fishing was all they could do. The police didn't have anything on him. As they stood up from his kitchen table to leave, the older officer seemed to remember something he wanted to ask.

"Bob, do you recall hearing about some marks on your wife's neck when she was found?" The officer asked, looking directly at him.

"Um, I think I heard something like that. I can't really

remember," Bob stammered.

"Are you sure? I think somebody must have talked to you about that. Do you mind holding out your hands there for a second, Bob?"

Bob raised his hands in front of him for a few seconds before replacing his arms by his side, not fully understanding their request.

"You have some big hands there! Did you used to play football in school?" The officer smiled as he asked the questions.

"I did play some ball, yes." He said, looking confused.

"Big hands like that could wrap themselves around a woman's neck with no problem at all, wouldn't you agree, Earnest?" Looking over at his partner for confirmation.

"Yes sir, they rightly could." Nodding his agreement.

"Bob, the size of those thumbs of yours look just about the size of the marks on each side of Catherine's neck. What do you think about that?" The officer was goading him now.

Bob's face had turned white in the last twenty seconds, and his gigantic hands began to tremble.

"I don't know what you guys are talkin about. I didn't do nothin' to my wife."

"We'll see about that. I'm going to head on over to the

funeral place and get those pictures that Mr. Bishop took. Maybe I'll come back by and see if we can match them up. How would that be?"

"That be fine, because 'I didn't do nothin'." Bob's color had returned to his face. His fear had been replaced with anger.

"We'll see you real soon, Mr. Davis." With that, he winked and headed for the door.

Bob couldn't open his mouth as fury radiated all over his body. There was only one person he could get his hands on which to direct his anger. Fucking, Bishop. He was the one who saw those marks in the first place and probably reported it to the police. He pretended to be consoling him, when really all the asshole was doin was goin behind his back.

Ansel finished sweeping the front entryway, considering what a loss Catherine leaving would be to him personally. The last month had been healing for each of them. He had ensured she was ready to return to the world, but they had developed a close friendship in the meantime. He was getting used to someone being home when he got there each day. It was time to let her go, though. Keeping her locked up any longer was both cruel and dangerous. It would be better for everyone if Catherine were as far from Texas as possible. New York would accomplish that nicely. At least after she left, he would have time to figure out what all of this was about and how he was able to bring her back in the first place. With the broom safely back in its place, it was time to make his departure official by locking the back door and turning off the lights. Mind occupied, he was taken by complete surprise when he turned around to see Bob Davis' fist coming straight toward his face.

"You son of a bitch! You think I killed my wife, huh?" The fist connected just as Bob began to speak, sending Ansel to the floor with a spray of blood hitting the wall, floor, and ceiling. He was conscious but unable to speak. His jaw wouldn't move, and Ansel suspected it was probably broken.

"Where are the pictures at?" Bob screamed.

Thinking it may be safer to stay quiet and still, Ansel didn't respond.

Bob's anger was at its peak, and this asshole had decided to be difficult.

"If you ain't gonna tell me, I will fuckin kill you," Bob screamed again while spitting in Ansel's broken face.

"STOP IT BOB, right now!" Catherine shrieked from the foyer, immediately observing what was happening, relieved she had made it before Bob killed him.

Bob's face went slack and paled faster than when he spoke

to the police. She could tell he wasn't sure if he was hallucinating or if she was really standing right in front of him. He had never seen her in slacks, hair pulled back, and she was at least fifteen pounds lighter, not to mention happier than she had ever been. The improvements had altered her appearance, but she knew, deep down in his tony black heart, he realized it was her.

"Who are you?" Bob whispered, almost inaudibly.

"Who do you think I am, Bob? I'm your wife."

"No, you're not. Catherine's dead and buried. I know she's dead."

"You were never a good husband, Bob, but I guess you didn't do a very good job of killing me either." Her tone was even and firm, absent of fear. Ansel was proud of her despite his agony.

She moved toward him one small step at a time, conquering every fear she ever had with each movement. She thought about every time he towered over her. Ansel, forgotten, Bob attempted to withdraw, moving left then backward to avoid her coming any closer.

"You bitch, you stay away from me, whoever you are. Stay away!" He shouted, grabbing the wall for support with each backward step he took as she persisted in her advance.

Ansel understood that it was only a matter of time before

Bob lashed out. He worried it would be at Catherine this time instead of him. Bob's fear would turn back to anger soon enough. As Bob blindly retreated, Ansel took his chance, moving his leg just in time for Bob's left boot to catch it, throwing him off balance. He tumbled sideways, reaching out for anything he could get his hands on, grasping at the air frantically. Catherine and Ansel stared as if in slow motion as Bob's head hit the edge of Ansel's desk, hearing the crack of his skull as he bounced off and then hit the floor face first.

"Hail Mary, full of Grace, the Lord is with you; blessed are you among women, and blessed is the fruit of your womb, Jesus…" Catherine recited, but Ansel couldn't hear it. He was in sensory overload. His jaw hung off center, sending throbbing pain throughout his head and neck, and his brain was just now registering the fact that he had just killed a man. Meticulously, he got to his knees, crawling to the side of his desk, not knowing what he would see when peering around.

Bob's eyes were open, glassy, but somehow alert. A small trail of blood dripped from an apparent crack in the side of his skull. Blood was pooling around his head, turning his once light hair dark beneath him. He was still alive.

"Wha he hll am I gon to do, Cathrin? Hs not ded!" His words came out with only half the sounds as his mouth refused to cooperate.

Still, in mid-prayer, Catherine didn't respond. Red-tinged bubbles began trickling out of his mouth, his tongue convulsing. The only thing to do was to wait. He was dying, and nothing was going to stop that now.

Catherine seemed to snap out of it, stopping in the middle of a Hail Mary.

"Is he in pain?" She asked, finally peering around the desk.

"He got a be," Ansel did his best to respond.

"Good."

Chapter Thirteen

Shelby sat alone in her living room, looking around and constructing a mental plan for tackling this move. She told Jeremy that she needed a few days to sort through her things and determine what was going to his house and what was staying. The house would be rented out semi-furnished, at the very least. The real reason she needed a few days by herself was complicated. It's not like she would never have alone time again. He did travel occasionally. The guilt had begun to creep back in as soon as the realization hit of how truly happy she was. Her daughter and husband were out somewhere going through God only knows what, and she was in perfect heavenly bliss. It didn't make her just a bad mother…it made her a terrible human being. The reality was challenging because she had loved Steve with her whole being, and Maja was everything she could have asked for in a child. While she had been forced to leave them when she died, a heart-retching relief had set in over the last several years. It wasn't them that she was glad to leave behind, but herself. As a wife and mother, Shelby had become a version of herself that she secretly despised and didn't even realize.

She had always been good at sales, but as her income continued to increase, so did the responsibility that came with it. The constant travel, meetings, and increasing goals had begun to weigh on her. If someone had asked her six years ago if she was happy, she would have gushed with pride about her family and all she had accomplished. If she wasn't working, she was wife-ing or mothering. She couldn't remember the last time she had time for herself during her marriage or completed a personal goal just for her. If she hadn't died and had a chance at a second life, she never would have known what she was truly capable of. She was literally living the life of her dreams. The only thing missing was the people who thought she was dead.

Wasn't moving on with Jeremy like giving her first life the proverbial finger? Maybe it was, but she had to make a choice: move on and forgive herself or wallow in self-loathing and miss out on living this life at all. She needed a swim… getting up from the couch, she threw her blouse and jeans on the bed and slipped into her suit. Shelby slipped out the back patio door, took in the afternoon air, jumped into the pool, and let the cool water wash over her head. Swimming lap after lap cleared her mind, washing her of at least some guilt. Finally, needing to catch her breath, she surfaced and let the Arizona sun soak into her skin.

The actuality was that she hadn't seen her husband or daughter for six years, and to them, she was dead. For all she knew, they both had moved on. Shelby would never know, not only because that was one of Ansel's sacred rules but because she could never get past whatever she may learn. When she died, any commitment she made to Steve was broken. Unfortunately, the same had to be said for Maja, too. She was going to have to let them go.

Shelby spent that evening watching a Twilight marathon, drinking wine, and eating popcorn. This was her quiet way of saying goodbye to her first life and the last five years of solitude. It was after 1:30 AM when she heard her phone vibrating on the coffee table.

"Hello, babe. Couldn't sleep?" She answered.

"Scarlet, there's been a break-in at the house. I'm at the hospital."

Oh God, no, she thought as chills spread across her arms and neck.

"Are you okay? What happened? What hospital are you at?" Shelby stammered uncontrollably.

"Yes, I'm hurt, but I'll be okay. They tied me up…" Jeremy's voice trailed off.

"Jesus Christ, I'll get dressed and be there as soon as possible. Where are you?"

"Saint Joseph's, I'm still in Emergency. Scarlet, I love you. All I was thinking about when trying to get free was you." She had already made her way to the bedroom and was yanking on a pair of jeans as he spoke.

"I love you too. Give me twenty minutes, baby, and I'll be

right there," hanging the phone up before he could even respond. She was terrified of how hurt he might be. His voice sounded more than just strained; he sounded mortified. She tugged a t-shirt over her head, slipped her feet into the Berk's on her closet floor, and was out the door. Saint Jo's was right off the highway, so she didn't have to map her route. Driving way too fast, it only took her eight minutes before her car was in the closest available spot near the Emergency entrance.

"Hi, I'm here to see Jeremy Locke," the words came out before she reached the reception desk.

"Just one second, let me take a look. Okay, yes, he's in room eleven. I'll buzz you through the door on your right and take the hallway all the way down. Eleven is the last room on the left."

"Thank you." She uttered as she rushed toward the door.

At 2:00 AM, the hospital was noisier than she thought it would be. Three nurses walked across her path to other rooms as she approached Jeremy. Everything about the hospital was too bright and vibrant to be so early, with strikingly white floors reflecting the fluorescents. Shelby braced herself as she approached the door to room eleven. She steeled her face to ensure he would be incapable of reading her emotions at the sight of him, then closed her eyes and went in.

He was sitting up in the hospital bed, his face red but

otherwise unhurt, although both arms were bandaged. Jeremy looked relieved at the sight of her.

"Oh God, baby, how are you doing?"

"I'm better now. I don't know why I was so scared that something may have happened to you, too. I'm just so relieved that you weren't there. I must have fallen asleep on the couch. I'm not sure, but I didn't hear anything. I woke up when they put the tape around my face."

"What? Why did they restrain you? What the hell happened?" Shelby was astonished.

"I think they came in to take things. I don't even know what's gone. I called 911 when I got my hands free. I didn't even check." Jeremy seemed to become agitated again as he recounted the events of the evening.

"Don't worry about it. We can figure all of that out later. Just tell me what happened as best you can."

"I was asleep. I think it must have been after 8:00 PM or so. I know it was dark. I felt someone wrap tape around my head and then pull me forward and put something around my wrists so I couldn't move. They must have turned off the lights because I could only see dark images. I know there were at least three of them. I felt something hit the back of my head, and by the time I woke up, they were done."

"Fuck!" To think she was watching her silly movie about the time he was being knocked out was a horrific thought. Anything could have happened.

"I tried to get my hands free, but I couldn't. It must have been at least a few hours before I could rip my hands free."

"What do you mean to rip your hands free? How bad is it, baby?" Teeth clenched, she waited for his answer.

"I just pulled both hands as hard as I could over and over again until they came free. I lost a lot of skin, but I had no other choice."

"Oh, fucking, Christ, Jeremy. I should have been there, I should have called, I should have checked on you, something."

"I don't even want to think about what would have happened if you were there, Scarlet. Stop, don't do that. It wasn't your fault, and it wasn't even mine. People can be really shitty. If I hadn't been home, it's possible that they would have just taken what they wanted and left. I'm hurt, but I'll be fine."

"What have the police said so far?" She asked.

"I'm supposed to go to the station in a few days and give a statement after I have a chance to take inventory of what's missing. Someone at the hospital took pictures of my head and hands before they bandaged me, which will also be used as evidence."

"Okay, What can I do? I feel awful. I was sitting at home watching movies when this was all happening."

"Just sit with me for a little while, then go back home and get some sleep. I had to see you to make sure you were okay. I was more worried about you than about me."

"You have got to be kidding. I am not going anywhere. I'm not letting you out of my sight. They can haul my ass out of here if they want me to leave."

"I don't think they are going to keep me overnight. I had to be checked for a concussion, and then they did X-rays on my hands and wrists, but no breaks. The nurses had just finished bandaging my arms when you came in."

"I'm waiting right here, and then we are going to my house tonight to get some sleep. We won't worry about what happened at your house until you're rested and able tomorrow."

"You mean our house, right?" Winking at her as he spoke.

"You are crazy, and you should have your head checked again for brain damage. How can you try to be funny at a time like this?" She couldn't help but smile and kiss his forehead gently before sitting down in the most uncomfortable black metal chair she had ever seen. They better get out of here soon. This place was the worst. He felt it, too. She could tell.

"When is the doctor coming back in?" Shelby asked.

"The nurse said soon. In Emergency Room speak, that could mean forty-five minutes or four hours."

An hour later, Shelby made her way down to the gift shop and bought a pack of cards and two Gatorade's. They played rummy, laughing at what Jeremy tried to pass off as a straight, finally reducing the adrenaline of the evening. The nurse poked her head in only once to check on them and offered a second dose of pain medication, which Jeremy refused.

"You know you're entitled to just zone out today, right? I don't want to imagine what your hands look like right now, but you deserve all the narcotics they can give you."

"It hurts like hell, I'm not going to lie. I want to get out of here, load up on some Advil, and sleep for the rest of the day." His eyes were at half-mast. He was fading fast now that he was calm. His body was shutting down.

"I'm just going to turn off the lights for a bit. Close your eyes, babe." By the time she returned to her chair, his breathing had slowed, and his eyes were closed. It was already 3:45 AM, Jesus. All that worrying earlier this evening about her first life was long gone. The only thing she could think about was this man sleeping in the dark beside her. There was no going back now. She was all in. He would heal, but this was the first real challenge they would face together. The last three months had been nothing but wine and roses. This was real life, and she wanted to do it with him, come rain or shine. Just as her own eyes were closing, there was a knock at the open door.

"Hello, I'm Dr. Young. Do you mind if I turn on these lights?"

"Sure," she said, getting up and gently touching Jeremy's shoulder to wake him.

"I just wanted to go over a few things before we let you go home this morning."

"Okay, that's fine," Jeremy mumbled groggily.

"Your CT looks good. We don't see any significant issues there. You will want to watch for dizziness and headaches. Your X-rays show no breaks, but please schedule an appointment with a dermatologist in the next few days to create a treatment plan for your wrists and hands. Infection is likely if you don't get treatment soon, so make sure that you call later today. I'm sending you home with a prescription for Oxycodone and a list of referrals for the dermatologist. Any questions?"

"No, I don't think so…" looking at Shelby for anything he

may have missed. She shook her head at him and the doctor.

"Okay, the nurse will be in with your discharge papers in a few minutes." With that, he was gone.

"Want to take any bets on how long a few minutes is?" He laughed. Shelby was happy to see him smile but worried about what might be under those bandages. She wasn't smiling quite yet.

"I just want to get you out of here and in bed where you can rest." Shelby stood by his bed, refusing to sit until the nurse arrived about twenty minutes later. From the car to Shelby's door took less than ten minutes, and she didn't stop until she led him directly to the bedroom.

"Can you take off your clothes, or do you need me to help you?"

"You can take my clothes off any day, babe," Jeremy said with a wink.

"Not today, Mister. Seriously, can you lift your shirt over your head?" He tried but could not quite get his arm out of the hole. Shelby gently lifted it and threw his shirt on the floor. Anything that may have touched these people went straight into the trash after he was asleep. Seizing a pair of boxer shorts from the drawer, she handed them to him, glad he had kept a few things at her house.

"Let's get one thing straight right now," his voice straining under the exhaustion, "I'm okay. You don't have to worry anymore. Please?"

Her anxiety had gotten the best of her, and she was hovering. While he was sleeping, it would be a good time for her to collect herself and redirect her mood.

"I know, babe. Let's get you in bed, and I'll stop worrying."

She allowed him to put on his own boxers, not even bothering to pay attention for a peek when he took off his old ones. This was business. As soon as he was under the covers, she turned out the light and closed the door behind her, quickly snagging his dirty clothes. While his adrenaline had subsided, hers was still flowing through her like electricity. She was turning the corner on twenty-four hours without sleep, but for the moment, she was wired. The clothes went straight to the garage and into the trash can. Good riddance. Her next stop was the fridge for a bottle of water, draining half before sitting back on the sofa she had left just four hours ago when her rose-colored glasses had still been firmly in place.

It was always amazing how things could change so quickly in a matter of seconds. She wasn't thinking about what Steve must have felt like when she died in the middle of the kitchen floor. She was only thinking about Jeremy and how much she didn't want to lose him. She laid back, closed her eyes, and began thinking about the first time she saw him. Grey polo, broad shoulders, and that sexy smile. Only in the dark could she admit that she had never loved anyone as much as she loved him. The feeling was all encompassing. Three months or not, she was never going to let him go.

Chapter Fifteen

The police finally arrived only after they were called. Apparently, Officer Smith only threatened to come to the funeral home, as he had mentioned to Bob that morning. That or they had stopped for lunch. Either way, Ansel forced Catherine to run back to his house before he would pick up the phone to call for help. She donned his coat one more time, looked both ways, and then made her way to the backdoor unobserved.

Ansel pulled himself together, straightening the creases on his suit jacket. After waiting a few more minutes just to be sure Catherine had made it back, he dialed the police station.

"Hem lease, I ned hemp…." Ansel attempted, jaw refusing to move.

"Who is this please?" The receptionist inquired.

"Asel Bishep. Funra home." This was more challenging than he had considered. The pain was nearly unbearable, but his every action had to be planned out methodically. He wasn't concerned that anyone would suspect Catherine was still alive. However, considering the circumstances, he wanted this to be as open and shut as possible.

"Bishep… Bishep."

"Mr. Bishop? Are you okay?"

“Oh, Olice.” Blood began to drip on the phone, causing it to slip in his hand.

“Ok, Mr. Bishop, I will have the police come to the funeral home immediately.” Ansel was shocked that she understood anything he was attempting to convey, relieved help was on the way. Bob had already ruined the carpet in the entryway, not to mention his lopsided jaw; the least he could do was not cause any more trouble. Ansel pulled out his desk chair and sat patiently for their arrival.

The ambulance arrived moments after the police vehicles, ushering him away to the hospital while the police were left behind to sort out the scene. After an X-ray, the attending doctor used two hands with a firm grip to relocate his jaw in one swift movement. As an expert in shoulder and hip dislocations, Dr. Washington considered jaws almost effortless.

Ansel was beyond grateful that his jaw remained intact and that he was able to speak immediately.

“Thank you, Doctor.” Grasping both sides of his face, feeling the bumps and protrusions as they should be once more. It hurt, but not as much as he thought it would. There was no evidence at all of what had happened with Catherine at the Funeral Home, so his mind was free to worry about how she must be dealing with the situation. She would clearly see the police presence across the street and worry about him and what was happening. He needed to return as soon as possible.

"Your jaw may lock from time to time. That will lessen over time. The laceration on your cheek will need care over the next few days. Keep it clean and bandaged. I'll send you home with Percodan for the pain." The doctor removed a white prescription pad from his pocket, scribbled for a moment, and handed him the slip.

"Thank you again. Am I free to go?"

"Of course," Dr. Washington said, dismissing him with a wave of his hand.

Ansel moved quickly, taking a waiting taxi outside the hospital. He asked to be dropped off a street away, not wanting the police to know he went home first. The sun was setting, but the orange dusk did not offer enough cover. He would have to be careful in getting to Catherine first before returning to the funeral home.

When he walked in, the back door was open, and he saw Catherine sitting in the dark at the kitchen table.

"Are you okay? What happened after I left?" Catherine interrogated him.

"Yes, it wasn't as bad as it could have been. My jaw was just dislocated.

"I'm fine. I don't know what's happening at the funeral

home, though. I was taken to the hospital right away. How are you dealing with all of this?"

"I'm free, Ansel. I know God sent me to save you and maybe others that Bob would have hurt in the future. That is what I was meant to do. It all makes sense. Glory to God." Catherine lamented.

Ansel, not entirely certain of her righteousness, nodded. He wasn't sure what he would discover when he got home, but her elation was a bit surprising.

"I wanted to check on you before I went across the street. Don't turn on any of the lights, and try to get some sleep. I don't know when I'll be back." He snuck out of the back and took the long way around, migrating slowly to the side of the building without windows. It would be better if he could walk in unseen and get a feel for what was happening before they could change their attitudes with his presence. As Ansel approached, he could only see one remaining police vehicle, and through the west window, he saw Officer Smith sitting in one of his waiting chairs smoking a cigarette. He seemed to be the only one left.

Hurrying toward the door, he wished to be seen as returning straight here after the hospital. Officer Smith stood as Ansel came into the building.

"You look much better than a few hours ago, Bishop." Officer Smith offered as he smiled.

"Thank you, Officer. I came back as quickly as I could."

"I was waiting for you. I wanted to tell you that I'm sorry this happened. I think all this is partly my fault. I went to Mr. Davis's home early this afternoon and threatened to come to see you to look at some pictures. I was trying to rile him up, but not like this." Officer Smith looked at his shoes as he admitted his mistake.

"I understand, Officer Smith. You couldn't have known what would happen. He did say something about pictures before he hit me." Ansel placed his hand on Smith's arm in reassurance.

"Just glad you're okay. I could give a shit about him," Smith hitched a thumb in the direction of where Bob's body was previously lying. "It's pretty clear what happened, and I guess it's pretty clear who murdered his wife. Did he say anything?"

"He came in asking where the pictures were. Accused me of thinking he killed Mrs. Davis. I went down hard when he hit me, and then he tried to come after me again and fell. I saw him hit his head and tried to help him, but he died instantly. It all happened very quickly."

"That's what I figured. There's no doubt he was a mean bastard. I have a feeling you might get a call in a day or two about helping to bury him. Ain't that a kick in the stomach? If you don't want to do it, make sure you tell 'em what happened." Officer Smith took his cap off Ansel's desk and moved toward the door.

“Call if you think of anything else, but otherwise, I’ll write my report, and you won’t likely hear from me again.”

“Alright. Have a safe drive home, Officer,” shaking his hand as he left.

Ansel took a seat at his desk, staring at the blood and hair embedded into the corner of the wood, his eyes trailing the streaks down to the pool of tacky blood Bob had left behind. He was going to have to live with this. Ansel surrounded himself with the dead daily, but he had only ever seen one man killed before today. That was during the war, and it was the enemy from a distance. Whether he had intentionally killed him or not didn’t matter; he sat there and watched him choke to death on his own blood. Yet, Ansel had witnessed what Bob himself was capable of. Catherine had been dead for days when she was brought in, brutally murdered by the only man who was legally required to care for her. What was done was done, and his conscience wasn’t as heavy as he expected. His duty was to Catherine, and Bob was likely to have killed her again if he hadn’t made that momentary decision that ended Bob’s life. In this case, he felt this may have been the best outcome for everyone involved.

He made a note to call the carpet company on Monday, not that he would forget, but old habits die hard. Then he pulled out a clean sheet of paper, writing a “Sorry, we are CLOSED” sign in neat block letters. No services were scheduled until a rosary Wednesday night, although anyone suffering a loss was likely to come in before then. Unfortunately, they would have to speak over the phone until he could arrange to replace the carpet. Tomorrow, he would see Catherine off safely and then figure out how to make his face look presentable.

Her rear was at least two sizes smaller than two months ago. This may have been her first bus ride, but when she slid into the seat easily, that much she could tell. Looking out the window, Catherine could see Ansel attempting to peer in to take one last look at her. She waved from her seat, seeing his waned smile of acknowledgment. He was nervous for her, and she felt sorry for him. He was such a good and kind young man. All of the nerves had left her from the time Bob had seen her walk into the funeral home. God had given her this second life and then the strength to complete her mission, which she proudly accomplished. As the bus pulled away, she felt the butterflies briefly flutter. Ansel raised his hand in a final wave, and she gave him a warm and hopeful smile. That was the last time they saw each other.

Her suitcase was under the bus, but her satchel was on the seat beside her. She pulled out the parting gift Ansel had given her, The Count of Monte Cristo. He told her it would be difficult to read but that she would relate to the story and stick with it.

Three hours later, when pulling into the next bus station, she understood why it was so important to him that she read it. Dantès was already imprisoned for a crime he didn't commit, betrayed by those closest to him. Catherine could relate to that.

Ansel had carefully reviewed the instructions for her bus trips and wrote down the steps she would take to make it to her hotel in New York in three days' time. She would be on this bus until Little Rock, Little Rock to Indianapolis, and then Indianapolis to New York City. Restroom breaks were every three to four hours, and there were places to buy food and drinks at least once a day. Catherine had packed three days' worth of sandwiches and snacks and wouldn't have to subject herself to roadside food poisoning. She had her book, notebook, and pen, which Ansel had also given her. When she wasn't reading, she would write a to-do list of the things she needed to accomplish to establish herself in the Big Apple.

Finding an apartment, buying furniture, and securing a job were all things she had never dreamed she would have the opportunity to do. She smiled unconsciously as she opened her book once more, hoping Edmond would succeed in his escape as she had.

Chapter Sixteen

Jeremy's recovery was slower than either of them had hoped. Many of the nerves on the top of his hands were damaged when what turned out to be two zip ties ripped away his skin. His hands were often in an agonizing burning pain as the nerve endings repaired themselves. Shelby convinced him to stay at her house until their joint home could be cleaned up and inventoried. So far, his two Mac Books, a gold Rolex his father had given him at college graduation, some cash he kept in his top office drawer, and a set of keys were missing. There had to be more, but he wasn't in any condition to search through every closet and drawer in the house. Shelby continued to ask him and herself why he would have been targeted, considering they had taken so little. The police were meeting them at the house this afternoon to make a formal statement. When he didn't make it to the police station, they offered to meet him at the scene.

What else could be happening here? It was possible that it was just a random break-in, especially considering they had left him alive. Wasn't there more of value to take, though? The vehicles were left in the garage untouched, and they didn't even take his iPad or other electronics besides his laptops. She was probably being paranoid, but she did love this man. If he was the target of something, she wanted to know about it, especially the cause. She could forgive about anything at this point, but if something dangerous was happening, she wanted to know about it. He was so concerned about her safety now that she thought about it. Why? When she wasn't even there. Stop, stop, stop… she told herself. They would get all of this behind them in a matter of weeks. His hands would start feeling better, and the police would probably file his report away, and no one would get any answers regardless. At least she had made the appointment for the dermatologist.

"What time is it?" Jeremy asked.

"About time to go. The police will be at the house in twenty minutes."

"Got it. I'll throw on a fresh shirt, and then we can go," wincing as he rose from his chair."

He was putting on a brave face for her, but Shelby knew he hurt like hell. The faster they could get all of this over with, the faster they could get on with their lives.

The police were in an unmarked car in the driveway when they pulled in five minutes early. After they parked the car in the garage, the officers climbed out of the vehicle to greet them.

"Hello, Mr. Locke. I'm Detective Preston, and this is Detective Merle," introducing the tall and skinny man standing to his left. Det. Merle made Shelby think of one of the characters from her favorite childhood movie, Grease. The guy they called "Ratface". Not only did he have pockmark scars on each side of his face, but the skin was drawn a little too tight around his jaw and eyes, creating a perfect silhouette of his skull. They exchanged pleasantries and then went inside to sit down and discuss last weekend's events.

"How are you feeling, Mr. Locke?" Preston started the conversation.

"I've been better," Jeremy scoffed, "It will take some time."

"I understand. We won't take much of your time. Please walk us through what happened on Saturday night. We have read your initial statement but need to review it again and ask you some questions."

"Okay…I fell asleep watching TV sometime between 7-8:00 PM. I woke up to a noise, and then the tape was placed around my mouth and head. Someone hit me over the head, and I was out. I woke up at some point later in the dark, not hearing anything. I assumed they had left, so I did my best to get out of the flex cuffs, and when I couldn't, I ripped my hands free and then called 911." Jeremy recounted, almost as if reciting his story. He seemed exhausted. The detectives gave each other a look before proceeding with their questions, careful to keep their expressions blank.

"Have you been able to complete the inventory of missing

items?"

"No, I've been at my girlfriend's house since the weekend. Besides the computers, cash, and watch, I haven't been able to go through everything."

"We plan to go through the rest of the house together this afternoon." Shelby offered.

"Excellent," Det. Merle handed her a card, "Can you send me a complete list to my email?"

"Yes, I'll do it tonight."

"Were you able to get a good look at anyone?"

"Not really; I think there were three people, though. I had my eyes open for less than twenty seconds, but I saw three shadows."

"Did they have short hair or long hair?" Det. Merle interrupted.

"I don't know. I think the one over me had short hair, but I can't be sure. It was very fast, and I was barely awake." Now, Jeremy was irritated. Shelby had never seen him so out of sorts.

"You have been through a terrible and traumatic ordeal. It's possible that something may come to you later that you don't remember now over the next few days. Please call me right away if you remember something. Will you be staying here tonight?"

"No," Shelby interjected before Jeremy could speak, "Once we go through the house, we are going back to my place."

"Okay, that's good. I will send over the print crew tonight and get that part out of the way. I have to warn you…the process is messy. I would have the whole place cleaned before you decide to come back."

"We had planned on doing that anyway. I'll schedule something for tomorrow afternoon." She smiled at Jeremy to reassure him she would take as much off his plate as possible.

Det. Preston put his hands on his thighs, making a move to get up.

"Well, I guess that's it then. Cases like these can take some time, so I'll reach out with an update in a week or so." Preston and Merle were both on their feet and headed toward the door. The whole encounter was surreal to Shelby; it seemed like one of those episodes of CSI or Law and Order where the first interview with the police was always so cordial, but they had their suspicions the whole time. It would only ring true if they stopped at the door and suddenly remembered a pivotal last-minute question to ask in some unassuming and off-handed way.

She and Jeremy followed them to the door where Det. Merle opened it for himself. Shelby guessed neither of them felt uneasy finding their way around a stranger's home anymore. Just then, Det.

Preston turned to Jeremy.

"Oh, I will need both of you to come down to the station this week so we can get copies of your fingerprints. We need to exclude yours from the prints we find in the house. Just call me before you come, and I'll ensure you get in and out." Well, there it is, Shelby thought. Not really a question, but somehow, Preston wanted to leave them with this last thought. She wondered, not for the first time, if they suspected Jeremy of something.

"Sure, no problem," Jeremy said in that same exhausted tone.

They spent the following few hours traveling from room to room. Shelby carried a notepad and pen, listing anything he felt was missing. The list was undoubtedly shorter than it should have been. iPads, gold cuff links, and a watch case full of designer Invicta's were all left behind. With Jeremy unconscious, the intruders had plenty of time to be thorough. His office had assuredly been the target. She had already sold her soul to this man, and there was no going back on it. Knowing she was keeping a monumental secret from him about her real identity and former life, she recognized it was possible, if not probable, that there were things he was keeping from her. And why in God's name did that man not have a security system, anyway?

"I think that's it, babe. We only added two items to the list.

You really think that's it?"

"That's all that I can think of that's missing. I guess something must have scared them off before they could make it to the rest of the house."

She wasn't sure if this was the right time to ask him about what was hanging in the air between them. Shelby hadn't felt a single secret being held by him, yet he hadn't thought she was lying through her teeth about her past either.

"Baby… do you think there could be any other reason they were here? A few computers and a watch hardly seem worth it when breaking into such a nice house."

They both let the question hang in the air. His head had been dangling down, but now he looked at her directly. It seemed as though he wanted to tell her something but wasn't exactly sure how. Shelby got on her knees and craned her neck up just enough to kiss him lightly on the cheek, hoping that it created a safe space between them.

"Why would you ask me that, Scarlet? Do you think I have something to do with this? Seriously?" She had never heard his voice raised and angry before. He lifted both of his arms in front of her face, waving them at her.

"You think I would let this happen to me? If I had something to do with this or even knew anything about it, I would do everything in my power to hold them accountable for what they did to me." His head dropped again as if that was all of the power he had left in him to get out those few angry and defensive words.

"I didn't mean anything by it, Jeremy. I'm so sorry. I believe you."

"The whole situation is fucked. It's not your fault." She rose from the floor and stood in front of him, lifting his face with both hands. "I love you. I love everything about you." It had been over a week now since she had made love to him. Too long. They needed to reignite their connection. She drew her face close to him and kissed his neck, lightly biting until she heard the tiniest moan of consent for her to venture further. She drew him out of the chair, leading him to the living room couch, forcing them both to reclaim the space. Careful not to touch his forearms, she pushed him down on the sofa.

"Scarlet…I don't know if..." He stopped the moment her hand found its way down his pants and around him. Her mouth firmly wrapped around his hardening cock while her hands took his pants the rest of the way down. She could already taste him. Jeremy needed this as much as she did. When he began to thrust into her mouth, she lifted her head swiftly to stop him from cumming. She needed him inside of her tonight.

She removed her jeans and panties, slowly lowering herself, allowing him to fill her up one inch at a time until the pressure was too much, and they began to move together. Shelby could feel him expanding and starting to pulse inside her. He came quickly, but she didn't mind. Her body collapsed on top of him, and he held her there against his fast-beating heart.

"I love you, darling. I'm sorry for the way I have been acting. I'm just angry and in so much god-damn pain. I'll be better, I promise," a tear ran down one side of his face.

"You don't have to be anything, babe. Just keep me close, please. That's all I ask. Trust me..." His mouth found its way to hers, all tongues and pure love between them. Shelby knew at that moment that things would be okay again.

"Can I take care of you this time, Scarlet?" Moving her to the side so he could place his face between her legs.

"Hello? This is the police. If someone is here, please identify yourself." A male voice called from the foyer.

"Oh shit!" Shelby laughed. They knew the forensic team was coming, but they lost track of time and didn't realize how late it was. Jeremy was on his feet in a flash, picking up his pants from the floor.

"Just one moment, please! This is Mr. Locke, the homeowner. I will be with you in a moment. Please stay where you are." He sounded so authoritative, Shelby thought. It just made him sexier. Her jeans were back on as quickly as she could manage, but there was no way she could conceal what they had been up to with her tousled hair and flushed face.

"You ready, darling?" His sly smile again demonstrated that everything was going to be okay. For future reference, she would have to remember that a good blow job would go a long way in improving his mood. She must keep that gem in her back pocket for a rainy day. They made their way to the entryway and explained to the police that they would leave them to their business. By the time they made it back to her house, Jeremy was sound asleep in the passenger seat.

She turned off the car and looked over his sleeping face. Despite his insistence and their lovemaking, he was lying. She had to ask herself what was important here. Was he trying to protect her, or was there something to hide, something bad? For now, there was nothing she could do about it. Maybe when he was feeling better, she could try again to get him to talk to her.

It was over a week before they received a call from Officer Merle with a status update that consisted of little more than excuses as to why they had no actual leads. She had taken Jeremy to the dermatologist six days ago. The doctor was hopeful that no surgery would be necessary, although they would know more throughout the healing process in the next few weeks. His bandages were replaced with thin sleeves covering the damaged skin, and he was in noticeably less pain. His mood improved dramatically, but still, she decided to wait for further questioning. Shelby hired a professional cleaning crew and moved him back into the house the next day, along with an alarm company. The whole system took less than three hours to install, and now they both had peace of mind. Delaying things would only hinder Jeremy's recovery, and he needed to get back to his routine and back to work.

She sat at the kitchen table with her Mac, watching him sleep on the sofa that had caused them so much misery, but where she had brought him back to life. He slept less and less but still required a mid-day nap most days. She took all this as positive signs. Shelby doted on him but was careful to give him space as well.

Her writing had taken a more solemn tone these last few weeks, with their trials being written into her characters' stories. She needed some outlet for the turmoil they had experienced. This scene was an emotional reunion, like the one she had orchestrated with Jeremy. She had even included the part where they were interrupted right before he attempted to go down on her. The reminiscing was both horrible and fun. With only a hundred pages written, she usually saved this type of reconciliation until toward the end, but everything about this book seemed different than the rest. Shelby wasn't convinced that it was a good or bad thing, fuck it… sometimes, you write a book for the reader, and sometimes, you write it for yourself. Looking at the clock, she was determined to close the laptop in an hour and return to her house for a swim. It was almost time to cover the pool for the winter, and she hated the thought of doing that. For the last month, she had relied on the heater to keep it warm, but December in Arizona was colder than most people thought. After her last swim of the season, then she would finish packing. This ordeal would not stop them from continuing with their plans, come hell or high water.

"Writing something juicy, my love?" He asked, startling her out of her thoughts. She had been on a roll for almost the last half hour and didn't notice when he woke up.

"As a matter of fact, they are busy making up as we speak, and yes, it's juicy."

"Oh… I may have you read it to me later. Right now, I'm starving. Did you eat?"

"No, I got caught up. Are you in the mood for lunch or dinner?" she asked, getting up and putting her arms around his neck, kissing him softly. She looked at the clock on the microwave, realizing it was past 3:00 PM, and they hadn't eaten since breakfast.

"I don't know. What are you thinking, babe?" He asked between kisses. The perpetual unanswered question about what's for dinner was perpetuated nightly by every couple in the world, she imagined.

"How about this? Why don't you have some of that leftover pizza in the fridge for now? I'll make a rez for us tonight somewhere. I think it's about time we got out and about again, and we can finally celebrate my moving in. I have to run back to the house and finish packing. You know the movers come tomorrow." She explained, reacting to his mild disappointment at the mention of leftover pizza.

"Yes, I remember, and I couldn't be more thrilled. I always want you here, enough to eat two-day-old cold pizza."

"No one is forcing you not to use the microwave, babe." Shelby laughed. "I'll text you in a few hours and tell you when to be ready. I'll pick you up." She closed her laptop, kissed his cheek, and left.

When Jeremy got the call that the police had found two fingerprint matches at his house, she wasn't there.

Chapter Seventeen

Ansel would never comprehend the significance of the life Catherine led in the last twenty-one years. When she sat down to write her letter seventeen years after the bus had dropped her off on the edge of New York City, there was no way he or she could have imagined all that would transpire. The morning she wrote the letter; she had visited the doctor. It was her third visit that month, and she knew the news wouldn't be good. Turns out her shortness of breath and the heart palpitations were more than just being out of shape and spending too much time at the shop reading instead of exercising. When the doctor explained she had congestive heart failure, the lack of concern worried the doctor. He thought she must be in shock at the news, although shock was the least of what she was feeling. Contentment and gratitude were closer to the mark.

The letter was the only way she knew how to tell him what a gift he had given her. She had to choose her words carefully just in case unknown eyes were to read them. Writing to him as an Aunt to her beloved nephew was the only way she could think to hide her identity. She was careful not to include specific details but general updates about her thriving bookstore and simple but happy existence. He would be proud of her no matter what she had accomplished, but owning her own business would be well above his expectations. It was essential to her that he knew she was more than alright. There is no need to mention the little heart issue. Not knowing how much time she had left was a little frightening, but worrying him was not the purpose of the letter. There would be nothing but joyful news. He may or may not find out about her second death sooner or later, but now, knowing her time was limited, thanking him was all she could think about.

My Dear Nephew,

I apologize for not writing sooner. I wanted to let you know that I am happy and well. The move to New York was the right decision, although I wish I could see you more often. The bookstore I own has become a grand success. If you could only see it.

More than anything, I wanted you to know how grateful I am for everything you have done for me. These past years have been a growing experience I never thought I would have, and I owe it all to you. I hope you are doing well. I love you with all my heart.

Your loving Aunt,

Catherine

She'd take it down to the post office before opening up the shop tomorrow. It made her heart lighter just knowing he would receive it and be relieved to hear from her. Not all of the last seventeen years had been easy, but there was no denying that she was a different person than she had been in her old life. She would hardly recognize that meek and subservient person today, the one who allowed her husband to run every facet of her life for thirty years.

When she arrived in the city, Catherine stayed at the Hotel Carter near Times Square for three weeks before she had the courage to lease an actual apartment that required her signature on a contract. She worried that the apartments wouldn't allow a woman to sign alone, or she would embarrass herself by not knowing what to ask or what to do. What they did require was proof of employment, which she did not have at the time. Sent away and near tears in her brand-new purple dress and smart black pumps, she walked down 34th Street, trying to figure out what to do next. Her eyes grew large as she passed the gigantic cosmopolitan buildings with massive store windows filled with merchandise she had only seen in magazines. Her gaze shifted to three mannequins standing in a window wearing swimsuits and holding beachballs. She had never seen anything so colorful and vibrant in her life. Before knowing what she was doing, she was inside the door and on her way to the customer service desk. When the day was through, she had a job and a new apartment, compliments of a kind old lady in the human resources department who provided her with a job in women's shoes and an employment letter.

"Us women of a certain age have to stick together," Catherine remembered her saying. The kindness caused her to tear up again, but she held herself together in front of her new employer. She was a top-tier saleswoman in less than six months, allowing her to save almost half of her income for the seven years she worked there. By her third year at Gimbals, she had signed up for a few classes at the City University of New York, which had just opened the year before. Basic accounting, business, and a writing course were all she could handle on top of the thirty-five hours she was working each week. Catherine felt like an imposter sitting through her first non-credit college course, but from the look on the other student's faces, she knew she wasn't alone. Even when the assignments got more difficult, she stuck with them.

Her income, along with her confidence, continued to increase. When the old Italian couple closed their grocery a few blocks away from her apartment, that was the only sign she needed to know she was finally ready. Every move she made in the last seven years prepared her for what came next. She negotiated the rent, but it was still slightly increased from what the Italian couple had been paying. Then, she organized a carpenter who was married to one of her co-workers at Gimbals to renovate the place and build shelving throughout. After that she wrote letters to book wholesalers in New York and Maine to purchase as many copies of last year's best sellers as possible. Finally, she put up a sign in the front window advertising that new authors would have the opportunity to showcase their writing in her store. She encouraged her patrons to bring back their old copies of books they had already read, and she would give them credit for purchasing something new.

Catherine had no intention of creating a cultural hub for young and up-and-coming artists and authors, but somehow, that's what happened. She let folks bring in snacks and drinks and even took suggestions on the type of music to play. Eventually, she could afford to put up a permanent sign outside, changing the simple banner from "Bookstore" to "Second Lives" in dimensional letters across the top of the building. The name fit for so many reasons. Perfect!

Then, of course, there was Jack. Something she would never have told Ansel about but was part of her fabulous new life. Jack came in looking for a book on the American Civil War and ended up asking her for a date. He was five years younger, but to Catherine, it might as well have been twenty. She could never fully allow herself to believe he was really interested in her. The casual dates and conversations were more than she could have hoped for. It was hard to believe that a man like Jack would pay her so much attention. She let it go on for as long as it seemed friendly, but after a goodnight kiss that lingered a bit too long, she broke it off. He wanted more than she would ever be prepared to give, and it wouldn't be fair to him to drag it on. She couldn't lie to herself, though. She wanted him, too, but her faith was far too strong to give in to temptation. Jack took it hard, and he didn't come back to the store for almost a year. When he finally reappeared, they were both tentative at first. But, within a few visits, they were back to being old friends. He came in at least once a week with a cup of coffee or a trinket of some sort. Jack was the best friend she ever had, next to Ansel. Even though Jack would never know the real her, he understood the new her. This is who she was meant to be all along, and God had given her this second chance.

It was time to start preparing for what came next. There were no illusions of a third chance. She would die sooner rather than later, and the store needed to be in good hands. It was the only legacy she had to leave behind. After opening the top drawer of her desk and pulling out another piece of paper, she began to write.

Preparation for the Inevitable:

1. *Call a Lawyer— write a Will.*
2. *Add Jack Knowles to the bank account.*
3. *Create an inventory of items to donate.*
4. *Research estate tax.*
5. *Create trust for the bookstore.*

She reviewed the list and realized it was much shorter than she thought it would be. Her life seemed very small on paper, but in her heart, it was bigger than her imagination would have dared to dream twenty years before. Everything would go to Jack on the contingency that a percentage of profits from the store would continue to go to the battered women's shelter she had been supporting for the last several years. The girls she employed would also need to keep their jobs. He was retired, but she knew he would be honored to take over for her and the extra bit of money. The girls at the store did all the heavy lifting these days. She handled the accounting, inventory, and ordering. In the next few weeks, she would devise an excuse to start training them on those tasks and throw in a little more on their wages to compensate for the additional responsibilities. When she reviewed the list one last time, along with the letter to Ansel, all she felt was gratitude and love.

The last month of Catherine's life came in the winter of 1974. She was hospitalized for three months, and when she felt like her time was close, she requested permission to go home and die in her own bed. Jack came every day of those last few weeks, and there were far more laughs than tears. Her final thought was of Ansel. She hoped he was doing well and wondered if he had been able to use his gift again. Catherine hoped so. Hope was the last and fleeting thought as Catherine passed away. This time, her death was peaceful and on her own terms.

Her funeral was larger than anyone who knew her anticipated. The women's shelter residents were all in attendance, along with a few of the most successful non-residents who had moved on years ago and were able to end their personal cycles of abuse. She had remained anonymous in life, but in death, the shelter's manager felt the need to ensure she was honored. She may have been the one who was brought back, but her generosity gave a second chance at life to countless women in the city, and her legacy would live on through them.

Jack sat in the front row and wept like a child.

Chapter Eighteen

When she picked Jeremy up, she could hardly believe his mood. He seemed like his old self again. She made a reservation at a restaurant neither of them had ever tried before, attempting to light a spark in their celebration and usher in another phase of newness with their living together.

“I’m not sure I can make it through dinner without keeping my hands off of you.” Jeremy growled at her while running his half-covered hand up her thigh as he settled into the passenger seat of her car.

“Reminds me of our first date.” Shelby laughed.

“The danger now is that I know how to lower your resistance.”

“Who said I would be resisting?” Spreading her legs slightly wider to invite his hand.

“What do you think you’re doing, Scarlet? If you think I won’t do it, you are wrong.”

His hand moved up her inner thigh, lightly touching the cloth that covered between her legs with the tip of his fingers. Goosebumps instantly rose across her legs and upper arms. There was no way she would let him stop now. Wetness was already spreading inside her panties. She hadn’t seen him this way in weeks, and this was the man she knew and loved.

As his fingers continued to tease her, her concentration on the road was shot. Shelby slowed down when she saw a shopping center on the right. She pulled in and parked the Genesis in the back as fast as she could safely maneuver. Before the vehicle was in park, he snapped her seatbelt free with his left hand as his right moved her panties to the side and slipped his middle and index finger inside of her. Their faces crashed together, tongues twisting and exploring each other as if they had never experienced each other before. Something had changed in him. For some reason, he was free from whatever darkness had wounded his spirit. He was free to express his love for her once more. His thick fingers methodically worked inside of her. He shoved them deeper with each forceful thrust. The intensity of his passion for her is what sent her over the edge. She came before he was able to quicken his pace as he usually did when he was pulling the orgasm from her. The front of his trousers was taut with the pressure she couldn't wait to set free. Without unbuttoning his pants, she pushed her arm down between his skin and slacks, feeling for what she wanted. Shelby's hand moved frantically when she grasped his hardness, already wet, causing her hand to glide easily. She felt his groans in her mouth as he got closer, never stopping their fervent kisses. All at once, he was pulsating underneath her grip, dousing her hand with his wetness. Jeremy jerked his head back and gasped for air, huffing until he could get his breathing under control.

Shelby laughed while she removed her soiled hand from his pants, "I guess we aren't going to dinner now!"

"Not unless you brought wet wipes and a change of clothes, you temptress. I'm afraid these pants are soaked through."

"Can you open the glove box?"

"Yep," He opened it and immediately saw what she wanted. He handed her three drive-through napkins to wipe her hands.

"Now I can at least get us back home."

"Yes, to our home, baby. It's official! We never have to live alone again."

"What are you implying, Mr. Locke?"

"For the court transcript, I would like the record to reflect that I plead the fifth," he said, reaching for her now clean hand.

"I love you, Scarlet. I love you more than I say. All I can do is show you as time goes on."

"That is good enough for me," raising his hand to kiss his knuckles, "I vote for delivery," she said, lightening the mood.

"Just not pizza," Jeremy pleaded.

"Ha! I know, I made you eat a two-day-old pizza already today. I'll drive us home, and you take my phone and find something to DoorDash for us. I'm starving."

"As you wish," Jeremy crooned in her ear as she placed the car in drive.

"I can't believe it's wintertime already. I hoped yesterday's swim wouldn't be the last of the season, but I think it may be."

"I know. Why live in Arizona if you have to deal with the cold anyway? Maybe we should move to Cozumel or somewhere like that." Shelby was safely snuggled into Jeremy's lap under a blanket, stomach full and feeling content from their earlier adventures.

"I think we can deal with a few months of below-fifty-degree weather, babe. It gives us an excuse to light a fire and get under the covers together."

"So true! How did I find a woman who is so smart?" Jeremy tilted his head to kiss her forehead. "I know I haven't been myself, Scarlet. Even in the last week. I was trying to put on a brave face and act like everything was okay, but I felt like I was under something I just couldn't shake."

"Yes. I know. I don't blame you, babe…"

"I got a call today right after you left. It changes everything, and I feel so much better. I don't know exactly why, but knowing they have suspects means these guys might not get away with it. I've been thinking all along that what happened to me would just be another unsolved case and that the guys who did this could be walking past me on the street, and I would never know."

"You mean they caught the guys? Why didn't you tell me?" Shelby's voice became shrill.

"No, they haven't caught anybody yet, but it seems likely they will soon. I wanted to tell you at dinner, as part of our celebration, but you distracted me."

"Oh, babe, I'm so happy. That's terrific news! Tell me what they said."

"They ran the prints from the office and the bedroom. They found one set of prints of a man with a record for breaking and entering. He served two years in Texas, which must have been where he met the other one. The second set was a woman's, weirdly enough. They asked me if you ever lived in Texas, and I told them you hadn't, so they knew it wasn't you. Anyway, this woman's last known address is in Texas. I never got a good look at them, so I guess it's possible that one of the three was a woman. I'm just glad there are some leads to go on… Scarlet, are you okay? What's wrong?"

Shelby was in shock. Part of herself was convincing the other that he couldn't be talking about her. The other part was absolutely certain that he was. How in the fuck? She hadn't even remembered getting fingerprinted for that short stint of student teaching. Did the police even keep those? Considering the possibilities and her own stupidity, that's when her whole body began to shake. She couldn't move or speak. This was the end.

"Scarlet, seriously. You're scaring me. What's wrong?" Jeremey shoved her off his lap and jumped up from the couch, getting tangled in the blanket and having to yank it out from under his legs. She slid off the sofa onto her knees, vomiting on the floor between her hands.

"Jesus Christ! Oh my god, Scarlet, do we need to go to the hospital? Is it something you ate?" He got on his hands and knees next to her, placing a hand on her back. She heaved again, and this time, he grabbed her hair to hold it back from her face.

Should she make some sort of excuse to go back to her house and then make a run for it? How far could she get before the police would track her down? It was only a matter of time until the police connected her as being the dead woman from Texas. For now, they didn't even know the woman from Texas was dead, but soon, they would. Then, they would review photos, circumstances, etc.... Surely, they could already see her previous driver's license photo. It was ten years ago, and she was careful to keep her hair styled differently, but soon, someone was bound to see the resemblance.

Her mind raced round and round with possibilities. Scarlet's life is over…Did she even have the strength to start again a third time? Her fear was paralyzing.

"For Christ's sake, Scarlet. Is it food poisoning?" Jeremy nearly screamed.

"No, I don't know. Maybe. I'm sorry. I just feel sick all of a sudden." Now that she was talking, Jeremy noticeably relaxed.

"It's okay, baby. Let me take you to bed, and I'll clean up in here." He lifted her gently from the floor and put his arm around her, guiding her slowly to the bedroom.

"Do you want to stop in the bathroom first?"

"Yeah, I better. I need to brush my teeth, too."

After taking care of her business, he tucked her into bed, pulling the covers close to her chest. The room was dark, but the light from the hallway shone on his face as he gazed down at her.

"I'm sorry, Jeremy. I'm so sorry."

"Don't be ridiculous. Everybody gets sick. One day, I'll stand up in front of everyone we know and make a pledge to you, in sickness or in health. Until then, you'll just have to believe me. I'm not going anywhere."

Shelby's eyes filled with tears. Everything they had built was able to come crumbling down. Even if she decided to tell him the truth, he wouldn't believe her. He would probably accuse her of abandoning her family and changing her identity as a way out. She was fucked… they were fucked. Her whole existence was at stake, all because she had procrastinated going down to the police office to place her prints on file. They would have simply matched them up with the prints in the house and been done with it. Now, because she had applied to be a teacher so many years ago, she couldn't even remember; her prints were in some sort of national database. They weren't expecting it to be her, that's why they hadn't recognized her yet. But they would. Soon. She had to come up with some sort of excuse to get away, think things through, and observe from a safe distance. There was a possibility that they couldn't figure it out, as slight as that possibility may be. She refused to throw everything away without finding out what happens next.

"Babe? What's wrong? Are you still feeling sick?" His voice was thick with concern.

"I'm okay. Just thinking about how lucky I am." Wasn't that the truth? That's all she could think about.

"Get some rest. Tomorrow is still a big day. The movers will be at your house early, but I will handle everything if you're still under the weather. Don't worry about anything. I love you, Scarlet."

"I love you, too." Oh God, did she ever.

Chapter Nineteen

Morgan hurried to the laundry room. The stain on Maja's uniform hadn't come out, and she needed it for tonight's basketball game. Somehow, Maja had gotten grass stains all over the front and back of her skirt from last week's game. How that even happened during an indoor game was beyond her imagination. She had just over an hour to try stain remover and scrubbing before Maja would be home for a quick change, and then the three of them would be off to the game. At least she didn't have to work anymore—the perks of marrying a wealthy man. She had hated the dental hygienist gig. Steve didn't care what she did during the day. He hardly cared what she did at all. That's what I get for marrying a man who is still in love with his dead wife, Morgan thought. He had someone to take care of the house, pick up his daughter from her after-school activities, and give him head at least a few times a month.

Morgan had loved him since she first saw him push the garbage can to the front of the house almost ten years ago. She didn't care that he was married, besides, Shelby was a bitch. Work obsessed and a little too good for anyone in the neighborhood. Sure, she eventually came around, and they became friends, but Morgan always thought Shelby was being polite more than anything else. Three days after the funeral, she was in Steve's bed. He had cried for almost ten minutes afterward, but every moment was worth it.

She had him now.

First, she had made herself useful and appreciated and then began helping with the things she knew he would be incapable of handling on his own, namely his daughter. By the end of the year, she had begun divorce proceedings with Brandon and moved herself into the house. Her idea, of course, but he couldn't argue when she began taking over all the daily responsibilities. Three weeks after the anniversary of Shelby's death, they went to the courthouse and got married. She accepted that it would take him a few years to get over her, but after six, she had grown impatient and unsympathetic. Morgan had the lifestyle, house, and freedom she had always desired. Was it too much to ask for a husband who loved her?

The stains were almost unnoticeable now, so she was able to throw it into the dryer just in time. Now, she could take a quick shower and dress for the game.

Maja was right on time.

"Morgan, where's my cheerleading uniform?"

"In the dryer," Morgan yelled from the back of the house that Steve refused to move out of. Morgan had thought that after a year or two, they could buy something new and get away from all the old memories. At first, he could explain why it was so important to him that they stayed here, but now he simply refused to talk about it.

"Is Dad coming tonight?"

"He should be here any minute, and we'll all go together."

After the game, they picked up the Chick-fil-A drive-through. When they walked through the door, the three went their separate ways. Steve had been the dutiful father, cheering and yelling at the boys' basketball game and waving or shouting whenever Maja looked his way. She was growing up way too fast. In a few days, she would be fifteen. Only five years younger than when he had met her mother. Three more years of high school, and then she would be off to college. Maja was already the spitting image of her mother. Long dark hair and green eyes like the color of spring foliage. She would never have to wear much makeup again, just like her mother. She was a cheerleader, top twenty percent of her class, and she even volunteered at the pet shelter twice a month cleaning up shit. It was amazing how she could be developing into the person she was when he had been such a weak father.

What would Shelby think of the way she had turned out? How would she feel about how he had turned out? Married to her best friend and having an affair with a 23-year-old intern in marketing would have been as far away from what she would have imagined as possible. Morgan had been a mistake from the beginning, for him, in any case. Maja had the comfort of having her mother's friend take the reins, someone she trusted in the house. It was funny the way Maja had never asked any questions about his relationship with Morgan, not even when she moved in full-time three months after her mother's death. Steve had tried to, of course, but he couldn't get past the absurdity of it and his own guilt. Things had pretty much stayed the same since then. Maja grew up, and he remained the same bitter and lonely man he was since Shelby's death. It was embarrassing, but he didn't know how to fix it. Divorce at this point would devastate Maja. At the very least, he would have to wait until she was off at college.

Steve rested in his office chair with the door closed. Shelby's desk had been transferred to Maja's room long ago, but he refused to fill the empty space left behind. How often had he sat here contemplating the void on the other side of the room? He finally unlocked his computer and reviewed the notes from his recent meeting with the Reebok account. They had lost Nike a few years back. Reebok was the B movie of the athletic industry, but it still paid the bills. After a few hours, he found himself staring again until there was a knock on the door.

"Steve, you coming to bed?" Morgan's raised voice asked through the door.

"Yeah, in a few." He looked at the time on his laptop, 9:07 PM. How did he get to a place in his life where he went to bed at

9:00 PM?

Walking through the hallway, he heard familiar music blaring through Maja's closed door.

"Who's afraid of little old me..." was clearly discernable through the wall. She had been playing that and a few other songs on repeat since Swift's new album was released several months ago—another familiar homage to her mother. Steve stopped at her door and knocked until it shook. He knew better than to walk in on an almost fifteen-year-old girl. All at once, the music stopped, and the door opened.

"Hi, Dad. Was the music too loud?" Maja was already in her blue floral pajamas with her long hair pulled up.

"Not really, it's almost bedtime, though. Let's tone it down a bit."

"Okay, I will."

"You were terrific tonight at the game, honey. I'm very proud of you, you know that, right?"

Her brow furrowed. "Yeah, I know, Dad. Are you okay? You've seemed more out of it than usual lately." She said in a way that conveyed she is the resident attitude expert of their home.

"I'm good, honey. Everything is good. I am just checking up on you."

"Have you thought any more about my birthday present?" Her demeanor instantly changed from concern to teenage excitement, her legs bouncing as she spoke.

"I haven't decided yet, Maja. You have a whole year until you're sixteen. Getting you a car now is a little premature. We've talked about this…"

"But, Dad… It would be better to practice driving in my own car. Please think about it some more," she pleaded.

"I'll think about it, but no promises. Give me a hug."

They embraced quickly, and Maja kissed his cheek. She was already shifting away from the door, and already appeared to be moving on to her next thought by the time Steve turned back.

"Goodnight, honey," Steve said as he closed the door behind him.

"You know you shouldn't get her hopes up, right?"

Steve turned his head to see Morgan leaning in their bedroom doorway.

"I know you're not buying her that car. At least tell her now so she can think of something else she wants for her birthday," Morgan chastised.

"What makes you so sure I'm not buying her that car?" Moving her to the side by placing his hands on her shoulder as he walked through the threshold to the bedroom. She had already turned down the bed and lit a candle on the bedside table. That was her way of telling him that she wanted to fuck, or in her words, make love. That was the last thing he wanted to do tonight. As he passed by the nightstand on the way to the bathroom, he forcefully blew the candle out, a grey puff of smoke filling his nose.

By the time he was done in the bathroom, the light was off, and Morgan was under the covers. He slipped into bed quietly, turning away from her. Morgan's hand began caressing his back, entering the back of his boxer briefs and between the crack of his ass. He jerked his body forward, locking his hand around her wrist and dragging it out of his underwear.

"Morgan, I'm tired and not up for this tonight. Go to sleep," he said, his voice on edge.

"I thought you liked that," she sulked. He wasn't going to indulge her neediness tonight. He was going to pay for this over the next few days, but right now, he could give a shit.

"Goodnight, then." She scoffed. He offered no response.

Morgan began another day of holding on to what little reassurance she had of continuing this life. She was trying too hard, and as her grip tightened, Steve became more distant. She prepared a breakfast of eggs, toast, sausage patties, and fruit salad.

Steve sat at the kitchen table digging into his breakfast but thinking about what he was going to text Lexi to convince her to take a long lunch with him today. He needed someone else's hands grabbing his ass, not Morgan's. While she stood at the sink scrubbing the eggs from the pan, he pulled out his phone.

Lunch at the Hawthorn? *I have a surprise for you.*

Less than twenty seconds later, she replied. That's what's wrong with the generation. Always on their phones.

What kind of surprise?

You will just have to wait and see.

Ok! 11:30 (Heart Emoji)

There was no surprise, but he knew she would show. He'd pick her up a single red rose… he could tease her with it. The young are easy to please. It wasn't until you got older that expectations ruined your excitement for the little things. He left for work in a much better mood, knowing what awaited him in a few hours. Her pretty pink ass in the air was just what he needed today.

Morgan glared at the closed door. He hadn't even bothered with a kiss or to say goodbye. Whatever was happening was getting worse. She would think of something special to do for him tonight. He loved a good steak cooked perfectly medium rare. She could run to the store later and pick up some scallops and the fresh green beans he liked, and then they could have a romantic evening together. Maja didn't have a game or practice. It would be perfect.

Maja came to the table, her usual chipper self.

"Smells good! Why such a big breakfast? Is it a special occasion?"

"I'm glad someone noticed. No, no special occasion, just wanted to have a nice breakfast."

"Go easy on Dad. He's been working a lot lately." Maja's voice was firm but not angry. Morgan should have known better than to make a snide remark about her father. He could do no wrong in her eyes, even though she was doing all the work.

"Sorry, hon. Thanks for noticing, was all I meant. Leave for school in ten minutes, then?"

"Sure."

Morgan finished cleaning up while Maja scarfed down the rest of the eggs, a small bowl of fruit, and two patties. Like her mother, the girl could eat whatever she wanted and not gain a pound. If she weren't such a good kid, it would be easy to resent her. Morgan had to stick with a single egg portion, a fruit cup, and black coffee. Even with that, she might gain five pounds.

After driving Maja to school, Morgan decided to treat herself to a massage. Before going home, she stopped by her favorite spot to see if they had an opening and booked the appointment for 1:00 PM. She'd be back an hour before Maja got home, relaxed, and ready to cook up Steve's favorite foods. She swung by the store and collected all the needed supplies. Then, she made one last stop at the liquor store for a bottle of red wine. This evening was going to be perfect.

After unloading the groceries, she climbed back into their unmade bed with a book. Sara Winters has become her favorite author these last few years. Morgan needed all the inspiration possible for this evening, and Sara always had a way of adding an element of adventure to the love scenes. A few chapters later, she resisted the temptation to touch herself. She did not want to spoil the anticipation of what was coming, forcing herself to put the book away for now. After a shower and chores, it was time for her massage.

As Morgan drove home, she decided that neither Maja nor Steve needed to know what she had been up to today. She was sure Steve had his own little indulgences that he failed to tell her about anyway. He didn't need to know about her two-hundred-dollar weekly massage habit any more than the weekly pedicures or every four-week dye jobs to cover her roots. She always paid in cash for her extravagances, and he never asked why she took money out each week. Between his already sizeable bank account and the social security they got for Maja after Shelby died, they could afford it. Still, Steve wouldn't approve, and Morgan knew it. His perfect wife wouldn't have spent money so frivolously. If he found out, he might make her get a job or something, and that was the last thing she wanted.

She was home by 2:30 PM, so she had plenty of time to season the meat and take another quick rinse before anyone came home.

When she heard the doorbell ring from the bathroom after her shower, she assumed Maja had lost her key again. She ran to the door with her big grey towel wrapped around her, unlocked it, and opened it a crack before running back to the bedroom.

"Hello, this is the police. Are you there?" A deep male voice called out.

Holy fuck, Morgan thought, almost dropping her towel. She raced to the bedroom to throw on a T-shirt and leggings as quickly as possible.

"Just one second, I'm getting dressed. I thought you were my daughter, forgetting her key again."

"Are you Shelby Wise, ma'am?"

Morgan pulled the shirt over her head and froze. All she could think about was Shelby today and now this!

“No, I’m not. Just a moment!” Morgan yelled, tugging the leggings on as she jogged toward the front of the house. Two policemen in uniforms were standing in the entryway waiting for her.

“I’m afraid I’m going to have to ask for some identification,” the taller cop in a cowboy hat said.

“What’s going on here?” Morgan asked, making no move to her purse.

“We need to speak with Shelby Wise. Are you Mrs. Wise?”

“No, I already told you I’m not.”

“Then that’s why we need to see some ID.” The shorter cop remained silent but stared at her without removing his mirrored sunglasses.

“Shelby is dead. She’s been dead for six years. Surely, you can see that on your computer. I’ll ask again, What is this about?”

“If you could show me some identification, I'd be happy to tell you,” Officer ten-gallon hat hotly retorted.

“Fine,” Morgan deliberately stomped her way toward the kitchen. Both officers followed three steps behind her. She reached into her wallet and opened it, showing her ID encased in plastic to the man in the hat.

The officers glanced at each other, silently deciding what

direction their interrogation would take in light of who she was and her apparent resistance.

"What is your relationship to Shelby--- Ms. Wise?" the hat man asked.

"I am the wife of Steve Wise. We were married a while after Shelby died. Again, I will ask you, what is this about?" Morgan's natural impatience was coming to the surface.

The officers once again silently questioned each other, concluding that they would have to give up some information to get some.

"We are here on behalf of the Phoenix Police Department investigating a crime committed there. My name is Officer Curry, and my partner is Officer Mundy. We have reason to believe that Shelby Wise may be related to that crime. At the very least, we need to question her."

Now, Morgan was more than annoyed. Cops are getting more incompetent all the time, Morgan thinks.

"I am not sure if I am making myself clear, but Shelby is dead. She died six years ago. There is no way she could be related to a crime in Phoenix. You have clearly made a mistake."

Officer no hat removed a piece of paper from his pocket, unfolded it, and handed it to his partner. The hat man handed the paper to Morgan, who snatched it from his hand.

"Is this Shelby Wise?"

"Yes, it's an old picture, but yes."

"Do you have a copy of Shelby's death certificate?"

"Yes, actually. It's in the office. Let me get a copy." Morgan felt like she was finally getting through to them. She jogged to the office and rummaged through the bottom drawer until she came to the file heading that clearly read "Death Certificates".

"Here." She simply handed a certified copy to the silent officer to throw them off.

"Can we keep this?"

"Sure. Do you need anything else?"

"Not at the moment. We may be back in touch with you, though." Officer no hat removed a small notepad from his breast pocket, ready to take notes. "What is your phone number?"

Once she gave it to them, they both produced cards with their contact information. Officer Todd Curry was evidently the cowboy hat aficionado, and Officer Jared Mindy was his silent partner.

"Thank you for your time, Ms. Wise."

Morgan watched as the police car pulled away from the curb and considered how much, if any, she should relay to Steve. The matter was essentially closed with the death certificate, so there was really no need to get anyone riled up about it. Steve would get upset, and their whole evening would be ruined. She made an executive decision that no one need know about their visit until there was something to know about. If they called for more information… then she could cross that bridge when it came.

She was still standing at the door when Maja walked through.

"What are you doing? Were you waiting for me?" Maja asked, confused.

"No, a salesman just left. I was getting dressed, and the doorbell scared me."

"Oh, okay."

Chapter Twenty

"Scarlet! It's fantastic to hear from you. Can you believe *Fever Dreams* is still in the top 100 after six months? Amazing! Anyway, what can I do for you?" Patricia, her agent at the publishing company, enthusiastically asked.

In Patricia's mind, it was imperative to flatter her. That was her primary job, among her other responsibilities. She had never actually met anyone from her publishing company face-to-face, so a request for a visit from one of their top but most elusive authors would be welcomed.

"I was wondering if you could arrange a meeting this week with the publishing team? I would love to come and make a visit to your offices, meet everyone, and maybe we can put our heads together about this next book."

"AHHHH!" Patricia screamed into the phone, "Yes, we would love to! When will you be here?"

"I'll be there tonight, actually. Could you arrange something for Tuesday?"

That would give her the chance, tonight and tomorrow, to wait for any news from Jeremy about what was happening here. Either the other shoe would drop… or it wouldn't.

"I can make Tuesday work, no problem. I'll get everyone

together; they are dying to meet you. We'll bring in lunch. It will be fabulous!" Patricia's excitement was already wearing on Shelby. If she ended up going through with this meeting, it would be the ultimate exercise in patience. "Just send me an email with your hotel info, and I'll send a car for you."

"Sounds good. I look forward to meeting with all of you. Thanks, bye."

Now that was arranged, she could break the news to Jeremy that she was leaving for the week. The movers had finished unloading last night at about 6:00 PM, and she was exhausted more from the endless hours of holding her breath every time she heard Jeremy's phone ding or buzz than from moving the furniture around. Most of it was boxes she would have to wait to unpack until she got back… if she ever got back.

When he said he had to go and meet a business partner, it was the best news she had heard in two days. She barely held it together, but he would soon stop accepting the "I don't feel well excuse." Her leaving would raise more red flags, but she had no other choice. If the police or some sort of secret CIA organization showed up at the door, she would have no potential means of escape. Distance was the key.

She tried to busy herself with unpacking the bathroom boxes before he returned home. A perfect soundtrack to her mood played in the background. How did such a happy occasion turn into such a shit show? She should be thrilled at placing her toothbrush next to his in the holder by the sink, once and for all. The least she could do was pretend. Shelby owed him that much. She would put on the show of her life this afternoon, making him believe they would be back together and ready to start the rest of their lives in mere days. Fuck! If only it could be true. She finished the bathroom and most of the master bedroom closet unpacking before she heard the faint sound of the garage door opening. She jumped up from the closet and ran to the bathroom to assess the hair situation before briskly making her way to the garage door. As he opened it, she reached for his hand and pulled him close to her, pressing her lips to his.

"I could get used to that! I guess you're feeling better!" He laughed, still holding her hand. She immediately noticed something was different.

"Oh my God! Your arms look amazing! You went to the doctor?"

"Yep. I did go and meet with Joe, too, but I also had an appt with the doctor. I wanted to surprise you. My arms look a little like Hamburger Helper, but she said it will continue to get better over time."

"They do not! A little bumpy is all. How do they feel?

"Weird, but better. A ton better. She is weaning me off of

the pain meds over the next two weeks. I still get the burning nerve pain. Not as bad as before, but it keeps me up at night sometimes."

"I know, babe. I'm just so glad you are feeling better. This is a huge step." She kept ahold of his hand, leading him to the kitchen. "Sit for a minute, have a drink with me."

"Um… Okay," he pulled out his chair, removed his coat, and draped it over the back of his chair, watching her pour two glasses of chilled pinot grigio.

"Sit!" Shelby commanded, smiling wryly.

"Yes, Ma'am! Are you going to tie me up again?"

"You wish! I want to make a toast. I kind of ruined it the other night being sick." She handed him his glass, which he instinctively raised. She lifted hers to meet it.

"To a very long and happy life together, filled with love and understanding. To us."

Their glasses clinked; they each took a sip and then leaned in to seal it with a kiss.

"I have to tell you something."

"What is it?"

"I got a call from my publisher. They need me to come to California and meet with them about the new book. They have these new ideas about a series they want to try, and I have to meet with them before I get any further in the writing process to adapt it to their vision."

For a long moment, he was silent.

"I thought you did everything over the phone or virtually." She should have given him more credit. Jeremy was no idiot. This is going to have to be convincing, and by the sound of his voice, he was already doubting the circumstances.

"Evidentially, book series are the new thing, and authors have been doubling or tripling their sales by splitting up the books. This week, they have assembled a whole team to walk me through the details and timeline for releases over the next year. I won't be gone long—a few days."

"Just when I was looking forward to having you here...," he said while taking a sip of his wine, starting at her.

"I know, babe. It won't be long, but I do need to go. We have the rest of our lives... I hope."

"I would never hold you back from your work. You know that. When do you have to leave?"

"My flight leaves in four hours. To be safe, the Uber is scheduled for about an hour and a half from now."

"What? Right now? When did they call you about all of

this?" Jeremy's tone betrayed his skepticism.

"They called me while you were gone. I guess some people from other offices are going to be in town, and they asked if I could make a last-minute flight. The meetings are tomorrow morning," she said, feeling like a grave digger standing in the hole, scooping out dirt and finding herself deeper and deeper. She had lied continuously about her past, although she had never lied to him about anything pertaining to her new life or their relationship. It hurt her to think he knew she was lying.

"Okay," he said as he turned and shuffled toward the bedroom. Shelby stood there in silence for a moment, contemplating what to do before going after him. The last thing she intended was to push him away before she knew what would happen.

"Babe, Are you okay?" Shelby called after him.

"Yeah, I'm good. Don't need you need to pack?"

"Jeremy, don't do that. Don't make me leave thinking you're mad at me. I'm not doing this because I don't want to be here."

"It's not that, Scarlet. It's just that the last night we weren't together didn't go so well. I'm not worried about me. I worry about you." Jeremy's eyes searched her face in earnest. He really did love her. This was the moment she could tell him everything. The problem was that there was no way he would believe her, and the death sentence their relationship was already under would have a certain and instantaneous execution date. In truth, she didn't have the courage.

"Babe, nothing is going to happen to me or to you. I promise." Shelby took his hand in hers, "Let's not waste another minute talking about the what ifs… take me to bed, Mr. Locke."

His sly smile told her all she needed to know. She was forgiven for the moment.

"Anything you say, Scarlet. I would hate to make you late for your flight," he said wickedly.

"Give it your best shot."

Shelby looked out the window at the New York City skyline from her first-class seat. She had never been to New York before, so that was something. Tomorrow, she could spend the day walking around and soaking up the atmosphere; she may need a new place to live here soon anyway. She was mentally and physically exhausted… lying was not for the weak. After their bedroom escapade in which Jeremy attempted valiantly to keep her in bed, she rushed to pack and then hid in the bathroom for a few minutes to research a hotel in San Francisco where she would be "staying". She had already used her Marriot app to book a hotel in New York and settled on the W. She needed to at least off-handedly mention where she was staying, or his suspicions would be raised again. He would never call her there anyway. This was the cell phone age.

She just needed to be careful to turn off all her location services on her phone, and then she would be essentially untraceable. Moving the money had been her first priority. At least half of it went into the Cayman account she opened over five years ago, where she kept the original one hundred thousand in case of a rainy day. Well, It was a fuck'n torrential downpour. After she began making money with her books, she added more and more to it until she reached the amount Ansel had given her when she left. Leaving it at that threshold was like honoring him in some way. That amount wouldn't be enough now if she needed to leave permanently, so she transferred half of her entire holdings, amounting to just over three million dollars. With a push of a button, she could access the money from almost anywhere. It was also unseizable by the authorities, to boot. Who knew she would end up a criminal mastermind in her new life? However, Shelby didn't consider herself a criminal, just someone trying to survive. This is what she gets for forming an attachment and allowing herself to be vulnerable out in the world.

As the plane touched down, Shelby shook her head, physically attempting to shake off these self-deprecating thoughts. This was survival mode. Beating herself up wasn't going to solve anything. For the first time in six years, she had a whole life now, complete with a home and the love of her life. This was GO time…

Even at 1:00 AM, the streets of Manhattan were packed with cars with taxis honking their way through traffic cones and one-lane roads. She had never seen so many pizza joints on one street before. When the Uber pulled up to the hotel adjacent to Times Square, it was as dazzling as she imagined it would be. The gigantic signs flashed and moved in fluid motion, lighting an entire four-block section of the area. She was disappointed that she couldn't even take a picture. The less evidence of her location, the better. Checking into the hotel was fast and easy, but as soon as she made it to the room, it was clear there was no way she would get to sleep. She dumped her luggage and went back downstairs to explore. One block later, she was standing in the middle of what she had only seen on TV every single year on New Year's Eve. It was exhilarating and depressing all at once. Tears began to fall from her eyes as she gazed up at the humungous billboards. After walking around and gazing into shop windows for the next half hour, the day's weight could be felt all over her body. She made it upstairs and into bed, falling asleep within minutes.

Shelby awoke to light flooding the room all around her. She had been too tired to remember to close the curtains, and her panoramic room didn't disappoint with the view or the sunlight. Walking toward the windows with the intention of closing them, she halted instantly as she looked out over New York City. From the thirty-second floor, there was nothing she couldn't see for miles. It was breathtaking and beautiful. She could see herself writing from here… maybe she would after taking in the sights today. It was cold as hell, but she would still check out Central Park and the 9-11 memorial. Other than that, she would play by ear. If her life was going to be over, at least she could check off a few items from the bucket list while she was at it, silently congratulating herself for being so stoic during a time like this.

It was only a quarter after eight when she was dressed and ready. Less than five hours of sleep. She would feel it later, but for now, she felt great. After a few minutes of Googling, she determined her first destination would be the Blue Dog for breakfast. It was only a six-minute walk from here., but it would be a cold one. The sweatshirt she wore last night would have to do. She couldn't have gotten away with bringing her fluffy coat when Jeremy thought she was going to San Francisco. If she walked a brisk pace it would warm her up on the way.

An hour later, she walked through Central Park and across the bridge she had only seen in movies. Granted, it was cold, overcast, and lightly dusted with snow, but she could still feel its magic. This was the kind of place you were supposed to walk around with your dog or significant other while holding hands. Other than the joggers, there were no single strollers here, just her. After a mile or so, she was chilled to the bone and needed another cup of coffee to warm her up before attempting any further sightseeing. She hauled out her phone again and looked up coffee shops near her. She found a bookstore and coffee shop combo less than three minutes away. Jackpot!

Shelby could see her breath as she trotted in the direction her map took her, finally seeing it across the street. The sign read *Second Lives*, how ironic, she thought. No matter the circumstances, it was always fun to find her own work in new bookstores. After getting some warm coffee in her, she explored their romance section. She stood in line and ordered a vanilla latte, which was delivered to her with an exquisite flower design on top. There was something so special about drinking coffee surrounded by walls of books. When she realized that the shop took in used books and re-sold them, she finally understood the store's name. It was a wonderful play on words.

At a table in the corner, a group of young college students were studying and quizzing each other. Just in front of them, an elderly couple sat bent over a shared book. It seemed like this place had been here forever and was an engrained part of New York City life. How cool, Shelby thought. After warming and downing her coffee, she perused the romance section, noting that three of her five books were sitting on the shelves. From the looks, they were well-worn. Just the way she liked it, an old book was always better than a new one, especially to an author. Just as she was able to continue her journey around the fiction section, her phone began to buzz. It was Jeremy…

Chapter Twenty-One

"Steve, want to get some lunch this afternoon, dude?" Jason, the sales director, asked.

"Nah, I made plans for lunch that I can't break. Maybe next week."

"Plans, huh? I get it." Jason winked at him as he walked out of Steve's office.

This would be the third time this week. He should win a fucking Academy Award for his performance as the doting lover. The two-dollar and seventy-nine-cent rose had done the trick, allowing him to get laid by a chick seventeen years younger than him three out of four days this week. God bless the young and ignorant, he thought. He managed to hold Morgan off with a stick, but just barely. She broke down crying the other day when he refused her advances two nights in a row, claiming he hadn't been feeling well. The truth was he had no taste for her anymore and wasn't sure why he ever did. She was a needy, conniving woman who left her husband at the first sight of something better, and the worst part was, he let her. When she convinced him to marry her, he was so blinded by grief that he wasn't thinking clearly. At least, that's what he kept telling himself. He would have to figure out something quickly because Maja was bound to notice what was happening sooner or later.

Steve glanced at the time on his laptop. Thirty minutes before lunch was perfect timing to do a little research before heading over to the Hawthorn. The biggest question was should he buy her a new or used one. If he bought her a new car, she could keep it through college. If it was used, it may not make it that long. He quickly searched “safest cars 2024”. Luxury cars were immediately marked off the list. He firmly believed that fancy cars went along with European vacations, only for people who could pay for them themselves. In the mid-size and moderately priced categories, two vehicles came out the winners, the Honda Accord and the Hyundai Ioniq. He hadn’t raised a tree hugger so the decision was clear, the Honda Accord it would be. The only decision left was the color, which he would leave up to his daughter. After scrolling through hundreds of pictures his favorite was metallic grey. It seemed to fit her perfectly but wasn’t too flashy. Morgan would be pissed, and honestly, wasn’t that why he was doing it?

He’d never been such an asshole to his first wife, nor did he ever have an affair. She would hardly recognize the man who sat in this chair as her husband. Of course, Shelby was different. They were a team and deeply in love, even after so many years. He knew there would be no happiness like what he had known with her. All that was left was this wife cheating, almost pedophile, asshole. When you’re having sex with someone who is only eight years older than your daughter, you have some serious problems on your hands.

Speaking of assholes, he had pretty one waiting for him at the hotel… it was time to go.

Steve watched her wiggle her ass back into her black skirt while he remained naked under the covers. Her backside was the best part of her. He also preferred it when she wasn't talking.

"What are you doing this weekend?" Lexi asked, turning around.

"Why do you ask?" he said, crawling out of bed to grab her tits before she was able to button her shirt. He pulled her left breast out of her bra and quickly nipped at the nipple."

"Owe! Stop! I have to get back to work!" She yelped.

Steve ground his groin against her thigh in protest before acquiescing and then walked around the edge of the bed to find his underwear and pants.

"I ask because we are going to see Billie Eilish this weekend, and my roommate's boyfriend bailed, so we have an extra ticket if you want," She said hotly.

"Lexi, you know I can't. I'm married! I can't be seen out in public with you. You know that."

"This is stupid. Why did I even agree to start doing this with you?" Lexi's voice had become shrill.

Steve grabbed her forearm and turned her to face him, "Stop that. You like fucking me, that's why. I like fucking you. I don't care what you do on the weekends. It doesn't matter to me." She stared at him expressionless.

"You're a shit. You don't give a shit about me. I am such an idiot," breaking free of his grip, she collected her bag and was gone before he could respond.

Steve stood naked in the center of the room, wondering what had just happened. He had always been transparent with her. Did she really storm off because of a concert? God, dammit. He really enjoyed these afternoons, which were a very welcome distraction from work and especially his home life. Now, he would have to resume jerking off in the shower in the morning, knowing that was as good as the day was going to get. Maybe he could order some flowers and have them delivered to her apartment. If the rose worked, she was bound to swoon over the flowers, and she would forget about whatever happened. He didn't have time or capacity to find a new mistress at this point, and he was pretty sure most of the guys at the office knew he was fucking her anyway. It would be easier to try and get her to forgive him. The only other options were to fuck his own wife, which wasn't really an option at this point, or he could join some sleazy website like Ashley Madison. It didn't turn out too well for those guys when a cyber-attacker released all their data. No, he would have to stick with it.

As Steve drove back to the office, the thought of going home and dealing with Morgan was nauseating. He devised a plan that would exclude and infuriate her at the same time, finally feeling a bit better after the rotten ending to his afternoon rendezvous. As soon as he arrived back at his desk, he texted Maja that they would spend some quality time together tonight. When she asked what they were doing, he decided to keep it a secret. Making her happy was lifting his spirits tremendously.

The moment Steve drove up to the curb, Maja ran outside, ready to go, just as he had instructed her by text. She was still wearing her school clothes, jeans, and a purple sweatshirt with some floral design on it. Even when she was dressed down, she managed to look adorable. She really was a great kid. She had never been in any serious trouble and was always on top of everything she was a part of. She didn't even have her nose glued to her phone like most of the teenagers he witnessed in the last few years. He and Shelby discussed technology use when Maja was around six. TV time, YouTube, iPad games, etc.… they agreed that nothing could be better than a good old-fashioned book with actual pages, swinging or climbing at the park, and even family board games. He bitterly recalled what Maja had said after the funeral. Mom wouldn't have wanted her to miss school, and she was right about that. It dawned on him that his daughter was continuing to live by that same principle all this time later. It was as if a simple light switch had been flicked up to illuminate an otherwise dark corner of his mind. Maja studied hard, participated in school activities, practiced her cheerleading, and even practiced kindness with her volunteering because that is what her mother would have wanted. God, he felt like such a shit. Oblivious to how amazing his daughter had turned out to be and the continued influence of his long-dead wife, she was a better parent from the grave than he had been living in the same house.

Why shouldn't he buy her a car a year early? In fact, as she claimed, it would be the wisest possible decision to allow her to learn in her own car. Maybe it would be a step in the right direction for their relationship and his attempt to be a more integral part of her life. She sat for a moment before he greeted her, pulling himself out of his snowball of realizations.

"Hi hon, How was school?"

"Pretty good. We are getting ready for finals, so it's boring this week."

"When are finals again?" Steve asked.

"Dad! They're next week!" Maja exclaimed.

"Oh, I know, I was just making sure you knew," he said with a wink. Maja rolled her eyes in her father's direction.

“Where are we going?” Maya asked as a matter of course. By her tone, she had no idea what he was up to, and that was just how he wanted it.

“I figured we would get something to eat real quick and then do a little shopping. Your birthday and Christmas are coming up, after all. What are you hungry for?”

“Um… Chicken fingers and a shake.”

“Wow, that is very specific. You got it. Will Press Box work?”

“Yes! Yum!” Maja shouted. Perfect, and only about five minutes from the Honda dealer, Steve thought.

As they sat and ate their chicken fingers with white gravy and fries, Steve thought about the last six years. He was a pretty shitty father for the first year. He knew that. When Morgan came along to take some of the responsibilities, he welcomed the chance to grieve without having to worry about the day-to-day job of raising a nine-year-old girl. He had allowed her to leave her husband of ten years to come take care of his kid and to eliminate the empty spot in his bed. He absently wondered if he had bothered to change the sheets before he had sex with her in his marriage bed? The mattresses Shelby had picked out just a year before she died. He hadn’t been fair to her, and he hadn’t been fair to his daughter.

"Dad, can I ask you a question?" Maja quietly asked, dragging him back to reality.

"Of course, Hun. What's up?"

"What's going on with you and Morgan? She has been acting really weird lately, and you have been locked in your office every night." Maja searched her dad's face as she asked. She wasn't sure if he would be honest with her or not.

"Um, well, it's complicated," Steve decided to offer her as much candor as he was capable of. It's possible I moved a little quickly after your mom passed, and lately, I have been thinking about that a lot. I'm not sure I was thinking clearly, and now that I am..." He had a hard time finishing his sentence because he wasn't even sure what all that signified.

"Dad, I can see you're not happy, not like how you were with Mom. I like Morgan, but I can tell that you don't." Oh, geez, Steve thought, out of the mouths of babes. Steve thought he was holding it all together, and now he knew he'd been wrong. He was wrong about a lot of things lately.

"I'm sorry, Maja. I don't know what to say… it's not that I don't like her. I just need to figure some things out," Steve tried to explain.

"Please talk to her then. She's been walking around the

house like a crazy person these last few weeks. I have never seen her so…so weird. It's like she can't sit still." Steve knew exactly the words that Maja was trying to come up with. Morgan had so much anxiety about what was going on that she was unable to control her behavior. For a moment, he felt guilty. He watched her dip her last crisper in gravy and eat it before responding.

"Yes, Hon, I know I need to talk to her. I will, promise."

"Okay, good," She seemed relieved.

"Let's talk about something else. How about where we're going shopping?"

"Okay, you mean I get to pick?" Maja asked hopefully.

"No, you don't get to pick. You don't even have much say in exactly what we're getting, except for the color."

"What do you mean?" She asked. Steve waited for her to make the connection before answering her question.

"OH MY GOD, you mean we are getting a car?" Maja screamed. Several tables in the restaurant turned to gawk despite the music but turned back when they saw it was a scream of joy, not terror. "Are you kidding me?" She asked, still in shock.

"Yes, but I picked out the kind of car based on the safety rating, so there is no negotiating there. We'll go to the lot and check out any of the ones with less than 30,000 miles. Sound good?"

"Yes, Dad! What kind of car is it?"

"We will get you a Honda Accord, they are super sharp looking cars that are safe but also have good resale value."

"Ok, let's go!"

"I do have to pay first, then we can go. Don't worry, we have plenty of time." Maja was already standing next to the table, slightly jumping up and down. She was still a kid, Steve reminded himself. She was turning fifteen, not twenty-five. He would have to set down some pretty strict ground rules, but he didn't want to put a damper on the evening. He would go over them in a few days when she'd had time to enjoy the surprise.

They spent almost an hour walking around the car lot, and he quickly realized new or used he wasn't getting out of there for less than $25k but more likely around $32k if they decided on a new one. On demand, the salesman was hanging back until they had time to peruse the inventory. Steve could tell she was trying to stick close to the pre-owned section, not wanting to spend more of his money than she had to. Again, he thought about what a good daughter she always was.

"Dad! Come here!" She called from two rows over, "This is the one… I think." The salesman approached just as quickly and arrived at the car before he did. Irritating. She was standing next to the 2022 electric blue sport model. She had good taste. He would give her that. It was not quite loaded, but close, and had a grey leather interior and a sunroof.

"Let me run inside and grab the keys. Can I see your ID?" Wes, the overeager salesman, said. With his driver's license in hand, Wes ran inside while Maja got situated in the passenger seat.

"Is this one your favorite?"

"Yes, I like the inside and outside of this one the best."

"Okay, I'll drive it around, but you will have to trust me if I feel like something is wrong. It doesn't mean we won't get a car; it just means we need to find a different one. Okay?"

"Okay, Dad." She sounded like a kid, and he was glad. She was already growing up too fast, and he had basically missed the last six years because his head was up his ass.

Wes returned with the keys and dealer plates. Steve found no issues with the car when it was all said and done. They only had to wait another thirty minutes to get into the finance office, just to be pressured into buying the additional warranties he knew he was going to buy simply because it was his only daughter's first car.

"Can someone drive this to my house tonight? We only live about ten minutes from here." Steve inquired.

"Of course, I'll ask if the lot attendant can follow me over there, and I'll take it for you." After another forty minutes, seventeen signatures, and a car detail later, they were off on a three-car caravan back to the house. Steve glanced at his phone for the first time in the last several hours, seeing three missing calls from Morgan and at least a few texts. He still couldn't stand her, but the guilt he felt earlier was just behind that, rearing its head. She would have to wait; whatever she wanted could be dealt with in ten minutes. He didn't want Maja to hear.

"Thank you so much, Dad. I didn't really think you would get me a car this year. I love it, and I will take good care of it."

"I know you will. I'll take you out driving tomorrow, and in a few days, we will sit down and go over the rules. You are still not able to drive it by yourself until you get your full license next year, and if I catch you driving it, even once before then, I'll be forced to sell it."

"Okay, Dad. Understood. I'll have the whole year to practice with you and Morgan. Can we go get my permit on my birthday?" She pleaded.

"Yes, we will. You can't go out on the roads until we have that. Tomorrow will have to be parking lot practice."

When they arrived home, Steve could see Morgan at the window pulling the blinds back when she saw the three vehicles pulling into the driveway. Steve parked his car in the garage and got out to meet the guys and grab Maja's keys. He noticed that she did not come outside and was no longer at the window when Wes and the attendant drove away. Maja was inspecting her new car again, walking around to the back and pressing the truck pop button.

"Maja, when we go inside, please go to your room and hang out for a little while. I'm going to talk to Morgan and explain about the car and then clear the air. Will you do that for me?"

"Of course. I'll go now," she lowered the trunk and then went straight inside without having to be asked a second time. When Steve walked in the living room was empty. Not a good sign. He wandered into the office, put down his backpack, and then went in search of his wife. As he entered their bedroom she began to speak before he could even see where she was.

"So, you take her to go get a brand new car without even telling me and then don't answer your phone or texts?" Morgan was sitting on the floor against the wall and between the bed. Steve had to walk around to her side of the bed and look over the side to see her.

"Morgan, get up please," he offered his hand to help her off the floor.

"No. I'm fine where I am," she said, sulking.

"You are not fine, Morgan. Please get off the floor, and let's talk. I want to apologize."

She looked up at him with hope in her eyes, taking his hand. Steve hated that look. She looked like a kicked dog that had just been given a scrap from the table. He hated himself even more for letting this continue as long as it had.

"Sit down on the bed, please," he directed, "We have to stop playing games with each other, Morgan."

"Exactly what kind of games do you think I'm playing?" Morgan asked.

"You are pretending that everything is fine when it's not. So have I. I'm not blaming you. I'm simply stating a fact. I'm sorry for everything that has been going on these last few months. I know it's my fault, but it doesn't mean that everything is going to be okay."

"What do you mean?" Morgan's eyes widened in anticipation of what she knew was coming. She had known for weeks and fought it with every fiber of her being.

"This isn't working for either one of us anymore. I think we both got carried away after Shelby died. We missed her so much that it helped to have each other, but I don't think there was any real love there."

"You shit! Are you kidding me, Steve? You mean to say that you never loved me? Is that what you're saying? Not only did I leave my husband for you, but I also take care of your kid, and the house, every little detail that goes into keeping things running goes through me… and you're saying I did all of this for nothing? Thank you very much. That's great!" Her eyes had welled up with weeks of pent-up tears she had not allowed herself to shed.

"Hey… I don't mean that I never loved you. I mean that it's been hard to know what was real and what wasn't. We've grown apart these last few years, and it isn't fair to either of us to deny that." Steve's foot was in his mouth again, and he did his best to backpedal as quickly as possible before Morgan did anything rash.

"You're an asshole, Steve. Pathetic. You don't even want to try and make things work with your wife of five years, who has turned her whole life upside down for you. What am I supposed to do now? You want a divorce!" She wiped tears from her face each time they fell, causing her cheeks to redden and her hands to become wetter and wetter.

"I never said that. I said it wasn't working, that's all." Steve sat next to her on the bed, touching her with the same hand that held Lexi's breast just a few hours before.

"What do you want? If you want me to leave, say so. Don't keep dragging me along." He had to give it to her, and she was right; it wasn't fair to drag her along. However, he had to figure out some things about Maja before kicking her to the curb. His work schedule was always hectic, and he counted on her to ensure Maja was always picked up, made it to cheerleading practice, and even doctor's appointments. He would need to hire someone to help before he cut the strings completely.

"I wanted us to clear the air. That's all for now. We need to recognize problems, but I'm not saying it is completely over. You need to stop trying so hard, and I need to do better at talking. Can we get through Maja's birthday this week and then Christmas and talk more about our next steps in the new year?" He moved his hand from her shoulder to her chin, tilting her head to the side and lightly kissing her lips. "Okay?"

"Okay. Will you lay with me for a minute?" Morgan asked, attempting to press her advantage.

"Yes, I will."

He forced himself to kiss her again, and when she began to unbutton his shirt, he reluctantly allowed it. If this is what she needs to continue on for the next few weeks, so be it. She worked feverishly to get him hard, and finally, when her goal had been achieved, she bent down to put him in her mouth.

"Stop!" He demanded a little too loudly, "I want to be inside of you instead." Her brow furrowed, but she turned on her back and spread her legs wide to allow him entry. If her mouth made it to his cock, he knew what she would have tasted, and the game would be up. He caught her just in time.

When it was finally over, she clung to him, silently sleeping with her head on his arm and a faint smile on her lips. Steve would have to pay the price to keep the family together for a few weeks longer, even if it meant trying to keep her happy. She disgusted him, but at this point, he had no other choice. When she began snoring, he knew she was in deep enough sleep to escape for a few minutes. He tip-toed to the bathroom, locked the door, pulled out his phone from his pocket, and jerked off until he accomplished what he couldn't manage inside of her. After washing his hands, he quickly changed into his night shirt and boxers and crawled back into bed. If misery loves company, they must be the perfect couple.

Chapter Twenty-Two

"Hi, babe. How's it going?" Shelby answered.

"Lonely without you. How's California? What's the weather like?"

Shelby hadn't looked at the weather since she got here, and if he checked, he might know she was lying. Ugh! Would he check, or was he just making small talk?

"It's good here," she claimed as ambiguously as possible. How are your arms feeling?" she asked, attempting to take the spotlight off her.

"Pretty good, actually. When are you coming home? It's strange having all your stuff here finally and for the house to still be empty." Jeremy lamented.

Over the last several months Shelby began to think of Jeremy as the perfect man. Hot as hell, great in bed, smart, educated, thoughtful, and caring. It was like she had made him up in one of her novels. Here she was, lying to him and using his trust in her to create an alibi for her whereabouts this week. She knew that if the police came asking, Jeremy would tell them exactly where she could be found, and that would throw them off track with enough time to make her final escape if needed.

"Babe, I've only been gone for a day so far. I'll be here at least a few more days, but I'll get home as fast as I can. I don't want to be away any more than you do. Were you okay at the house by yourself last night?" That was the truth. Shelby would give anything for all of this to blow over. According to Ansel, none of the others have ever experienced these types of problems. That's what I get for living in the age of technology and being too lazy to go down to the police station and give them my goddamn fingerprints; she chastised herself.

"Yep, I was fine, slept like a baby. I am a grown man, after all." Shelby noticed that he sounded a little annoyed.

"I was just asking because of what happened. I'm sorry."

"It's fine. I really am feeling better, and I am eager to get on with our lives. The last month has sucked, Scarlet, and I wanted to tell you that I'm sorry for putting such a damper on everything. If you felt like you had to escape for a while and clear your head or something, I understand."

"Jeremy, no! That's not it at all." Shelby pleaded for understanding. "This is work and nothing more than bad timing. I love you more than you will ever know. You are my everything."

"I'm glad to hear it because you are the love of my life, Scarlet. I'll do anything and everything to keep you."

The tears flowed freely down her face, and as she looked

around the bookstore, she was relieved that no one was taking any particular note of her. She hid in the back of the fiction area near the fantasy section to compose herself.

"We are on the same page, babe. Me too. I gotta go for now, but I'll call you tonight when I get back to the hotel. I love you."

"Love you too. Bye, Scarlet."

"Bye." And he was gone. How could she feel any more guilty? Walking around New York looking for books when her man was home alone just weeks after being horribly attacked. She could tell he was still feeling vulnerable, and she didn't blame him one bit. What he needed was a supportive partner who wouldn't cut and run at the last minute, someone reliable. Well, beating herself up wasn't going to do any good. She would wait out the next few days and interject some curiosity into the next conversation about if he had heard from the police. If he hadn't, she would have to come back and face any potential consequences that may happen down the road. What choice did she have?

Shelby drank the rest of her coffee and decided that this bookstore was far too exceptional to walk out without purchasing a new book. Besides, she needed something to do to fill the hours in the evenings at the hotel. Even though she wrote Erotica, it wasn't really her reading genre. She preferred a good mystery, thriller, or horror novel any day. She approached a young female employee stocking books in a baggy NYU sweatshirt and faded jeans.

"Excuse me, is there a section for local authors here? I love would to support someone while I'm in town." Shelby asked.

"Absolutely, I'll walk you over there. I'm really glad you asked." The girl began walking toward the front of the store by the entrance. Her blonde ponytail swayed as she went, pointing out the first large display as a customer would enter the store. "My great-grandfather ran this store for many years before passing it on to my grandmother and then my mom. He was passionate about ensuring the New York writing community was featured above anything else."

"That's amazing! Are you going to take over the store one day?" Shelby smiled at her as she inquired.

"I hope so! I have an older brother, but he's more into sports than books. I think Mom will pick me." Shelby was instantly saddened by this young girl's innocent and hopeful face. She spent so many years away from people that she hadn't spent much time speaking to children or teenagers. This girl couldn't be more than a year or two older than Maja was now. This young lady was almost grown, so beautiful and full of life and promise for the future. What would Maja be like today? Ambitious with hope for the future or the opposite?

"I bet she will pick you too. What would you recommend for

a good mystery story?" Shelby asked.

"Jim Toner's *Intercepted* is phenomenal. You won't be able to put it down."

"Fantastic, thank you."

"When you make a purchase here, a portion of our profits goes towards helping women leave domestic abuse situations. Since we started keeping track in 1975, we have assisted over twelve thousand women in the New York Area to find new homes and start new lives." Shelby could see the pride in her eyes as she spoke about the store's secondary mission, wondering if somewhere along the way in the store's history, someone had been a victim.

Shelby picked up a paperback copy, thanked the girl, and went to the register to pay. It's amazing how sometimes life can come full circle, and the past hits you right in the face, she thought.

Spending the following day with Patricia and the team was just as irritating as she assumed it would be. They booked an entire day of meet and greets, vision planning, and new distribution concepts. In more than one meeting, they attempted to talk her into an international book tour, to which she politely declined without explanation. There was no need to justify her rules to them, considering how much money she was making everyone seated at the table. At least she had something tangible to talk to Jeremy about when they spoke in the evening. She told him about the new marketing strategy and how obnoxious Patricia was, laughing together for the first time since she left. As the third day rolled around, she was beginning to think she had overreacted. It was possible that once they found out about the owner of the fingerprints being dead, they would assume that she had been in the house prior to her death. If they hadn't put two and two together with a picture that they surely had access to, they might not be looking that hard. The waiting was the worst part. Every time her phone buzzed, she continued to jump and imagine the coming apocalypse. The worst part was that she missed Jeremy. She should be home right now. Two more days, she decided, would be the limit. Whatever happened after that, she would be home for, come hell or high water. Today would be another day to play tourist and wait around.

True to his word, Steve took Maja to get her driver's permit on the day of her birthday, and they spent the evening practicing with her in her new car. They had already spent a few hours in a parking lot previously. This time, she was ready for the open road.

"Dad! I'm not going to crash. Calm down!" Maja yelled from the driver's seat as Steve held onto the dashboard with both hands. His anxiety had gotten the better of him, although she was doing an excellent job for her first real driving experience with other cars on the road. Whatever happened to those cars with a brake pedal on the passenger side that driving instructors used to use? If they made those for the general public, he would have bought one of those instead.

She drove in the parking lot again for a few minutes and then sat through a series of lectures about safety, cell phone usage, mirrors, and turn signals. When Maja finally talked him into getting out on the road, Steve felt like he might throw up. He was nervous about her driving but also began to realize how grown-up she really was. This was a major milestone for his only child. After spinning around the neighborhood up to 40 mph, she drove them the two miles on residential roads back home. She managed to navigate a few tight spots and even avoid a few cars that were going way too fast in the opposite direction. Maja had picked up more on her first real day of driving than he had in his first few weeks. When they pulled up to a police car parked on the curb, Steve didn't think much of it at first. He assumed the vehicle must be there for a close neighbor or even a family event.

"What should I do?" Maja asked, sounding agitated.

"Put it in park and hop out, I'll pull it into the driveway. I don't think that car is here for us. If it was, Morgan would have called." He was careful to put his phone on the ring before they left just in case she called. He would have to be more careful with her these next few weeks before any final decisions were made. Morgan was like a bomb waiting to go off.

Maja got out of the car and walked toward the garage door while he finished parking just in case she was to run into the door. She had done such a great job that he doubted she would have, but better safe than sorry. Safety never takes a vacation, he thought. As soon as he parked, Maja began entering the code for the garage when they saw two police officers, one in a large cowboy hat, walk toward them from the direction of the front door.

"Mr. Wise?" The officer in the hat asked.

"Yes, hi. Can I help you?" He noticed that Morgan didn't follow them outside.

"We came here to follow up on the inquiry we made earlier this week about your previous wife, Shelby Wise." Steve glanced quickly at Maja, seeing the startled look on her face.

"I don't understand. What do you mean?" Steve asked, confused.

"We talked to your wife on Monday, and she gave us a copy of the death certificate, but we have a few more questions for you."

Steve's anger peaked instantly. They had been here before talking about Shelby and Morgan never even mentioned it. No wonder she wasn't out here, she was probably in the bedroom packing up her shit because she knew that hell was going to break loose once these guys left.

"You are going to have to back up and tell me what's going on. Who are you, and why are you here?"

The policemen were obviously as confused as he was, sharing bewildered looks with each other. He could also sense some embarrassment on his behalf, which only made it worse. Your new wife not telling you about the police coming by to discuss your dead wife was beyond embarrassing, it was inexcusable.

"I apologize, Mr. Wise. I am Officer Curry, and this is Officer Mundy. We work for the Dallas criminal investigations unit, but we are here in coordination with the Phoenix Police Department to ask some additional questions about your late wife…"

"Maja, can you please close the garage and go inside?" Steve interrupted. The officer remained silent as she moved slowly past them into the garage and then watched as the door closed. "Go ahead," Steve commanded.

Curry began again, "When we spoke with your wife on Monday, she told us that Shelby had passed away about six years ago and provided an original death certificate. We had some reason to believe she could have been involved with a crime in Phoenix about a month ago. Now that we know she has passed, we just needed to clear up some loose ends."

"How is it possible that you thought my wife could have been involved with something over five years after her death? I don't get it. It doesn't make sense." Steve blurted out.

"We have some physical evidence that suggests she was at the scene at some point… her fingerprints were located at the scene of a burglary and assault."

"That is impossible. Not only is she dead, but she has never even been to Arizona. I have known her since she was twenty years old, and she barely traveled. You must have her data mixed up with someone else. All of this is impossible. Don't your computers tell you when someone's dead?"

"I understand your frustration, Mr. Wise. One of the problems I mentioned was determining whether Shelby had ever been to Phoenix before. If we can establish that she was there prior to her death, then we can simply close this portion of the case and move on. Fingerprints can remain on a surface for many years if they are undisturbed, so while hard to imagine, it is plausible the evidence had been there for over six years. If you are claiming that she has never been to Phoenix, that brings up an entirely new problem for us, as you can understand," Officer Curry explained as plainly as he could.

"Where in the hell did you get Shelby's fingerprints, anyway? She has never been arrested… never even had a speeding ticket. I still think there has been some sort of mix-up on your end."

"When Mrs. Wise was in college, she applied to student teach and was required to submit her fingerprints during that process. She was photographed and fingerprinted at the time, and the photo matches up with her driver's license picture taken during the same year."

Steve vaguely remembered her deciding to move from education to psychology but hadn't known her at the beginning of the term when she began the education program. None of this could be happening. His anger was burning so brightly that he couldn't think of another question that would change all of this into making sense.

"Mr. Wise, now that we have an official death certificate, all we need to do is confirm that she was in Phoenix at some point. That's it. Please take a few days to think about any past business trips, long weekends, or anything that would have put her in the area, and we are happy to close the books on this entire situation."

"Hold on… where were these fingerprints found?" Steve asked. This was all getting too much to handle. If they said she had robbed a bank or something, it was going to be the last straw.

The officers made eye contact again for less than a second but long enough for Steve to notice. "Where?" he asked again.

"Inside of a private residence," Officer Curry offered coolly.

"Inside of whose private residence?" Steve asked, his voice barely above a whisper.

"A private citizen. He was attacked in his home and burglarized just over a month ago, and the prints were found inside the home. Initially, it was thought the prints could be associated with whomever illegally entered the residence. That is why we visited your home on Monday. Now that we know she is deceased, we are simply trying to establish her potential connection to the scene, perhaps at another time."

Steve's mouth hung open. If they were so confident of their evidence, there were only a few possibilities on what could be happening here. The one that was flickering on and off in his head like a neon sign was obvious, and he could tell the officers suspected it, too. When Shelby had traveled for her job, had she always been honest about where she was going and who she was seeing? He was so blind in his happiness with his wife he never suspected her of having an affair. Why else would her fingerprints be inside of someone's home a thousand miles away?

"Was this a family residence?" Steve framed the only question he could think of to try and figure out the circumstances.

"No, sir. A single resident lives and has lived in the home for a number of years."

After a few moments of silence, the much shorter cop spoke up for the first time. “Mr. Wise, why don’t we leave you with our contact information and follow up with you in a few days? Sometimes, we don’t remember insignificant details clearly and need time to recall what happened several years ago. When you have some time to think about it, I bet you will come to the conclusion that your wife had a very legitimate reason to be in the area.” He pulled two cards out of his jacket pocket without looking and handed them to Steve. Without formally dismissing themselves, they began to retreat to the cruiser parked on the curb.

“Wait!” Steve called after them. “Didn’t you ask the guy?”

They both turned around and stared at him without replying.

“Did you ask the guy who lives in the house about Shelby? If she had ever been there?”

“According to my phone call this morning with the team in Phoenix, they were going to speak with him today to try and close the gap on their end as well,” Curry responded.

“Can I get his phone number, too, please?”

“Unfortunately, we can’t hand out the victim's contact information, but I can forward you the information for the people working the case at the Phoenix police department.”

“Give it to me now, please.” At Steve’s insistence, Mundy

removed a pen and his notepad from inside his jacket pocket along with his phone. After a few minutes of searching, he wrote down the detective's contact details, ripped off the sheet of paper, and handed it to Steve. Until now, he hadn't felt the cold of the December day, but all at once, he began to shiver. "Thank you," Steve muttered.

Before they could respond, he swung toward the house and went inside through the unlocked front door, closing it gently behind him. He told himself to remain calm, exaggerating his movements to ensure his anger didn't get the best of him. Now, he had to deal with Morgan.

Chapter Twenty-Three

Maja did as she was told by closing the garage door, although she didn't go inside. There was no way she was going anywhere out of earshot after the policemen explained why they were there. No one had breathed life back into her mother in such a way since she was a little girl, and her father didn't like to bring up the subject of her mother anymore. It made him too sad, even after all this time. She was like a perfect memory everyone was trying to forget, and Maja never understood why. What harm would it be to talk about her mom?

Being dismissed meant that whatever her father didn't want her to hear was precisely what she should be listening for. Maja tip-toed to the metal garage door, carefully bending down below the four square windows so the men outside would not see her. As they continued to talk without her presence, the more uneasy she became. Why would her Mom's fingerprints still be in someone's house after six years? She and Stacey, her best friend, went to the science museum for school last year, where her class participated in several CSI-like crime lab activities. One of those activities was manually dusting for fingerprints. The instructor of the exhibit explained that, depending on the surface, fingerprints could last more than forty years. The issue was the surface had to be uncontaminated for that entire length of time. Were there surfaces in someone's home that they hadn't touched or cleaned for over six years? That didn't make sense. Who was the guy who lived at this house?

The endless possibilities surged through her mind as she continued to crouch and listen. She tried to recall when and if her mom traveled, certainly not often and usually not without her father. As far as she remembered, her mother had read her a bedtime story every night since she could remember. She could still recite some of the books they would read from memory, and she would never forget the look on her mom's face when she read her first word. It was as if she received the biggest surprise of her life.

Maja could sense her Dad's anger in his voice as the conversation continued. She knew he was mad at Morgan, but there was something else too. When the policemen offered to call him in a few days, it was time to go back inside and attempt to make it to her room unnoticed. As soundless as possible, she moved her way to the door leading to the main hallway, opened it, briefly looked around, and then went straight to her room. Success!

Maja hadn't heard her father's last question, and if she had, it may or may not have changed the plan she was beginning to formulate. All she knew was that there was a verified location where her mother had been, and no one who knew her seemed to understand. Something wasn't right. Maja decided she would need more information before she calculated her next step.

Steve found her on the bed, this time not bothering to hide on the floor as she had a few days before. Once again, she played the part of a whipped dog, her head hanging down and long blonde hair dangling in her face. He stood two inches in front of her, glaring at the top of her head, waiting for her to speak, unwilling to be the first one to break the tension. The minutes seemed to pass like hours as beads of sweat began to form on his brow. This bitch better speak up, he thought. Just as he lifted his right leg to move, she gave in, unsure of what he may do.

"I'm sorry," Morgan said in barely a whisper.

"The fuck you are," Steve replied, not wanting her to get away with another one of her excuses. In the last few years, he stopped listening, but early on, it seemed like all she brought to the table were excuses. It all boiled down to a series of pathetic excuses, why she couldn't get a job, why she needed to buy this or that, and why it would be best if she stayed in the house. He was done with all that.

"I knew it would upset you, so I just thought it would be best… and since she was gone… I answered their question, so you didn't have to worry about it." Her rambling was a giveaway, and she knew Steve would be furious if he ever found out. And she made the choice to keep it from him anyway.

"Morgan. I am only going to say this one time. Stay away from me. Do not ask me any questions, do not expect me to sleep next to you, and for God's sake, do not touch me. I am done with you." Instinctively, she reached for his hand, and Steve recoiled as if he had just been touched by a flame. "Don't. Don't even think about it. I am going to talk to my daughter and then make some calls. I don't want to see you." He was gone before she could stand up. There were no tears this time, nothing but the slightest sense of relief. Now that she was certain it was over, she could stop worrying about when it would end.

Steve knocked on Maja's door and entered without waiting for an invitation.

"I feel terrible that you had to be here when that happened. I know how much you miss your mom."

"What did they say?" She asked.

With no hesitation, Steve began to lie. After all, he had become quite the expert in how to lie to those closest to him in the last few years. He still wasn't sure how long after his wife's death he had become this version of himself. Was he always this way, or did it take losing her to unbury this subhuman part of himself? He and Shelby used to tell each other stories of friends or celebrities who had cheated or betrayed their spouses or loved ones as if they were outsiders, trying to understand why these foreign creatures would do such a thing. Now, he realized that he was the only outsider. His wife had been pretending, too, just as he had been with Morgan. Had she ever really been happy, or was his memory of their perfect marriage an empty shell?

"There has been some mix-up. Your mom couldn't possibly be where they thought she was, so there isn't anything left to do. They know she's gone, honey, so they won't be back."

"That's it? Where did they say she was?"

"I'm not sure. They could have said, but I don't remember. I am so sorry you had to deal with that, especially on your birthday. What can I do to make it better?"

Her eyes seemed to examine his face for several seconds. Steve couldn't read her expression, which exacerbated his anxiety. He got worried when she turned away and sat down in her desk chair. "Hon, what are you thinking? I want to make sure you are okay."

"Of course, I'm fine. If you say it is nothing, then it is nothing." Since when did she grow up enough to sound like a woman who knows her husband or boyfriend is lying to her? A perfect cold tone and disinterested gaze to go with it. No matter her tactics, he would refuse to tell her. She was too young to understand, and no matter what Shelby had done, he also refused to tarnish the perfect shine that Maja had created in her mind of her mother's image.

"You don't seem fine. This is a big deal, Maja. Someone coming to ask questions is bound to bring up some memories. Are you sure you don't want to talk about it?"

"No, Dad. If you say it's nothing, then it's nothing." She turned her body in the chair toward her laptop screen and turned it on. He had never been dismissed by his own daughter, but that is exactly what she was doing. She was understandably upset, and today was her birthday. The entire situation sucked!

"I'll leave you alone for a while then. Remember, we have dinner tonight at The Cheesecake Factory at 6:15 PM. It will be just us." With the last statement, she tilted her head to look at him, and raised her eyebrows, but said nothing. She was more intuitive than he gave her credit for. It was as if she knew half of what was going on---she would be a mess, he thought.

Steve walked directly to his office, immediately searching for the Phoenix Police Department's contact information, and then he remembered that he had it in his jeans pocket. Unlike most days where he paused for a moment to consider the extra desk that used to occupy the space next to his, this time, it didn't even register. All he could think of were the last six years of misery. How long had she been unfaithful to him? When she said she was going to her friend's bachelorette party in Vegas the second year they were married, was that it?

Steve took a deep breath and thought about his strategy for finding out who this guy was before he proceeded. As he considered the approaches, he thought about how much he loved his wife, even still. Was it possible he was wrong, and she had a legitimate reason to be in Phoenix? Before he called the police, he owed it to her, and more importantly himself, to consider all the possibilities. Steve opened the top right-hand drawer of his desk, the one where he kept nothing but notepads. Ever since his first job, he had a habit of writing everything down and keeping the notepads just in case he ever needed to look over them again. Going through a yellow legal pad every few months for the last twenty years, he had accumulated over a hundred of them, most in a big box in the garage that Shelby had labeled "Obsessive Compulsive" in black Sharpie with a big smiley face next to it. His desk drawer contained this year's, so about three or four, and then there was a copy paper box lid on the floor next to his feet that included the previous few years. He would have indeed written down any trips she made after Maja was born because he needed to make a list of additional responsibilities for the time she was gone. Before he went digging, he took out a notepad. He began jotting down the approximate year and reason Shelby had traveled alone during their fourteen years together. The bachelorette party was the first time he could remember. That would have been about 2006, but to Vegas. She went to training in Austin before their move to Texas… in 2009 or 2010, probably 2010, because Maja had just been born. Then there was her reward trip to Orlando for being the number one sales representative in the funeral business when Maja was almost four so, 2013. Since then, he couldn't remember anything…. But there had to be. What about a time when he was gone? Would she have left, too? Could she have? Just because he couldn't remember didn't mean it didn't happen.

Exasperated, he pulled his cell out of his pocket and dialed the number, reading it from the scrap of paper Officer Mundy had given him. After two rings, a deep voice answered.

"Detective Preston."

"Um, yeah, hi. My name is Steve Wise. Two officers visited my home today and asked questions about my late wife…"

"Yes, Mr. Wise, I am familiar with the situation. How can I help you?"

He seemed tight-lipped, and he guessed that's how he would have to be due to his profession. He was going to have to be specific, and that is what he was trying to avoid. "Officer Preston said you were aware that my wife is dead." It was not really a question, but he was checking the temperature of the water.

"Yes, they sent me a copy of the death certificate."

There was nothing else. The detective was no armature.

"Officer Mundy said you were going to speak with the victim today. He was unable to provide me with any direct contact information, but he said you were going to ask him if she was ever in his home," Steve said carefully.

"Did you have a question, Mr. Wise?" Fine, Steve was going to have to come out with it.

"Yes. Did you speak to him, and if so, did he give you any answers? I would really like to know that all of this is settled, as the police have been to my home twice this week."

"I did speak with him, and he provided me with an answer of sorts. He claims that he never knew anyone by the name of Shelby Wise. Since you called, I do have something you could help me with. I was going to stop by his house tomorrow and show him a photo of your wife, but all I have is her driver's license photo. Would you mind emailing me a few other photographs of your wife, that may make identification easier. If he sees a picture of her, that may jog his memory. We are just as anxious to close this portion of the case as you are to get us out of your hair. Once we eliminate her as a suspect, we can get on with finding out who the actual assailant was."

"Shelby is a suspect? She's dead!" Steve was astonished by what he was hearing. His mouth was hanging open, and his brow was furrowed. Unbelievable, he thought.

"We must do our due diligence in eliminating the fingerprints as those belonging to a suspect. I apologize. I should have been clearer. Would you please help us out with the photographs?"

"Sure, I can do that." As he agreed, Steve had made up his mind about his next step.

"Would it be possible to contact this man myself?" Steve asked. There was a pause on the other end of the phone before Detective Preston replied.

"Is there a specific reason you would like to speak with him?"

"To be honest, Detective, this is a bit strange. After all this time, someone shows up at my door about fingerprints in a man's house I have never met who lives a thousand miles away. I don't think it's too much to ask that I speak with this man and find out what's going on!" Steve's voice rose unintentionally as he explained.

"I understand, Mr. Wise. You want to know if your wife had an inappropriate relationship with Mr. Locke."

Detective Preston had let it slip and didn't even realize it. Now he knew the fucker's name. His last name, at least. That was all he needed.

“Yes, I am,” Steve admitted.

“I can’t help you with that, Mr. Wise. The faster you send me those pictures, the faster we can all get through this.”

“Yeah, ok, fine. I’ll email you the pictures.”

Steve wrote down the detective’s email and made a promise to send them quickly, thanking him for his time. It was a promise he had no intention of keeping. According to Google, there were fourteen male Locke’s in the city of Phoenix, most of them were named John. Evidentially, these Phoenix folks knew their history. If he narrowed down the list to those living in houses as opposed to apartments and then limited the age band from 38 to 48, there were three: Two Johns and a Jeremy.

If this were a movie, he thought, Steve would be able to pick up the phone and dial a friend of his who worked at the FBI or even a local police station. His friend would run the name in the computer and spit out the last known addresses, disregarding the rules and federal consequences to help him out. He would have to do his best with Google. That’s all he had…. Glancing at the top right-hand corner of his computer again, he realized he had just enough time to book his flight before they would need to leave for Maja’s birthday dinner.

Chapter Twenty-Three

After Jeremy hung up his cell and pulled up the sleeves on his long-sleeved green and yellow striped Polo shirt, something told him not to call and tell Scarlet about the recent developments in his burglary case. Something was going on with her. Initially, he suspected that she had found out the real reason his laptops had been stolen, but even then, she wouldn't have just left. She may have been a little angry that he was keeping things from her, but not enough to jump on a plane. If Jeremy was sure of anything, it was that Scarlet was in love with him. They each felt it in a way that was hard to describe. He definitely didn't intend to or believe he would be in this situation with Scarlet. His last several "relationships," if you could call them that, ended with a complete lack of communication on both sides. More often than not, they ended when he found the next woman he wanted to sleep with.

Jeremy never made any promises and felt his conscience was clear. Settling down wasn't in his plans, but here he was, shacked up with a woman like no one he had ever met. He opened the fridge, surveyed the two boxes of leftover takeout, and decided to order Chinese.

As he reviewed the online menu on his iPhone, his mind continued to wonder about what the hell was going on with her. The information he collected on his former boss over the last several years wouldn't have mattered to her as much as his lying about it. All he was trying to do was protect her and himself. If he had learned anything, politically connected, wealthy, and powerful men don't hesitate to eliminate those that get in the way. He had never spoken to anyone in authority or otherwise about his knowledge. That was why he was still alive. When he realized his laptops were pretty much all they took, he knew it had been Barlowes' people who did it. When the police came up with fingerprints, he assumed they were some idiots he hired who deserved to get caught if they weren't going to wear gloves. His hired help could have been anyone, and that was frustrating. He wanted those guys caught, but the true identity of the man responsible had to remain anonymous. All Jeremy had on those hard drives were investment records of his companies, although those investments were made with laundered money. If the records were destroyed, then there was no more evidence. Mr. Barlowe liked him, and there were no hard feelings when he left the company. It must have taken him a while to realize the kind of information Jeremy had brought with him, or maybe he wasn't even sure and was playing it safe. He must be running for office, Jeremy mussed. That's the reason he was trying to clean up any potential pitfalls from his past. If he had spilled his cookies to the police, then the next break-in would have resulted in a bullet in the head instead of just a knock-out. Scarlet knew something was off about the break-in, and most likely, the police did too, but he was thankful she hadn't pressed it.

He was able to shake off his funk of guilt and pain from his arms, but just as he did, she ran. After eliminating his small deception from the list, he assumed her strange behavior the few days before her departure was just nerves. Moving almost everything into his house, giving up her independence, and co-habituating with a man she had met five months ago was a huge step. Jeremy thought it might be similar to cold feet. His best friend at college, Jason, had cold feet so badly the night before his wedding that he couldn't stop shitting water all night. As his best man, it was his job to pump him as full of as much Pepto Bismol every hour as possible. The funny thing was he never saw someone so in love when they were that young. He adored his bride-to-be in such a way that sophomore year he and the boys were effectively declaring him "pussy whipped." Jason didn't even care, just smiled. He wasn't sure he ever had that kind of devotion to his first wife, and he didn't have cold feet before the wedding, either. He understood it, though.

When she decided to cut and run on such short notice, he knew in his heart, it would only be a few days, and then he should come back, fuck his brains out, and things would go back to their normal, if not blissful, state. When he discovered she had lied about her whereabouts, that was a whole new matter to consider.

After he had read her incredibly sexy novel and she had

come clean about the nature of her writing, they began teasing each other with sexier and more explicit pictures when they were apart. He talked her into downloading Snapchat so they could send even raunchier photos to each other that would disappear after the other person viewed them. He had used it in the past for the exact same reason with that waitress he had met while traveling to Seattle. They had a two-month internet tryst after the live-action two-hour event. At first, it wound down slowly, but then, one day, he forgot to respond. He never heard from her again.

What Scarlet didn't realize, and he never thought he would need to use, was the feature that auto-enables location services through the app. All he had to do was send her a Snap, and when she opened it, her location would appear in a separate part of the app. He Snapped her the first night, and he looked up her location out of curiosity more than suspicion. He wanted to see exactly where she was in the city, what was around her, etc… When her location registered smack dab in the middle of Times Square in New York City, his heart broke more than he could admit. He had been lied to before by girlfriends and even his wife, but he had never been lied to by Scarlet… or so he thought. His love for her was so consuming that his chest ached at the thought of this level of deception. But---he refused to call her out. He was convinced that she would eventually tell him whatever was going on. The way she was acting, and the haste of her departure meant it wasn't an affair, so he pushed that thought from his mind. Whatever it was, It was going to be worse.

When the police called with an update on his case, he was relieved but confused to know that the potential woman suspect couldn't have been involved in the robbery. He didn't like the thought of Barlowe hiring a woman, but he did like the thought of the guys who knocked him out getting caught. He wanted someone to pay for what had happened, at any rate, and for this whole nightmare to go away. It seemed like a whole new nightmare was beginning. The woman being dead for several years was a wrinkle he didn't expect. He had only lived in the house full-time for a little over a year, even though he had owned the house for over a decade now. He wondered if it was an old cleaning lady's fingerprints or something. As far as he knew, those were the only people in here over the years. Det. Preston would send him some pics tomorrow, and they could both mark that Shelby woman off the list.

He was tempted to fly to New York tonight, find Scarlet, confront her, and bring her home. Maybe she would tell him what she was running from, and then again, she may need more time. Either way, he was willing to give her that time and space to figure her shit out if she would just come home. He decided to wait until tomorrow to decide what to do. It was getting late anyway. Tonight, he would let Scarlet call him. In the meantime, he ordered his Chinese dumplings and moo goo gai pan, then waited in his office for the food to arrive.

Shelby had a bad feeling. She had promised herself no more than two days, and since those two days had passed, it felt like someone was constantly walking over her grave again and again. She laughed hysterically aloud in her empty hotel room, unconsciously running her fingers through her long dark hair several times. Well, she had a real grave out there somewhere, didn't she? It was worth a laugh. How in the hell did this life get so complicated? Her second life was supposed to be simple and carefree, which was carefully built just the way she had always wanted. No matter what her intuition was saying, it was time to go home… tomorrow or maybe Friday. Something told her that leaving now would be the end of her and her new life. She needed to call Jeremy and tell him one more day, maybe making some excuse about getting a flight out. Better yet, she decided that if she booked a flight now, it would force her to stick with her timeline of leaving Friday. Let's not bother with the fact that a flight could be changed in a matter of seconds online. Once she had the flight set in stone, it was time to bite the bullet and call Jeremy.

Her excuses were getting harder to believe from her own lips, she wondered how they sounded to another person. By this time, he had to know she was full of shit. Either way, it didn't matter.

Whatever was going to happen was very close now. Shelby took her finger out of her mouth, hardly noticing that she had ripped her thumb nail off down to the quick.

"Hi, Babe!" Shelby said a little too cheerfully. "I booked my flight home, I just have to stay another day, and then I'll be there, okay?" She was rushing it, and her voice was shaking.

"What time do you get in? I can pick you up," Jeremy offered without missing a beat, seemingly not noticing her anxiety.

"Don't be silly. I'll Uber. It will be easier. I get in about five Friday night and will be home for dinner!" She was an old pro at lying but couldn't shake the feeling that her number was finally up.

Steve decided he had no time to waste. After taking Maja out to dinner, he went to the bedroom to pack, expecting to see Morgan cowering in the corner of the bed again, but she wasn't there. He grabbed his black hard-shell carry-on from the top shelf in the closet. Two pairs of slacks, two button-downs, two pairs of underwear, and a few T-shirts. There was no way he would be gone more than a day or two. As he was filling his shaving kit, he felt eyes on his back. Looking up, he saw Morgan's familiar grey SFA sweatshirt in the mirror. He liked her better silent anyway; today, at least, she would serve a purpose.

"Go sit on the bed. I need to talk to you," Steve ordered.

"Where are you going?" She muttered.

He went on digging through the second drawer of the bathroom vanity for a box of disposable razors he was sure he still had. A few moments later, the sweatshirt disappeared from view, but he was able to focus on the task at hand. When he was finally ready, he went to face her.

"I'm going on a business trip. I'm leaving tonight. I need you to stay here with Maja and make sure she gets to finals this week. After I get back, we will discuss what comes next." He was afraid to tell her exactly what he knew was going to happen next. She might bolt, leaving Maja unattended while he searched for the answers he desperately needed. "Tell me you understand what I am saying." She continued to look like someone who had undergone a shock and could not comprehend what was happening around her. When she finally gave him a slow nod, still avoiding eye contact, he was content that was enough. Without another word, he wheeled his hard case roller bag to the hallway and knocked on Maja's door, barely registering the unique absence of music. He was so consumed by his own thoughts that he didn't notice her quiet stares throughout dinner or the fact that she barely touched her chicken parmesan.

"Honey, I have a work emergency. I have to head out tonight to see a client. I'll be back in a few days. Morgan is here if you need anything. I gotta go, or I'll miss my flight." Steve bent down to kiss her on the forehead as she sat at her desk, not bothering to notice what was on her computer screen either. Maja made no attempts to ask questions.

"Okay, Dad. See you soon."

Steve was out the door moments later, snagging his brown leather jacket. He just made it to his 9:00 PM flight on time.

Maja expected a knock on the door anytime, suspecting precisely what her father was up to. In the meantime, she used Google to research the forensics of fingerprints, reading stories about how fingerprint evidence could be easily removed and stories about the technologies that lift prints from almost any surface. What she couldn't find was a situation that fit her own. Just twenty minutes into her search, the knock at the door she had expected came. After he was gone, she'd have to make several decisions. Regardless of the lying, any typical newly fifteen-year-old would wait until he returned in a few days to confront him, but she prided herself on being her mother's daughter. Her mother would not wait around, she told herself.

After hearing the garage door close behind her father, Maja trekked directly to his office and closed the door behind her. She powered on his Mac Book and, without hesitating, opened Chrome and clicked on the History tab at the top. If she were right, everything she needed would be here.

She started from the beginning and realized that her Dad had homed in his search to three potential addresses from a list of many. He searched for those three names on a few "find it" sites and then for five addresses in the Phoenix area on Zillow. Reviewing his printer history, she discovered he had printed all five addresses, just as Maja was doing now. A quick check of his email gave her his flight info: a one-way ticket to Sky Harbor International leaving tonight. Why was it so important to him to find this guy's house? The question circled in her mind like a vulture before a horrific realization began to form in her mind.

Chapter Twenty-Four

Getting out of the Uber in front of Jeremy's house, she finally felt a sense of relief for the first time in five days. Excuse me, her house… our house, she corrected herself. It was cold and wet, unseasonably so for Phoenix, even in December, but still warmer than New York. At least her flight hadn't been delayed. Small miracles. When she spoke with Jeremy this morning, he seemed thrilled to see her tonight, just as much as she was. They would put all of this behind them and move forward; Thank God. The Uber driver, a quiet, older Asian man, hopped out of the driver's seat and unloaded her bag from the truck, giving her a polite smile and a nod before driving away.

The garage door began to open before she even had a chance to text him of her arrival. Jeremy was waiting at the door with a big grin. So, this is what it would be like to come home to him? She could get used to this! Even after five days, she had forgotten how devastatingly handsome he was, especially when he wore that grey polo shirt. She loved the way the arms clung to his biceps, forcing them to stretch the fabric. She remembered it from their first date. Offhandedly, she wondered if he chose that specifically for tonight. How long was long enough to say hello before they could head to the bedroom? Her inner thighs tingled just thinking about it.

"How was your flight, babe?" Jeremy asked as he took the

handle of her roller bag out of her hand. "I'll put this in the bedroom for you. I just poured you a glass of wine. Go ahead and sit on the couch and relax for a minute." His voice trailed as he disappeared down the hallway toward their room. A glass of wine sounds heavenly right now. She removed her combo ballet flat and loafer shoes by the garage door, peeled off her jacket, flung it over the side arm of the couch, and then plopped herself dramatically into the middle of it. It was good to be home! There was no more running. She picked up the glass of red sitting on the coffee table, assuming it was that delicious merlot they picked up a few weeks ago after having tasted it at that little Italian bistro they had recently discovered. Yum, it was the very same, she thought, as the cool liquid circled her mouth. She placed the glass back down on the table before closing her eyes as she heard his footsteps coming back down the hall.

"Looks like you're glad to be home. I've been lonely without you." He lifted the wine glass and held it out for her.

"Yes, I am. And this wine is fantastic. I forgot we hadn't opened the bottle."

"Tell me about your trip." Jeremy inquired, laying back on the corner of the couch, intently watching her take another sip.

"Oh, Patricia is a nightmare, but overall, she came up with some good ideas for the next book. The series will have a different leading man in each one, with a sneak peek at the end to entice readers to preorder the next one. I got to meet the publishing team I had been working with for the last five years, which was fun. But Patricia talks more than anyone I have ever met. She literally couldn't stop. I watched her team's faces while she was going over the review process for *Fever Dreams,* and they couldn't stand her! I can see why they stay, though. She is good at what she does."

As she told her story, she realized how good it was to laugh. Sitting on pins and needles for the last week had set into her bones, laying on the couch next to the man she loved was all the medicine needed to snap out of it. Shelby scooted her butt a few inches to the right, close enough to reach for his hand, lifting it and then kissing each knuckle as she did when they first met.

"I love you.. so very much," Shelby whispered between kisses.

"How was the sightseeing? Did you do anything fun while you were in New York?" Jeremy asked coolly.

"Yeah, but only a few places. Visited Central Park and Times Square but didn't have the energy to do much mo…." Shelby froze. Her number was up. He knew she had been lying and let her dig herself into a nearly unsurmountable grave. There was no denying it now. He made no move to pull his hand away. He was leaving the ball firmly in her court. Maybe even allowing her to explain?

“Jeremy, I’m sorry I lied to you. I have no good excuse other than that I was running from the possibility of never seeing you again. I felt like if I didn’t… my past would catch up with me, and it would keep us apart forever. After everything you have been through lately, I know this is the last thing you need: me lying to you. You have to believe me when I say there is no one else. I wasn’t there to cheat or get away from you.” Shelby’s words came out like released steam. There was so much to say and explain, but she didn’t know how to do it. She couldn’t tell him. He wouldn’t believe her, and she would come off like a lunatic. Not to mention the promises she made to the man who had given her this life. There were others out there she had to protect, too. It wasn’t all about her.

“I need you to tell me everything. This is your chance. Look at me,” he lifted her chin. She saw both eyes brimming with tears. There was no doubt that this man loved her. He was conflicted about giving her a chance to explain but couldn’t help his feelings for her. “This is it. If you don’t tell me the truth, then we are over. Do you understand?” Despite the tears, his voice was calm and firm. She was startled enough to forget the wine glass was still in her hand before spinning a yarn that would get her out of this mess, she needed another swig. With all her careful planning, she hadn’t bothered to create a backstory other than the simplest one about where she grew up and the places she lived. Never in a million years did she think she would need a separate cover story, and there would be no time to fact-check or research, so she had to be as brief and ambiguous as possible. She was an author, after all, coming up with plausible fiction was worth millions in her bank account.

“Okay, babe, yes. I’ll tell you the truth. Before I tell you, I need you to know how much I love you. I never expected to find someone like you, ever. I never expected to fall so deeply in love. You are the only man I have ever been so afraid to lose. I don’t know what I would do without you.” She wasn’t allowing herself to cry. All she needed was for him to understand the intensity of her feelings for him. As she spoke, she could see the doubt in his gaze.

“If you ever loved me, I deserve the truth no matter how bad it is. I can get past just about anything because I believe you when you tell me how you feel. I’ll believe it more after you tell me what the hell is going on.” Jeremy sat up straight against the right arm of the couch, ready to listen. His hair was a little too perfect for so late in the evening, but she guessed he must have dressed for the day just before she got home.

“About six years ago, I was hurt very badly.” Unconsciously, Jeremy moved his body forward, intently listening. “I had to leave in a hurry where I was because if I didn’t, I and several other people would have been in danger. It forced me to change my name and leave everything I knew behind…” How much more could she say?

That's all the truth she could give him, but it wasn't enough. "I was a witness to a murder; they hurt me, and I was able to get away, but…"

Shelby couldn't take her eyes off Jeremy's face. As she spoke the last sentence, the tears he had held back came flowing down his cheeks. He put his face in his hands and shook his head several times, finally screaming. Shelby jumped up from the other end of the couch and went to him, pressing his head against her stomach. She tried to cradle him as best she could. She couldn't imagine what set him off, but the hysterics scared her more than anything. Even after his injury, he hadn't behaved this way.

"Why the fuck, Shelby?" Her legs began to buckle at the sound of her name, her real name. She barely caught the side of the coffee table before her knee connected with the ground, sending a shock of pain up her leg.

"Ow!" Shelby yelled. She instinctively rubbed her knee, now sprawled out between the sofa and the coffee table. She stared at Jeremy from her place on the floor. What the fuck was she supposed to do now? The police must have come or sent him a picture or something. He knew, and she continued to lie to him! He won't ever forgive me, she thought. Endless contemplations spiraled around her head. Maybe if she tells the whole story and swears him to secrecy… it was the only way. Jeremy looked up, focused his eyes on her, and continued to shake his head, his eyes bloodshot. She followed his gaze as he seemed to fixate on something behind her. She turned her whole body around to see it just before she passed out.

"I'm sorry that it took longer than I thought. I didn't mean for you to have to hide in the guest room for that long." Jeremy apologized.

Steve was speechless. He knew she was alive in his mind, but seeing her solidified the reality that he never thought possible. Once Jeremy had confirmed he knew the woman in the picture, he got the shock of his life when he learned that not only was his wife alive, but she was also living here with this man. Seeing her spread out on the hardwood was reminiscent of the last time he looked upon her, seemingly dead on the kitchen floor. After the first few minutes of speaking with Jeremy yesterday, Steve realized there was no reason to be angry with him. He was a pawn in all of this, just as he was.

Third times is a charm, as they say, and Jeremy was the third and final Locke he tried. He practiced his little thirty-second elevator pitch in the mirror at the hotel a few times before knocking on any doors, feeling stupid for traveling a thousand miles just to find out if his dead wife had an affair probably a decade ago. He held up a photo of his beautiful wife grinning widely, holding a then five-year-old Maja on her hip. At first, he tried "I'm looking for an old friend of mine" and then realized that was not going to get him the information he wanted. He practiced a few others and then settled on a simple and direct approach.

"Hi, I'm Steve Wise. I was wondering if you have ever known this woman?" Short and sweet and to the point. The first John seemed genuinely confused, the second wasn't home, and when Jeremy answered the door, and simply replied with "Why?"

Steve knew he had something. Jeremy asked to see the picture and invited him in without even asking who he was. This guy must have really been broken up when she stopped calling, was all Steve could think of at the moment.

It took the men a few hours and several beers to sort out what must have happened. Once Steve produced several more pictures of their wedding and daughter, it didn't take long for Jeremy to open up about how he met "Scarlet" and the timeline of the last six months. He didn't need Steve to tell him the reason she left in a hurry on a plane. Once he said the name, Shelby, he knew instantly why she panicked. Her house of cards was on shaky ground, and a slight breeze was bound to blow it over. He kept that part to himself for a while, though. When Jeremy admitted he had seen this Shelby woman a week ago, that is when Steve lost his shit. At first, screaming that Jeremy was a liar, demanding that Jeremy "Stop fucking with me, man!" and then to complete silence.

Steve removed his phone from the pocket of his khakis for a second time, allowing Jeremy to review the photos of the funeral, including several shots of the presentation table with Shelby's pearl inlaid urn surrounded by framed pictures of her life and those she loved. It was Jeremy's turn to rant, which he did for almost ten minutes. Up until she left, he would have dismissed this guy at the door, but knowing she was running and already lying about where she was, had left doubt in his heart. After his tantrum, he offered Steve a beer, and they sat at the kitchen table, sulking, letting the new and mind-blowing information they had both received sink in.

Steve's anger renewed when he thought of the old funeral director… Bishop was his name. The son of a bitch must have been in on it, helping her while pretending to console him and his daughter. He could have sworn she was dead on the floor, though. That was the thing. She was dead. They pronounced her dead at the hospital, and then they did an autopsy, for Christ's sake. She must have switched the bodies or had help. That was the only possible explanation. That's all he could think of. When he thought about the last six years of mourning, raising his daughter without her mother and Morgan, he felt sick. She was everything to him, and she faked her own death to get away. Steve wasn't mad at Jeremy. Not only did he not know about the faked death, but he just met her less than a year ago. He was angry that this guy's arms could hardly be contained by his shirt and that they were sitting at a table inside his multi-million-dollar designer home. Shelby had certainly been living it up, he thought.

Jeremy was dumbfounded. He wanted nothing more than to find out all this had been a mistake. What if this clearly high-strung guy was the reason she had to run away from her family? After all, he was searching for her years after he thought she was dead. It's possible that she was afraid of him and lied to protect them both as he had with the burglary. He didn't know this guy from Adam, and he did seem quick to anger. Jeremy kept his hand close to his chest, eliminating the sharing of information about her status as an author or the money she must have made after she left him. No matter what he said, Jeremy made up his mind that he needed time alone to get her side of the story. If she had the opportunity to tell him the truth about what really happened and put her faith in him, as the man she loved, he could forgive her almost anything. They made no plans that first night. Jeremy offered Steve the guest room, and he accepted, not knowing what else to do. They both lay awake most of the night, thinking about the same woman. Steve, with a mix of unrequited love and deep-seated hate, and Jeremy, with a longing for someone he realized he barely knew.

The following morning, the men convened in the kitchen right after dawn, drinking coffee and implementing their plan. Jeremy laid out the ground rules, demanding that he meet with Shelby alone before confronting her. He felt he owed her a chance to come clean. If she didn't… then Steve would get his opportunity.

The day dragged on until around 11:00 AM when Detective Preston, unaccompanied, showed up at the door without calling ahead. Today, he wore a pair of pleated blue jeans and a black leather jacket that he didn't bother removing. Jeremy wondered if he came over here on his day off. Steve hid in the guest room while Det. Preston explained the call from Dallas about the woman's husband, who wanted to speak with him and how he was waiting for additional photos. However, he displayed Shelby's decade-old driver's license picture on his phone. Jeremy merely glanced at it before claiming he didn't know who the woman was and had never seen or met her before.

After the Detective left, the men discussed the timing of the plan again before Steve left in his dark blue Kia Sorento rental car to take a shower and change clothes. He was gone less than a few hours and was sure to park on the next street up in the cul-de-sac before knocking again on Jeremy's door. The sleet made the side roads slick, and he slipped a few times, but he managed to stay on his feet and walk back to his new friend Jeremy's house. They sat in the living room and watched the Coyotes beat the Caps like old friends until just after 5:00 PM when Steve, without being told, retreated to the guest room in anticipation of Shelby's arrival.

And now, here he was, standing next to her, and seeing her

face to face was surreal. Well, it's not technically face-to-face quite yet, but she did start coming around.

Chapter Twenty-Five

When she opened her eyes, she briefly wondered how it was possible for reality to exceed her worst nightmares. Her husband was standing next to the man she loved, and they were both looking down on her like some strange new insect. She rose from the floor, rubbed her knee once more, and then sat on the couch's edge without saying a word. She had never seen that blank expression on Jeremy's face before, his eyes still bloodshot, but whether or not he still loved her was the least of her problems now. Her husband of over ten years was clearly furious; no explanation would be enough for either of them. She was mildly surprised at her lack of feelings when seeing him, horror and surprise for sure, but nothing else for the man with whom she had spent most of her adult life. Mostly, she felt regret that Jeremy had to find out this way and that she hadn't had the guts to tell him the truth and trust his love for her.

"I think you better start explaining," Steve demanded, not bothering to sit down. Both men stood where they were, about three feet from the couch. A safe enough distance to examine the colorful yet dangerous new insect they had jointly captured. "Don't scrimp on the details about how you switched the body before the autopsy, too. I want to know if I was married to a murderer or just a grave robber. Oh! Excuse me, still married." Steve's hands were on his hips, and his words spewed like venom.

Of all the possibilities of what could go wrong that Shelby considered, Steve showing up in Phoenix was the very last of them. No matter the consequences to herself or the others, the only option she had in front of her was to tell them. Right now, she looked like a woman who faked her own death and abandoned her family in search of greener pastures. If they chose, and right now she wouldn't put it past Steve, they could turn her into the authorities. Spending the rest of her life in prison would be some form of karmic hell. Ansel would be disappointed in her, and how she handled all of this, that is, if he were still alive. Shelby straightened her black sweater, ran her fingers through her hair, and attempted to make herself as presentable as possible. It was time to take control of the situation. A sense of calm crept over her. Now that she was caught, nothing was left to fear. The worst had happened. Was this how murders felt the night they were apprehended, laying in their bunks, getting the best night's sleep in years once the anxiety of being caught was finally over?

"Please sit," Shelby gently ordered in a firm but quiet voice. Her men glanced at each other, evidently deciding it was okay to sit. How did they manage to find each other, let alone get so close in a matter of days? She would have to find out once she told them her side of the story. Steve took the loveseat adjacent to the couch while Jeremy chose the winged-back black leather chair the furthest away from her. It serves her right, she guessed. Once they were settled, she decided the only place to start was at the beginning.

"The truth is that I was the one who died that day, no one else." Shelby began, folding her hands in her lap as she admitted out loud for the first time what happened to her.

"Bullshit!" Steve spat out from the far-right cushion of the loveseat.

"Steve, will you let me tell you what happened or not? Lying is exhausting, and doing it for so many years, I'm bone tired. I have no ulterior motives here. I want to get it out, and then you can decide for yourself what you believe or don't. Whatever happens afterward will be up to the two of you." Her men again glanced at each other, nodding affirmation, agreeing to let her proceed.

"I heard the songs, Steve. Ansel wouldn't let me listen to the rest, but I did hear the songs you picked for my funeral. I cried the whole time," Shelby began.

"Who's Ansel?" Steve asked, his tone softening at the mention of the music he had put so much thought into.

"The funeral director, Ansel Bishop. He brought me back from the dead. He doesn't know exactly how he can do it, but he said it only works on some people. I was the twenty-third person he brought back, and one of the biggest reasons I couldn't tell either of you about what happened. From the very beginning, he was clear about the rules he set in place. His biggest fear was that the wrong people would find out and come after us. Several of us are still alive, and I couldn't risk that. I fought when Ansel told me I couldn't return to my family," Shelby focused her eyes on Steve's, willing him to understand. "I was dead, and everyone I ever knew thought I was dead too. He kept me for a month at his house when my body was healing, and he gave me a new identity. I had to pick somewhere far away and promise never to return, no internet searches, no turning back."

Jeremy asked a question this time, "What do you mean when your body healed?" She nodded understanding and then explained.

"I died of a brain aneurysm, and then because I was so young, they did an autopsy before dropping me off at the funeral home. My entire body was cut open. Ansel knew how to care for the wounds, and within a few weeks, I could start making plans for this life."

"You don't have any scars…" Jeremy said doubtfully. Steve's head swiveled to Jeremy, sick at the thought of the intimate knowledge this man had of his wife's body.

"No, I don't. Ansel told me they would fade over time, and they did. I haven't noticed the marks in years. He gave me enough money to get established, the identification to become Scarlet Winchell, and several other rules I had to follow. Once I got to

Phoenix, it took me months to figure out what I was going to do with my life. I shut myself in, trying to think of a way to stay inside my apartment and still make money without being seen. That's when I had the idea of writing books."

"You write books for a living?" Steve asked incredulously, switching his left leg over his right. Shelby realized Jeremy hadn't offered Steve much information about her current life. Maybe there was hope for them yet. When she looked at him, he turned away.

"Yes, I do. My purpose was to make enough money to stay in my little apartment, but when the books took off, I moved into a house where I could expand my life a little. I stayed inside most of the time, didn't use my real name or even my second name on the books, fake picture on the back, the works. It took me over five years to realize I needed to move on with my life. Five years before I started dating anyone, five years before I could stop crying myself to sleep each night thinking about my daughter. I know I don't have the right to ask, but how is she?" Shelby asked pleadingly, this time with tears in her eyes.

Steve could see real love in her for their daughter, but up until her name was mentioned, Shelby had expressed no emotion toward him. He hated her for that.

"She is perfect in every way." He wasn't going to give her the satisfaction of elaborating. He wanted her to know how much she had missed out on witnessing her daughter become the wonderful young lady she was.

"Good," Shelby wiped away the wetness from her cheeks before continuing. "All I wanted was for her to be happy." She hoped he would continue, but Steve was content to keep his mouth shut.

"I tried to keep myself busy, but I was lonely. I started dating and then shortly after met Jeremy. When we fell in love, it was unexpected. I hadn't even dared to dream I would find someone after… my first life was over." Shelby looked down at her hands; her fingers were red from twisting them so many times during her explanations. "When the house got broken into, and they found my prints in your office where the laptops had been stolen, I felt like I had no other option but to run. Either you weren't going to believe me, or I could be putting a lot of people I don't even know in jeopardy. I had no idea how out of hand everything would get or that Steve, you, would even be involved. I was going to wait until things either blew up or blew over to make a move."

"So, if they blew up, did you have an escape plan? You weren't even going to tell me or give me a chance?" Jeremy was leaning forward in the chair, elbows on his knees. His eyes were no longer red, but he had dark hallow marks under them, the color of bruises a few days after the injury. She thought that if she was going to tell the truth, she might as well tell it all.

"Yes, I transferred some money to the Caymans, just in case. I hadn't planned on what I was going to tell you. I didn't get that far. Once you figured out that I was some dead woman, I figured you would turn me in." Jeremy stood up and threw up his hands.

"Oh, really? Well, fuck you, Shelby. Fuck you. I don't believe any of this shit! What I have the hardest time believing, above all else, is how little you actually cared about me. That you could lay next to me every single night, lying to my face, and waltz onto a plane with no notice, secure in the reality that you may never see me again. After everything?" He turned and stormed down the hall, slamming the bedroom door behind him.

"It seems like I am not the only man you betrayed." Steve said, seeming to gloat at his new friend's misery.

"I didn't betray you, Steve. I died. There is a big difference." Shelby rolled her eyes, but at the same time, she realized that she didn't recognize the man who was acting this way.

"You used to work in the funeral business. Did you think I forgot? You switched bodies somehow before the autopsy. That is the only possible explanation."

"Was it me that dropped dead on the kitchen floor, Steve? Did I fake that? What about when they pronounced me dead? How long was it before they took me away to the hospital? Was it hours, Steve? I bet it was." Shelby was tired of this, tired of defending herself, and tired of Steve's petty shit. According to her Apple watch, it was nearing midnight. She was starving, thinking that after she got home, they would likely go out and grab a late bite together. She rose from the couch and went to the kitchen in search of food. While in the kitchen, she would make a cup of coffee to go with it. Switching from wine to coffee would be the wisest decision she made tonight. She found some pizza rolls in the fridge, dumped them out on a paper plate, and set the microwave timer for two minutes.

"You want some coffee?" She called from the kitchen. A few seconds later, Steve appeared beside her at the counter.

"Making yourself at home, aren't we?"

"This is my home."

"I wouldn't get too comfortable. He is going to kick your ass to the curb after all of this."

Ignoring him, she asked again, "Do you want coffee or not?" After a pause, he said he did. After retrieving mugs out of the cabinet, she set up the coffee maker for five cups, better safe than sorry. It could be a long night. Waiting for the coffee to brew, she turned around and leaned her back on the counter, crossing her arms across her chest.

“What happened to you?” She asked him.

Without asking, he knew what she meant. It wasn’t just seeing her alive that was the issue. It was him. Something inside of him was broken, and it hadn’t happened right after she died. It happened slowly over time.

“Seeing your dead wife walking around making coffee after six years will do that to a man,” He said softly.

“Don’t do that. Tell me what’s going on with you, and tell me about our daughter.” She dismissed his attitude as easily as she had when they were married, grounding him.

“After the funeral, she went back to school a few days later, claiming that’s what you would have wanted. She has pretty much lived her life that way ever since. She’s a cheerleader, a good student, and excels in English and drama classes. I bought her a car last week, and we went out driving. She’s much better than I was my first time.” He didn’t want to give her more than just the facts. She didn’t deserve that, so he kept it short.

“You bought her a car? She’s fifteen!”

“Yes, she is, but she used her powers of persuasion to convince me to let her learn on her own car.”

“So…she’s smart,” Shelby smirked.

“Very smart, scary smart. She’s beautiful too.” He

considered for a moment and then removed his phone from his pocket, mildly noticing he had missed over a dozen calls from Morgan. He pressed his photo app and selected the most recent picture of Maja standing next to her new Honda, handing the phone to his wife. She gazed at the beautiful, almost grown-up girl she saw in the picture and smiled, quickly handing it back to him. It was no use to linger. There wasn't any way she could ever see her child again. She turned back to the coffee and poured them both a cup, hers to the brim and his with plenty of room for sugar and cream.

"There should be cream in the fridge, and the sugar is right there," pointing to a small, lidded bowl on the counter. Once he had doctored his coffee, she removed her pizza rolls from the microwave and placed them at the center of the table, clearly indicating they were to share.

"Tell me about you," she said, biting into a roll, amazed she was sitting here so calmly having this conversation. He hadn't noticed until that moment what she was drinking her coffee from. When he saw the "I Drink Coffee and Know Things" mug she was holding, he started sobbing, years of emotions brought to the surface. She reached out across the table, placing her hand on his.

"Sorry," he sniffed, "everything just became real---at this very moment. I have been miserable, Shelby." His sobs were coming in waves. She waited for him to pull himself together, somehow feeling like it was no longer her place to console him. She had noticed the wedding ring he was wearing an hour ago, and it wasn't the one she gave him with the black diamonds. This one was a plain gold band she had never seen before.

"I'm a shitty father who lets his wife take care of his practically orphaned daughter. I'm having an affair with a twenty-three-year-old who got mad at me last week because I wouldn't go to see Billie Eilish with her, and I traveled over a thousand miles to find out if my dead wife had been having an affair before she died. All I need is a syringe full of heroin to have hit rock bottom."

"That is an awful lot to unpack," she said, laughing softly. He smiled at her and wiped his face with his sleeve.

"It gets worse," he said, refusing to look her in the eye, content to keep his gaze set on the swirling coffee in his mug.

"How could it possibly be worse?"

"I married your best friend," Steve finally admitted.

Shelby stopped mid-air as she lifted another pizza roll to her mouth, placing it back on the plate. She felt so much pity for him that it broke her heart. How many times had they laid in bed making fun of one of Megan's quirks or wondering what kind of marriage she and Brandon had with the way Morgan always had "a stick up her ass," she remembered Steve saying. Why else would he have married Morgan than to feel closer to her? It wasn't endearing. It was sad.

"How is that going for you, besides the twenty-three-year-old?" She asked, trying to lighten the mood again.

"You're not mad?" He asked, head still down.

"Steve, why would I be mad? After you buried me, your life was your own to do with as you see fit. All I ever wanted for you was to move on with your life and to be happy. I knew that would have nothing to do with me."

"I've really messed up my life. I can't even stand to come home at night."

"You sound like a man who knows he made a mistake, but all he needs is the courage to do something about it."

"Is that coffee I smell?" Jeremy asked as he entered the kitchen from the other side.

Shelby jumped up from the table, "Yes, it is. Let me pour you a cup." She pulled out a chair for him at the table on her way to the counter. He sat down, letting her bring his coffee to him.

Steve watched as he noticed how attentive Shelby was to this man, deepening his misery.

"You guys have a chance to catch up?" Jeremy asked.

Steve cleared his throat, not wanting it to sound like he had been crying. "We did, actually. She told me I needed to get a divorce."

"Not in so many words, but maybe I implied it. For your own good."

"Well, it's official, this is the most fucked up situation I have ever been a part of. I've had a little time to do some thinking while you guys were getting reacquainted." He picked up his coffee and took a large sip before continuing. "I can't swallow your story, Shelby. I believe that something happened to you, and I might even consider that you believe your own story. What I can't understand is why you had to lie to me this whole time, especially after the police were involved. If you had trusted me, this whole thing would have turned out differently."

"I know this is my fault. I should have trusted you, but as you said for yourself, it's hard to accept. Also, it's not only you. There are police involved. I could have ended up in prison or a lab with guys in white coats doing experiments on me. Not to mention the others like me…"

"Shelby, it's still weird to call you that, by the way. The police were here a few hours before you got home. They showed me your picture. I told them I had never seen you before, which is what I will continue to say. The thing is…you should have known."

Shelby had no words, for as much as she loved him, she had failed him by denying him the opportunity to love her for who she really was. Steve stayed quiet, understanding that he was no longer part of Shelby's story. They drank the rest of their coffees without further discussion until everyone at the table felt the tiring weight of the day.

"I suggest we get some sleep before the sun comes up, then figure out what to do with this mess tomorrow. Steve, you are already set up in one of the guest rooms. Shelby, you take the other one." He stood up from the table and walked toward the master bedroom. Shelby heard the door click behind him. When she found her way to the smaller two guest rooms, she saw her suitcase was already on the bed.

Chapter Twenty-Six

Things seemed better in the morning, as they often do in the light of day. For Steve, it was as if a weight had been lifted. The biggest bombshell of his life had produced horrific feelings of disbelief and betrayal, but what followed had given him more peace than he'd experienced in years. Admitting his shortcomings and misery to the only woman he ever loved was cathartic. She responded in the same way she always had, pushing him to be better instead of allowing him to wallow in it as he had been.

Now, it was time to pull himself together. He was sleeping in the guest room of a stranger he had just met who was sleeping with his dead wife. Things don't get weirder than that, although he knew that was the least of his problems. His problems were back home, and he needed to get to them. Even though he knew that future contact wouldn't be possible, he came up with the idea of creating a generic email address that Shelby could access so that he could send her important updates or pictures of Maja over the years. He would run it by her this morning before heading back to Dallas. It didn't mean that he believed her or that he wasn't angry. It meant that he was finally ready to move on with his life.

His bag was still at the hotel, so he redressed in yesterday's clothes, hit the attached bath, and then made his way to the kitchen for another round of coffee before telling them of his plans. Jeremy was already at the table, and for a man who was older than he was and going on less than five hours of sleep, he looked unsettlingly put together in a v-neck t-shirt, beige cardigan, and blue jeans. He got up from the table when he saw Steve coming, offering him a cup. To his dismay, he could practically see the six-pack sitting under his shirt. His wife could certainly pick 'em. After he made his coffee acceptable to drink, they sat together.

"What are you going to do?" Steve asked as if talking to an old friend.

"I don't know yet. This is uncharted territory for me, and I'm not sure I can move past it. She's going to have to go home. Maybe we'll be friends, maybe we won't." He sat back in his chair, holding his mug with both hands.

"I can see, at least in her mind, why she didn't tell you."

"I can, too, but that's the problem. If she loved me, she would have come up with a way to get past that, and she didn't. She ran." There was no use discussing it now, Steve realized. All of this was going to take time to process.

"Well, How 'bout them Cowboys?" Steve offered with a smile.

"Are you kidding me? They'll choke in the playoffs like they do every year. The real question is the Chiefs. Do you think they will pull off the three-peat?"

"I didn't take you for a Chief's fan. I think we will have to redefine the nature of our relationship. I thought you had good taste, but I guess that only goes so far as women."

"You, gentleman, seem like you're getting along," Shelby said as she entered the kitchen, fully dressed in fresh clothes from her suitcase. She did not want to enter the master to access her wardrobe from the closet. The men looked up and said good morning. Shelby sat without grabbing a cup, prompting Steve to get up and pour her one. It's amazing how quickly life can change in a matter of hours, Shelby thought. Nothing was solved between her and Jeremy, but her conscience was finally clear, and it had been a while. Steve walked back to the table, handed Shelby her mug, and explained his intentions.

"I'm going to head back to Dallas this morning. There is no reason for me to stay any longer. I got all the answers I was looking for and then some. I think it's time I figured my own shit out and went on with my life."

"You sound good, man. Better than you have in the last few days. I'm glad I met you, Steve, really." Jeremy stood up and reached out for a hand in Steve's direction. Steve took it, and they pumped several times before letting go. It wasn't a hugging situation, and they both knew it, but they had an odd appreciation for one another after all of this.

"I still feel like I'm in the Twilight Zone," Shelby muttered, still marveling at how they were all in the same room together. "Listen, you have to swear not to tell anyone, especially anyone who knew me. But seriously, anyone. I'm sorry to say it, but I have to."

"No one would believe me if I did. It's much more likely they would lock me up at the looney bin than you. It will help me to know you're out here and happy, though. It will." He glanced at Jeremy, who turned away at Steve's implication. "Will you walk me out, Shelby?"

"Sure, let me grab my coat. It's still cold as hell out there." She walked to the hallway, opened the coat closet, and followed him out to the garage after she was zipped in. She left the garage door open for her return, knowing that she would be facing the music with Jeremy when she got back. Her gut had already told her what was going to happen; he would keep her secret, but he wouldn't be a part of her life. She deserved nothing more, but the thought of losing him made her feel hollow inside, sending a chill up her spine caused more by impending loneliness than the freezing wind. They walked side by side down the hill until she could see a dark blue SUV parked alone in the cul-de-sac.

"Is it always this cold in Arizona?" He said, trying to make conversation, knowing this was the last time he would ever see her.

“Coldest winter I’ve seen. I can’t believe it,” Shelby answered, not knowing what else to say so she reached out her arms for a hug. They embraced for several minutes, Steve running his ungloved hand down the back of her hair, trying to remember the last time he did that. He pulled away first, standing back and looking at her. “Oh, I almost forgot. I had an idea. What if I send you some pictures or updates about Maya every once in a while? Her graduation, college, when she gets married, stuff like that.”

“I would love that, but it's probably not safe. I wish…”

“No, I know that. I’ll make a generic email, and I’ll send it to Jeremy with the address and password. You could even buy a burner to access if you thought that would make it safer.”

“Actually, that would be great. I might do that. I would love to know how she’s doing. You wouldn’t believe how much I miss her.”

“What I can’t believe is how you were able to stay away, but if what you say is true… I guess you did what you had to do.” Steve’s mind was more open than it had been before, although he still wasn’t convinced.

“Fly safe. I wish you the best, Steve. I’m sorry for everything. I really am.” Shelby leaned in and kissed him on the cheek, smiling. Still no emotion, she thought, very strange. He turned to unlock the SUV and saw a woman in a heavy coat and hood walking toward them. The coat looked familiar… and so did the face of the--- girl.

"Maja! What are you doing here?" Steve yelled, turning to Shelby, whose eyes were wide and panicked. She swung around and began trying to run. She slipped on the wet concrete, going down on the same knee she hit last night, screaming out. Maja stopped two feet in front of her mother, staring down at her, pure hate radiating from her face. Shelby could hear Steve continuing to shout, but the sound was drowned out by the sound of rushing blood in her ears.

"How could you do this to me?" Whirling around, she faced her father. "Both of you! How could you make me think she was dead and then replace her with the neighbor? I saw you!" Maja roared as anger came spewing out of her in an uncontrollable wave.

After Maja had made copies of the addresses from her Dad's computer, she went back to her room to think. She sat down at her desk, opened her school notebooks, and released a few pages of notebook paper from its claws. Locating her favorite hot pink pen, she carefully printed three questions using the lines to space them out.

1. How likely is it that fingerprints will stay on a surface after six years?

2. Why would my Dad go to Phoenix to locate three men with the last name Locke?

3. What else does my Dad know that he is not telling me?

After examining her list for a few minutes, she picked up her pen and wrote one last question.

4. What am I going to do about it?

That was the real question, wasn't it? Whatever her Dad found out in Phoenix, it was more than likely she would never know. He already fabricated a story to get out of the house, and she wouldn't be able to use her detective skills to find out what he had been up to like she did on his computer. The only way to find out would be to follow him. She had some money on her debit card, but not enough for a plane ticket, food, and maybe even a hotel room. She checked her account through the app on her phone. $81 in checking and $732 in savings. She could transfer money from savings with no problem, but still worried it wouldn't be enough. The only option she had was to drive.

I will be grounded for the rest of my life, she thought, but honestly, it didn't matter. She wouldn't even get halfway without Morgan realizing she was gone, and her Dad would know she was coming. Her phone would blow up, he would track her down, and she wouldn't find out anything anyway. That's exactly how it would go down. Except he had been distracted lately. More than distracted, he has been absent. It probably wouldn't make any difference in this situation, but it might. She may get there and learn something before he finds out if she played her cards right. After a brief review of Google Maps, she learned it was possible to get there in about 16 hours. With her less-than-skilled driving and most likely going under the speed limit, it would take her closer to twenty, give or take. If she told Morgan she would stay at her friend Rebecca's house, that would give her at least twelve to fifteen hours. A well-placed call tomorrow night could extend it at least another day. The car was a whole other matter. Would Morgan notice it was gone? Probably. Would she call her Dad about the car? Maybe, but maybe not. They were fighting, and the car would be the least of her problems. Any one of a hundred things could go wrong, but they were all chances that Maja was willing to take. She had to find out what was going on and how her mother was involved. The final consideration was convincing Morgan to let her stay with a friend during finals week. I will just make that my reason: we need to study for the exam. That will be that.

She quickly gathered a few long-sleeved shirts, her Taylor Swift Sweatshirt, some underwear, a pair of jeans, then leggings and stuffed them into her backpack. She grabbed her toothbrush, lip gloss, hairbrush, and a few hair ties and stuck them in her bag's small, zippered pocket.

It took her a few minutes to locate Morgan, who was not in

the living room, kitchen, or her parent's bedroom. When she crossed the living room a second time, she barely noticed through the blinds that Morgan was sitting in a chair on the back patio. It wasn't freezing, but it was cold, and she didn't have a coat on. Opening the back door and stepping out didn't seem to get her attention.

"Morgan, are you okay?" She asked.

Her head moved slowly toward her, a completely blank expression on her face. When she saw Maja, her face changed in an instant; a large grin appeared.

"Are you okay?"

"Yes, I'm fine. Just enjoying the crisp evening air. What have you got there?" Morgan explained a little too cheerfully.

"My backpack. I need to stay over at Rebecca's tonight to study for finals."

"How do her parents feel about that?"

"Fine, they are okay with it. We are in high school now. We aren't little kids anymore." Maja realized she may be going a bit overboard and tried to pull it back. "We have two of the same classes, Biology and American History, and we would feel better if we could quiz each other." She stood there waiting for Morgan to respond for what seemed like minutes, but that same look wouldn't leave her face. After a few more moments, Maja began backing away toward the door.

"I'm going now. I'll call you tomorrow."

"That's fine. I'll see you tomorrow," Morgan called after her. Jesus, Maja thought, she's lost it. Morgan was always off, but this was a whole new situation. Her Dad must have said something or done something. Another reason she needed to figure out what the hell was going on.

She snatched her coat off the rack by the door and headed toward the car, keys in hand. It was dark, and he had never been on the highway before. She didn't even have a valid driver's license, but the excitement coursing through her was exhilarating. Maja had never done anything impulsive or even remotely irresponsible before. It was thrilling in a way that was indescribable. She placed her bag in the backseat and then situated herself behind the wheel, plugging in her phone that connected it to Apple Car Play. Then, she added the first address to the map. Sixteen hours and four minutes, it said. We shall see about that.

The first four or five hours of the trip were somewhat uneventful once she found the highway and engaged the cruise control her Dad had shown her "in theory" how to use. Once she felt comfortable at sixty miles per hour, she pressed the buttons he showed her and felt a jolt of panic when the car seemed to lurch forward and the gas pedal depressed under her foot. Damn! She swerved a bit and hit the brake, just to be sure she could still stop the car if needed. The big black Ford truck behind her came baring down and honked, swerving to the right and offering her the one-finger salute as he passed. She had overreacted and almost got herself smashed into… you have to calm down, Maja! She yelled at herself inside the car.

After her heart rate returned to its normal rhythm, she summoned the courage to try it again, anticipating the feeling. Okay, now all she had to do was keep her eyes on the road and try not to get hit. Her first exit wasn't for one hundred and twenty-three miles. If she could get through the first part, she was confident she could get through the rest.

It wasn't until three hundred miles later that her first big obstacle came in the form of the gas light. That same panic hit her again when the bright orange light on the dash interrupted her inner monologue about what she would say when she saw her Dad. Oh, Shit, Gas! She had told herself to keep an eye on the tank for the last hundred miles, not realizing how long it had been since examining the gauges. Looking to her right, she saw a big green sign stating that it was five miles to Big Spring. That would have to do. The next relieving sign was blue with pictures of McDonalds, Holiday Inn, and, thank God, Exxon Mobile.

Her legs felt like jelly when she got out of the car next to the gas pump. She stretched several times, hands to her toes, before walking inside to pay, her hair blowing wildly in the frigid night air. She had seen her Dad do it dozens, if not hundreds, of times, but she wasn't confident enough to use the credit card reader attached to the gas pump. It was late, but not that late yet, and the inside of the station was still open. The attendant inside was an old man, older than her grandfather, with translucent skin and a whisp of white hair on the top of his head. He told her where the bathroom was, and once her bladder was empty, she paid for her gas, two bottles of water, a bag of Doritos, and a Red Bull, and then headed back to the car. When her Dad filled up his car, the pump usually read around fifty to fifty-five dollars. To be safe, and because her car was empty, she asked the clerk for sixty.

She opened the passenger door, dumped her purchases in the seat, and picked up the gas thingy. Within seconds, she knew she had a problem. There was a little square where she knew the gas should go, but it was closed. She tried to pull it open, but it wouldn't budge. Returning the gas thing to its holder, she went back to the driver's side in search of a button that would open it. Five minutes later, she was sitting in the car with the door closed, sobbing. Not only was this a bad idea, but now she was going to be raped and murdered in the middle of some small town in West Texas because she didn't even know how to get gas in her own car! A loud knock on the window made Maja jump and scream out before jerking her head to see the attendant from inside staring at her less than three inches from her face.

"Are you okay?" He yelled through the closed window, his voice being swept away by the wind.

She slowly opened the door, giving him a chance to back away. "Yeah, I think my gas tank thing is stuck. It won't open." She was trying desperately to stop crying, but her words came out in hitches.

"How old are you, young lady?" His light blue eyes focused in on her with apparent concern.

"Seventeen, going to see my Dad," she said, screaming into the wind. He stood there staring at her a moment longer before limping slowly to the other side of the car.

"Come here, girl, let me show you something." He placed his hand on the cut-out square and pushed it forward with two fingers, popping it open. Her feeling of stupidity was quickly overshadowed by a sense of relief that she wouldn't be stranded out here and killed by some weirdo in the middle of the night. He twisted the cap underneath and then pushed the nozzle inside.

"If you hold down the handle until it clicks, the gas keeps flowing until your tank is full. I'm not sure this car will take a full $60. If it doesn't, then come back inside, and I'll refund ya the difference." Pulling his jacket closed, he dragged his bad leg behind him and went back into the store. She watched as the numbers climbed into the fifties and then stopped at $58.76. She was momentarily proud of herself for being so close. The dollar something left wasn't enough to go back in and face the clerk again, so she put the thing back in its place, closed the tank, and went on her way.

Five stops later, she was in Arizona holding a Burger King chicken sandwich in one hand and the wheel in the other. She had been awake for thirty-one hours, and despite her victorious arrival, she was exhausted. Maja made it in just over nineteen hours, although while she was passing through New Mexico as the sun began to peek out from behind the clouds and offer the first real sunshine of the overcast day, in a little less than fourteen hours into the trip, Morgan received a message from Shepton High School reporting Maja absent from class. That was something Maja, at fifteen years old, hadn't accounted for. Her carefully laid dominos began to fall much quicker than she had been able to set them up. A call to Rebecca's mother a few minutes later revealed her lie about the previous evening, and that is when Morgan began trying to reach Steve. Fourteen calls and twenty-three text messages in two days were un-responded to, leading mother and daughter to see each other face to face for the first time in six years, three months, and eight days.

Before that, though, she needed sleep. Two miles away from the first address, she pulled into a Target parking lot, drove around back, and found a spot between two big trucks. Parking the car was no problem. She climbed out of the car, her body screaming at her, stretched, and then crawled into the back seat. She clicked the lock button on her keys, placed her hands under her chin, and was asleep in a matter of minutes. It was 3:00 PM on the day Shelby would be arriving back home to the confrontation of the two men who loved her, still feeling secure in her secret. Maja slept for ten hours undisturbed in her hidden spot, waking up in the middle of the night, mad that she had wasted so much time. It was too late to make any progress today. She checked her phone, expecting messages from her father, but there were none. Voicemails from Morgan and Rebecca revealed the game had been up for over half a day, but still, there was nothing from her Dad. Either something had happened to him, or he was preoccupied.

After reviewing the map and the three addresses, she figured she could at least drive by to see what she would be dealing with tomorrow. It's better than waiting around here. As she got back in the driver's seat, she noticed it had rained at some point in the night. She would have to be careful driving on the wet roads. In less than an hour, she had cruised by all three houses, one of them a gigantic, gated estate. She had at least four hours until it would be polite to knock on any doors. Maja parked across the street from the estate in a small parking lot attached to a community park and pool that was closed for the winter. No other cars were in the lot, but she turned off the car anyway. She didn't know how long cars should run, but she felt four hours would be too long. She hadn't gotten cold when she was sleeping only because it was daytime, and her utter exhaustion would have kept her asleep at any temperature. Because her phone was fully charged, she listened to music and played a game. In the back of her mind, she knew she was compartmentalizing… not the actual word for it, but understood that she had placed anything going on back home into a box to be dealt with later. It wasn't like her to disregard other people's feelings, especially her family and friends, although her internal motivation was stronger than her concern for what Morgan or Rebecca might be feeling right now. Her gut told her that her Dad still had no idea she was even gone, which proved her point about being distracted even more.

Instead of Taylor, she felt it was more appropriate to listen to Panic, one of her mother's favorites. Or, as she used to say, WSMFP, she thought and laughed. Even at nine, Maja knew what that meant. After a few minutes, she closed her eyes and sat back in the seat, letting the music take her back to when she was a child, holding her mother's hand and dancing as they used to do so often. Soon, she was asleep.

Light from the window and her own shivering woke her at

dawn. Glancing at her watch told her it was just after seven; she was hungry again and had to pee. Knocking on anyone's door before 9:00 AM wouldn't be received well, anyway, so she had plenty of time to find some hot breakfast and a bathroom.

Her belly full of Chick-fil-A mini's and a full box of hashbrowns made her feel ready for anything she had to face today. The roads weren't nearly as wet as they were the night before, and it even seemed a few degrees warmer without the wind. As she drove back to her spot in the small parking lot, she noticed the garage door opening and two people, a man and a woman, walking out. Her father's coat was instantly recognizable. He always wore that brown leather jacket. It must be at least ten years old. He had it since she could remember. Without turning off the car, she climbed out of the car, attempting to get a better look at who he was with. The addresses were all for men, not women. From the other side of the street, they were walking in her direction. When they stopped at an SUV parked across the street directly across from her, she could examine both of them clearly. Once she realized who it was, she held onto her car's side mirror for support. Her mother and father were standing in an embrace and laughing. She rubbed her eyes several times just to be sure, but she could still recognize her Mom after all this time. It was her.

He had been pretending all this time that she had died, and he came here to warn her about what was happening… there was no other explanation. The other addresses were a red herring, just like she had learned in English class when they read Agatha Christie's And Then There Were None. She wasn't sure which one of them had done it, but it didn't matter, they were both in on it! They lied to Grandpa and Grandma, all their friends… everyone. Anger rose within her like she had never felt, a quick anger she inherited from her father. Without thinking, she pulled the hood of her coat over her head and began charging across the street toward the parked car.

As her Dad turned around to open the car door, he reacted suddenly, "Maja! What are you doing here?" Her anger had the best of her, she would deal with him later. It was her mother she needed to confront. She witnessed the look of horror on her mother's face and her attempt to flee from the consequences of her actions. As she hit the ground, all Maja could think was that it served her right. Hate consumed her.

"How could you do this to me?" Whirling around, she faced her father. "Both of you! How could you make me think she was dead and then replace her with the neighbor? I saw you!" Shelby couldn't find words to respond or the strength to get up from the sidewalk where she sprawled. It was Steve who tried to set the record straight.

"No, you don't understand, Maja! I didn't know, and your Mom couldn't tell us."

"How did you even know she was here then? You came all this way, for what? Never mind… my entire life is a lie now. I have missed my mother for almost half of my life. There hasn't been a day gone by that I didn't think about you." Directing her venom directly at Shelby.

From across the street, Jeremy was watching from the cover of the open garage, unsure if he should intervene. His neighbors would most likely be calling the police by now with all the yelling from these apparent strangers. The mess just kept getting bigger. How in the hell did I find myself in the middle of this shit show? He asked himself.

"I can't deal with either one of you. I'm going back home, and I never want to see you again, whoever you are now!" The end of her sentence barely came out as Maja's screaming had strained her voice. She stormed across the street, making loud echoes with her feet against the moist pavement. She hopped in the running car, not bothering with a seat belt, before backing out of her space and speeding down the residential street toward the main intersection. Steve, Shelby, and Jeremy all watched intently as her car sped toward the stop sign, blowing through it. At the speed Maja was driving the homeowner three houses up on the right, he never saw her coming as he was backing out of his driveway. Her car smashed into his blessedly empty passenger side door at forty-five miles an hour, sending Jason's car, who had only been going out for donuts for his wife's and kid's breakfast, into a collision with another parked car on the opposite side of the street. Maja's body was lifted out of her seat, the top of her head crashing violently into her brand-new windshield, shattering both the glass and her skull instantly. Her body landed on the concrete nine feet in front of the pile of vehicles with a thud that Shelby could hear from a quarter mile away. That is when she began to scream.

Chapter Twenty-Seven

Jeremy was the first to react, running back into the house and snatching his cell off the nightstand.

"9-1-1, What's your emergency?" A man's voice asked. He gave them his address. It's close enough, he thinks. "Hurry, a young girl was in one of the cars."

Shelby was off the ground and speeding toward her daughter, her painful knee forgotten. "No... No! No! NOOOO!" was all she could scream as she huffed and puffed down the sidewalk for four whole minutes before she could see Maja's body in the middle of the pavement. The man in the sedan that Maja ran into was zig-zagging his way to her, determined to check for a pulse regardless of the world continuing to spin around him or the fact that he could see grey and red soft tissue through the tangles of her matted hair. Kneeling next to her, he saw bright green eyes blankly staring up at him. There was no reason to check for vitals. She was dead. He just hoped it was quick. He lost balance on his feet and toppled over into a pile of broken glass. The woman down the street was almost to them... in seconds, she barreled past him as if he weren't there.

"Maja! Wake up, honey. Maja!" Shelby wailed.

That's when they all heard sirens from a distance,

somewhere over the hill. Later that afternoon, Jason recalled to his wife that the woman's eyes became wild, and she began to make a low guttural sound in her throat. He was still on his back, observing as she lifted the girl's sneakers and began to pull her body toward the sidewalk. His mouth hung open in shock. He couldn't believe what he was witnessing. Another man in a dark brown leather jacket seemed to approach her cautiously.

"What are you doing? Put her down, now!" He commanded. The woman glared at him with that same wild look, continuing to drag what he could only assume was her daughter. He had never seen anything like it, mildly wondering if a concussion could cause hallucinations.

"Help me!" she pleaded to the man across the street and the one in the leather coat. "We have to get her out of here before they take her away. Neither of the men moved to assist her, each grappling with what had just happened minutes before. Fine, she thought, I'll do this all by myself if I have to. She'll come back, Ansel can help, and he will make her come back. I know he will.

Jeremy stood frozen in the driveway of their house, mesmerized by the blood trail Maja's body had left on the rain-slicked ground. Tiny rivulets of blood and water were mixing together to make a bright pink cascading stream that went in the direction of the road.

Shelby had made it to the truck of Jeremy's BMW X7. She laid her legs back down on the cement and ran through the open door to grab his keys, the trunk beginning to lift before she was even back outside.

"Help me, God, dammit! I can't get her up there by myself. Steve! We can bring her back! Please help me!" From the expression on Jeremy's face, she knew he was useless. Her only hope was Steve, and she could now see the firetruck turning the corner toward the mangled cars. He was at the bottom of the driveway, feeling as though he had finally lost his mind. His wife was back from the grave, and now his daughter was dead. It was like a cruel joke he couldn't comprehend, and then he felt relieved when he decided that it must all be a dream. He would wake up at any moment days before his trip to Phoenix.

It was Jeremy who snapped out of it first, lifting Maja's shoulders while Shelby raised her feet and legs into the trunk. Shelby quickly tapped the truck button and lowered it just as the firemen were jumping out of their truck cab and ran to the man who was still lying on the ground by the accident.

"Are you coming?" Shelby called to her men.

Without a word, they walked toward the car and got in, Jeremy in the front passenger seat and Steve in the back. Jeremy knew enough at the moment to realize he didn't want to be the one driving a girl's body away from the scene of an accident. As Jeremy closed his door, Shelby was backing the car out of the garage while Jeremy pressed the button to close it behind them. She went in the opposite direction of the accident, being sure to drive slowly so as not to arouse suspicion before they realized a victim was missing from the scene.

"What are we doing, Shelby? Your daughter's dead body is in the back of the car. You're not thinking clearly." Jeremy asked, trying to be the voice of reason in a completely fucked up situation. His hands and wrists hurt for the first time in a week, a slow but deep burning sensation.

But she was. Shelby had formulated a plan almost as soon she heard the thud a quarter mile away that could only mean one thing. If it worked on me, she reasoned, it would work on anyone in her bloodline. It had to. From here, they could be back in Dallas in less than a day. It worked on her after forty-eight hours with a fatal brain injury, granted not as bad as Maja's, but Ansel said that the injuries didn't matter. She was convinced that by tomorrow, this nightmare would be over.

They passed three police cars, all with sirens blaring, on their way out of the neighborhood. None of them paid attention to the BMW driving in the other direction. It would be Jason's responsibility to explain to the authorities what happened. He would do so later that day from a hospital bed once his MRI and CAT scan were cleared. The fantastical nature of the story required the police to double-check with the doctors regarding Jason's competence. A quick check gave them Jeremy's name within moments, but the other man and woman at the site of the crash were, as yet, unidentified.

Just outside the highway entrance, she pulled into a gas station to get her baring and set up the map for their road trip. She loved the man sitting next to her, but she also knew she needed to give him a chance to get out of the car before he had no other choice. This was her and Steve's duty, not his. Consulting the map, she told her passengers it would take about fifteen hours to reach their final destination.

"If you need the bathroom, the time is now. Jeremy, it's up to you if you want to continue. You didn't even know Maja existed until a few days ago." Her words were cold, but necessary. If he was with them, great, if not, she needed to know now.

Jeremy considered the options. They were already in his car, and he had no doubt the police already knew of his involvement. Despite what would happen between them down the line, Shelby was likely going to need him when they got to the end of the line, and she finally realized the reality of the situation. People don't come back from the dead, let alone ones with parts of their skull missing and brains splattered all over the road. No one in the car had killed her, and there was at least one witness to that, but probably more behind open blinds. By the end of the day, he would call the police and explain the actions of these half-crazed and bereaved parents and why they had crossed three state lines with a young girl's body. Until then, he would have to see this through for everyone's safety.

"I'm coming," he said, turning his head to look at Steve in the back seat. All he saw was a broken man silently sobbing. Yes, he would be coming on this trip. He had to. Again, she gave them a chance to go inside, but both men stayed where they were. The map directed her to the eastbound ramp, where she entered, cruising to over eight-five before setting the cruise.

"Shelby?" Steve could be heard from the back seat, his voice barely above a whisper.

"Yes?"

"Can you bring her back?" He asked in earnest.

"No, I can't. But I know who can. I know because I'm the twenty-third person he brought back. She'll come back, Steve."

"Why are there only twenty-three of you? If he can do this great thing, bringing people back to life, why aren't there more of you?" Jeremy countered, wondering how far off the mental cliff she had yet to fall.

Shelby hesitated. Steve might lose hope if she told them the truth. Hell, she didn't even understand the truth, and neither did Ansel. What could she say? That his hands chose? That when he began to tingle, he knew…

"He only chooses specific people. I know he'll do it for me."

Shelby coasted more than a hundred miles before another word was spoken. No one turned their attention to the back of the car, afraid to speak or even think about the condition of their fourth passenger.

By mid-afternoon, everyone at the station was talking about the missing girl who could neither be confirmed as dead nor alive, although the man involved in the accident claimed she died on impact and then her body was stolen. It wasn't until he overheard two beat cops who had been at the scene discussing where the accident occurred did he become interested in hearing more.

"Where did you say the accident was?" He asked the chubby one.

"In that rich neighborhood, Cherry Hills Village. North Wads and 54th."

That was just where he thought they were talking about. He

was there yesterday afternoon at Mr. Locke's residence. Was it a coincidence that a fatality accident occurred at an intersection close to a house that had been burglarized a few months before? Probably, he thinks, but worth checking out nonetheless, and a missing body certainly sweetened the pot of the coincidence. He decided to visit the building next door to learn more from his buddy in the traffic division.

"Dude, want to grab some lunch, he said as he approached Jimmy's desk."

"Sure, it will have to be quick cause we are all working that wreck from this morning. Super strange. I'll tell you all about it over tacos," he grinned, already heading toward the door.

Detective Randy Preston could always count on Jimmy for a few gruesome details from the accidents he was working. This time, it wasn't so much the goriness he was interested in, but the circumstances and who was involved.

"I'll buy," Preston offered.

"No, shit? Awesome, thanks!"

Jimmy was excitable whenever he landed an interesting assignment. The more dead bodies he scraped off the pavement, the more hyper he became. Preston wasn't sure if it was a coping mechanism or if he was a psychopath. In this line of duty, it didn't really matter either way as long as the job got done. We are all a little crazy, he thought. When he was a boy, he remembered a kid, Simon, who the liberal, treeing hugging, "you hurt my feelings," pussies would have called sensitive or imaginative. He would have gotten special treatment, not even requiring him to participate in school or follow the rules. The truth is that Simon was a psychopath. The side he showed the adults was defiant but quiet, and back in the 80's, he got whooped for it as he should have been. The side he showed the kids in the neighborhood was pure evil. His evil came in the form of mutilating any small creature he could get his hands on, including Preston's tabby cat, Sophie. When he found Sophie on the side of the house sans head, he knew quickly who had done it. The kid didn't need therapy as many of the libs would have demanded for him today; he needed an ass-kicking. That is precisely what Preston gave him. If Jimmy got a little excited when someone ended up in a grease spot on the road, then so be it. He had seen worse.

Sitting at City Taco, Jimmy was far more interested in doctoring his carne asada with every hot sauce they carried rather than talking. Preston pushed him a bit to get him going, but once he did, Jimmy didn't stop.

"What happened this morning at the accident everyone's talking about?" Preston asked.

"Oh, shit, yeah, man. Some girl crashed into a guy pulling

out of his driveway, going close to fifty. According to the guy who was hit, the girl torpedoed out of the windshield and went head-first into the concrete. She was dead as a doornail. This crazy woman came screaming down the road from a mile away. She dragged the girl's body all the way down the street and then loaded her into the back of a Black BMW and drove away. The vehicle's owner was in the car as they drove away, along with another man. Evidentially, the owner of the car lived in the neighborhood," Jimmy explained with a twinkle in his eye.

"Guy got a record?"

"No, some rich guy. Something… Locke." And there it was, the connection that he knew was possible. He felt it. Jimmy shoved half of a taco in his mouth before the next question.

"What about the girl? Who was she, and the two other people?"

"The car the girl was driving had temp tags from Texas, registered to a guy. We ran the plates of several vehicles nearby, and one of them ended up being rented. When I called the rental place, I found out it was rented by the same guy. Apparently, the driver of the blue sedan was his daughter. We have no idea who the woman is. George called the Texas guy's house, and his wife answered, so we know it's not her." Jimmy wedged the second half of the taco in his mouth, chewing vigorously.

Preston had a good idea who that woman might be. There were only two options: Locke's girlfriend or Shelby Wise. He had his money on the deceased wife of Steve Wise, who was also the mother of the driver of the blue sedan. If he had pushed his detective skills further, he could have ascertained that until sometime in the last forty-eight hours, Steve Wise was unaware that his wife had pulled a fast one. The most likely scenario was that Shelby Wise was the girlfriend. That is why her prints were all over the house. He felt dumber than a bag of hammers for not putting the pieces together until now. The question was, did Jeremey Locke know his girlfriend had faked her own death? Probably not, Preston considered. Luckily, Jimmy was working on his fourth taco, which left him to work out the rest of the details.

It was like Ted Bundy being pulled over by a traffic cop to finally put him behind bars. The unrelated break-in at Locke's house set the chain reaction in motion to find the biggest fish of them all, this woman who faked her own death and had been hiding out for half a decade undiscovered until he finally cracked the case. Not only was she guilty of that crime, she was also responsible for her own daughter's demise. No wonder she ran. It all made perfect sense.

Before he went off all half-cocked, he would need some confirmation of his theory, and he had a good feeling he knew exactly who to get it from.

Chapter Twenty-Eight

Six hours into the drive, they made their second stop. This time, it was Shelby who needed to pee. She was drinking too much coffee and knew it. Her anxiety was getting the best of her. When she ran in to pee, instead of coffee, this time, she replaced it with Gatorade. She would need to be at the top of her game for the next few days, at the least.

Steve stayed in the back of the car. He had no need to pee because he hadn't drunk a thing all day. His head hurt, and the body of his beautiful and newly fifteen-year-old daughter was about six inches away from him in the back of the car… eating, drinking, or sleeping was not an option. Everything he had ever done wrong in his life had just come to bite him in the ass. Karma was a fucking bitch. He knew it wasn't his fault when Shelby was taken from him. She had an unknown medical condition. There was nothing he could have done.

Maja's death, on the other hand, was on him. This wouldn't have happened if he had told her the truth or even cared to check up on her in the last few days. Speaking of that, he needed to check his phone. The last thing he remembered was missing a dozen calls from Morgan, but that wasn't out of the ordinary. It didn't take a genius to figure out why she had been calling this time, he thought. Instead of listening to the messages, he checked his texts. The last one from

Morgan came through a little over an hour ago.

The police are looking for you and Maja. They put out an APB. What is going on?

The one before it was short and sweet:

ANSWER ME!

Another before that one:

Maja has been gone for two days, and you haven't answered any of my calls. Where are you?

She was persistent. He would have to give her that, he thought wryly.

It's only a matter of time until the police assume they are headed back to Texas and track them down. Did he even believe this was going to work anyway? The pure insanity of the situation was hitting him like a MAC truck. He hadn't lost his marbles yet, but the lady driving sure had. Her complete calm frightened him more than anything. She should be crying, hysterical…something. Did her demeanor indicate that she truly believed everything was going to be okay, or did it mean that she had lost her ever-loving mind? He contemplated telling her about the text. What would she do if she knew they were being followed? Or was it best to keep it to himself and let the cops find them so they could give his little girl a proper burial?

Jeremy was asleep in the front seat, mouth hanging open wide. The last few days had taken a toll on him, and sleep was more of a retreat than an opportunity to rest. When Shelby slammed the door upon reentering the car, he was jolted awake.

"I got water for everyone, and we'll stop for dinner in about three hours." To her, it was all business. To them, they were careening down a slippery slope of body snatching and becoming fugitives from justice.

"The police know and are looking for us," Steve blurted from the backseat before he could stop himself. Even if there was only a twenty percent chance that she was right, hell, a one percent chance she was right… as a father, he had to take it. At the end of the road, they would know one way or the other and could make a move.

"Ok. I thought this might happen. How do you know for sure?"

"Morgan texted me. The police called her."

"What did she say about Maja?"

"Just that the police were looking for both of us."

"Okay, good. That means they aren't 100% sure she's dead. They think she may be, but they aren't sure. That could play into our advantage."

Jeremy turned to face her. "What advantage, Shelby? We have no advantage here. The cops are looking for us because we stole a corpse. Your *CHILD's* corpse!" he screamed.

She winced upon hearing the word. She isn't a corpse. She is just hibernating until we get to Ansel. Then she will wake up. Part of her knew she was in denial about Maja's death, especially the part where it might not work. She shook her head. No, stop, she thought.

"Jeremy," She said evenly, "If I didn't take her body, then I would never gotten access to her later. This is the only way. There is only one man who saw what really happened. When it turns out she's fine, who will they believe?" For a moment, Jeremy began to question how he had ever fallen in love with this woman. She was crazy, bat shit, rubbing yourself with peanut butter, crazy.

Shelby was already consulting the map and identifying potential back roads they could take that wouldn't add too much unnecessary time. Back in her own world she continued her planning.

"Now that they have identified everyone involved --except me-- then it's safe to assume they think you are on your way back home. Since we just made it past the Texas border, there are more small towns and options to get us off the highway. Six hundred and fifty miles to go, but we'll have to be careful." Shelby twisted the nob on the console of the BMW to put them in drive and she was off. In about a hundred miles, they could get off at Hwy 10, then cut over to 385, which turned into 67, and could cut through San Angelo, only adding about fifty minutes to the drive. She congratulated herself on her ingenuity, unaware that her men were making plans of their own.

Jeremy wasn't surprised when his phone buzzed twenty minutes later, and he saw a text notification from Det. Preston. The only part that surprised him was that it took so long.

Are you okay?

He was smart. Trying to draw him in. But that was alright; he wanted to be drawn in and saved from this nightmare.

Yes, we are okay. Except for the girl. She's dead.

A few moments later.

Where are you?

He hesitated, but only for a second.

Not sure exactly. Back roads, heading to Dallas.

OK. I'm getting on a plane. When you come to the next stop, send me your location.

Ten seconds later, another message appeared.

Is Shelby with you?

He clicked off the screen and put the phone back in his

pocket. Things were escalating quickly, and Det. Preston had figured it out. He didn't know how all this would end, but he knew he didn't want Shelby to end up in prison. At the same time, they had to get that poor girl's body out of the car. He pulled his phone back out and sent one more message.

I'll text you when we get to Dallas.

Preston had counted on Jeremy being a good man, and he wasn't disappointed. As long as he knew Jeremy was playing for the right team, he could hold off getting any other departments involved. He needed to tell his partner what was happening and about his trip to Dallas. He could be trusted not to give away the game until they were ready. He would be solving two cases for the price of one, and one of the cases no one even knew was open. It's not very often you get to catch a death faker. Not only was that a crime, but he could think of a dozen other charges they could file against her for insurance fraud, social security fraud, falsifying government documents, and using fake IDs; the possibilities were endless and tantalizing. He would get credit for it all. Although the genuine concern here was making sure that the little girl was properly cared for. Wasn't it?

Flipping to his recent calls, Preston clicked on "P in Crime."

That was the affectionate nickname given to his partner. They had worked together going on nine years. At first, he considered Merle a little squirrely. He was too skinny but ate like a fat man at a Chinese buffet, and he was a little awkward, especially around the ladies. But they had been through a few scrapes together that proved his loyalty. That's what the job was all about—loyalty. His wife thought Merle, or as she called him, Dennis, was creepy. But she had never been chasing an armed robber through the back ally of Roosevelt Row with only your partner for cover. When another guy shoots a man in the head for you, well, that was the pinnacle, in his mind.

"Dude. I figured it out!" Preston said before Merle had a chance to offer a hello.

"Which one, the Curry case or Locke? Where are you anyway?" Merle asked.

"I just got done at lunch with Jason from Traffic. You hear about that weird accident this morning in Cherry Hills?"

"Yeah, that's all anyone's talking about. From what the Lieutenant said, I think homicide is getting involved."

"Good, that means in less than twelve hours, we have a chance to show them up."

"Okay, I'm listening."

"What you don't know is that the accident was right in front of Locke's place. He is with the woman who took the body."

"Holy hot dog shit on a stick! How did you find out?"

"Jason. They know that Steve Wise and an unidentified woman are in the car with Locke and that little girl's body."

"Steve Wise? Do you mean the guy from Texas? The dead woman's husband?"

"Yep, and the girl who was killed in the accident is his daughter."

"Well, I guess reality is really stranger than fiction, as they say. So, what do we have to do with it?"

"Any guesses on who the unidentified woman is?"

"I don't know, Locke's girlfriend?"

"Yep! Who just so happens to be Mr. Wise's dead wife."

There was silence on the other end of the line as Merle worked it out for himself.

Finally, he said, "I guess that makes sense, doesn't it?"

"It does. That is the part nobody knows. They are all running around trying to figure out who the woman is. I texted Jeremy, and he confirmed they got the girl in the car. I'm going down there this afternoon. Can you cover for me?"

"Sure. I can do that."

"Once I take them in, I'll call, and you can send in the calvary."

"Be careful. Not sure anyone here is going to be too happy about you getting the jump on things."

"I will only be following up on a lead for the Locke case that took me to Dallas. Simple as that, and I know you'll back me up."

"Of course."

"Okay, talk soon." Preston said, hanging up.

He called his wife, explained he needed to make an overnight trip but would be back tomorrow, and then booked a flight to Dallas on his Southwest app. The flight left in ninety minutes. He considered taking a Lyft but remembered another sweet perk of being a cop: the free parking. He didn't need a bag, so he drove directly to the airport. He was ready and rearing to go.

Steve dozed for about twenty minutes before being jolted awake by a vision in his own nightmare. He checked his palms to ensure they were dry before placing them over his eyes, fighting back tears. He could still feel the sensation of wetness seeping through the back of the car and his seat. In his nightmare, he had discovered that his daughter's brain matter had soaked through, creating a stain and making his hands and back wet. He double-checked the fabric behind him to make sure it was dry. His fellow travelers in the front of the car seemed oblivious to his horror. Probably for the best, he thought. Nightmares were always best kept to oneself.

"Where are we?" He asked, projecting his voice to the front of the SUV.

"Just now past San Angelo," Shelby answered.

Steve knew that meant about four hours out. That would give him a while to figure out how to handle all of this once it was over. There was no talking to his former wife about turning themselves in at this point. She was so close to her goal now. For better or for worse, the shit was about to hit the proverbial fan. He was less worried about how to handle the Maja situation than he was about how to handle Shelby when the sandcastle she built in her mind began to wash away.

Jeremy turned to his new companion. If they knew each other just a little bit better they would have been able to turn the situation around and take control, but neither of them understood what the other was thinking. For all Jeremy knew, Steve was still out of his mind with grief. Their clear-headedness would have surprised them both.

"You doing, ok?" Jeremy asked him.

“No.” Steve retorted.

“I get that, man. I’m sorry.”

“I know. I am too, more than you know.”

Shelby had been careful to stay off the major thoroughfares, but once they got back to the DFW area, that would be all there was. She would just have to take her chances. She considered calling Ansel now to give him a warning of their impending arrival but decided against it for a few reasons. The first was plausible deniability, not that anyone would think to call him, but just in case. Second, third, and fourth was her fear that he would either say no, that he couldn’t do it, or the very worst, he would be dead.

Chapter Twenty-Nine

Preston had three missed texts when he landed at Love Field. The first was from his wife telling him to have a good trip and be safe. Righty-O. The second was from P-In Crime letting him know things back home were covered. A sentiment he trusted more than the first one. The last was from Jeremy.

An hour out. Bishop Family Funeral Home.

Shit… an hour out, who knows how long ago that was. It couldn't have been long, considering the mileage left when they last communicated. Whatever back roads she had taken, he respected the little lady for making such a good time. His wife was one of the slowest drivers he had ever witnessed. In his experience, women were never the drivers of the get-a-way cars, and for good reason. Why were they headed to a funeral home, anyway?

Maybe he had talked some sense into the parents and got them to go directly to the funeral home. Stupid people, Preston thinks. Bypass the coroner's office and autopsy, go straight to the funeral home, and collect two hundred dollars? Not enough people in this world understand how life really works. It's the red tape that makes it go 'round--- processes, procedures, that's where the magic is. There is no skipping a step!

As far as he was concerned, being a cop allowed him to bypass some of the red tape he so gleefully demanded others mitigate. After jogging down to the car rental counter, flashing his badge to the twenty or so customers ahead of him in line cut through about an hour of wait time and yards of red tape. It was good to be the king, he thought, chuckling.

Business done and keys in hand, he continued his jog to his vehicle, a white Chevy Impala. Beggars can't be choosers in a pinch. His map indicated a drive time of forty-three minutes. He could reasonably cut that down to thirty-five, maybe even thirty if he gunned it. This wasn't his city, but he'd never known a cop to bust the balls of another for a little speeding. He hit the tollway, going eighty-five on his way to glory and riches.

It was just after midnight as they drove into the funeral home parking lot. For all of the weariness of the day and the long drive, Steve and Jeremy were surprisingly alert. The adrenaline began hitting Steve's brain when they passed his neighborhood. It wasn't just the cops chasing them that had him on edge. It was the reality of the situation. When they first started this adventure, it was hope that got him in the car. As they drove, the hope disappeared and was replaced with repulsion and fear. Now that he could see the sign of the funeral home that he had avoided for six years, hope came flooding back. Was it possible that she wasn't crazy?

Shelby slammed the BMW into park and flew out of the car,

not bothering to close the door behind her, leaving the men behind. The front door was open. She swung it wide and ran inside.

"Hello?" She called when noticing Ansel's empty desk in his front office, "Hello!"

"Yes, Ma'am, can I help you?" A young man in a black suit with legs much too slim and tapered at the bottom walked around to the front. He hesitated when he saw the wide-eyed woman in the entryway. He hadn't been doing this for long, but he could smell trouble when it walked in. What he could smell was desperation, and that could be dangerous. He was only here because he had just accepted a delivery and was planning to close up shop and go home in a matter of minutes.

"Where's Ansel?" She demanded.

"Mr. Bishop?" he asked.

"Yes! Mr. Bishop!" Just then, Jeremy walked in the door, unsure of what to expect. His muscles felt tight with the anxiety spreading throughout his body. This could only go one way and all hell was bound to break loose, and he needed to be ready for it. He was just glad the doors were open, and they could get over with whatever was about to happen.

The boy eyed the new man on the scene with the same skepticism. They looked scared. "Mr. Bishop retired several years ago. He'd been ill. I'm sorry, did you know him?"

Jeremy watched as Shelby fell to her knees and then screamed out. For the first time, he noticed blood on the outside of her jeans, right above her left knee.

"Shelby, you're bleeding. Let me help you back to the car," Jeremy offered his hand and spoke as gently as possible. Her psyche was fragile, and he couldn't risk a complete break from reality, not with the police on their way. The only reason he allowed Det. Preston into their situation was for the girl, so that no more damage could be done, and they could minimize the repercussions. He didn't want Shelby to go to jail, and she obviously needed help.

"Should I call someone?" the boy offered, looking even more uncomfortable now.

"No, she has suffered a loss today. We need a minute."

This was something the young man was all too familiar with and could handle like a pro. He straightened his tie and moved into action. He kneeled next to Shelby, placed a hand on her back and then offered her his other. She took it almost instinctively.

"Follow me," he said as he led her down the hallway, looking back to indicate that Jeremy should follow him. He took her to the bereavement room, giving her the standard speech he learned on his second day.

"I am sorry for your loss. I can't imagine what you must be going through right now. Please take as much time as you need, and I will be right outside at the desk when you are ready to talk," he said, slipping out quietly before Shelby looked up from her lap. He would give them a few minutes to collect themselves and then book an appointment to make arrangements tomorrow after he got some sleep. This day had been a long one.

"Shelby…we have to get Maja taken care of. We got her back home, but now it's time to hand her over to the people who will take care of her. She's not coming back," Jeremy tried to convince her, soothingly. His eyes were fixated on her leg, and he began wondering what that knee looked like under those jeans. The fabric was tighter around her left one, showing obvious signs of swelling.

Shelby knew better. She knew better than to believe Ansel was still alive, but she drove all this way anyway. He was practically a hundred years old six years ago, for Christ's sake. She hadn't let a shred of doubt into her mind on the way here because it would have started to bloom once it was there. He was dead, and all of this was for nothing. She would go to prison, and her barely fifteen-year-old daughter would rot in the ground while she went on living a life behind bars that she never should have been living in the first place. For what? So, she could make a ton of money and have the best sex of her life… it only cost her Maja's life. A bargain, she thought, a laugh escaping her lips.

Jeremy jerked his head toward her face again at hearing that laugh, finally realizing she was lost for good. Both of them looked at each other when they heard voices coming from the lobby. At first, he assumed Steve eventually had the courage to get out of the car, but then he heard another familiar voice.

"They're in there, you said?" Det. Preston asked as he walked toward the curtains that separated the room from the hallway. He pulled them back and gave Jeremy a wink before sitting down next to Shelby.

It took her a moment to realize what that wink meant. There was no way he could be here without someone telling him, and she knew Det. Preston from the first time they met in Jeremy's house the day after the attack. Jeremy had betrayed them before they even knew Ansel was dead. He had most likely told the cops everything within minutes of telling her he wouldn't. The whole day he was keeping his secret from them and just waiting until they arrived. He didn't even believe her enough to give her a chance. Even if Ansel was alive, they wouldn't have had the chance to help Maja because the police would have already been there. Fuck him!

"Hello, Shelby, Jeremy." Tipping his hat in their direction.

"I saw your husband out there, Shelby. He's a mess, but I don't think he'll try to run, not with his daughter's body in the back of the car. She looks even worse than him." He reminded himself to be respectful. After all, a little girl had been killed. He could gloat all he wanted later.

"Did you think all of this was going to work out for you? Lying to your husband, your kid, creating another identity in another city, duping poor unsuspecting men… did you really think it was going to work?" Det. Preston asked as he walked around the room with the look of a man performing a sermon. "I don't know what you are thinking, lady, but you were bound to be caught sooner or later. After the accident this morning, it took me a while, but I figured it out when no one else could. At least Jeremy here is on my side, knowing the priority was that little girl in the back of the car. Right, Mr. Locke?"

Jeremy couldn't look at him, nor did he want to see the look of disbelief on Shelby's face. He hung his head low, refusing to acknowledge Det. Preston's assertion of collusion. Shelby stared at him, too heartbroken to be angry, but knowing it was coming.

"So, here is what we are going to do, guys," Det. Preston began again, he seemed like he was starting to pick up steam. "We are going to wait a few minutes while I call my partner, and he is going to send some guys down here to take care of the girl. You, Shelby, will be coming back to Phoenix with me, where we can find out why you decided to ditch your old life along with any other crimes you may have committed along the way. My guess is that there are plenty. Jeremy, I also assume you will change your mind on that photo identification from the other day. Then, my man, you can move on with your life."

He removed his Samsung from his inside jacket pocket and made the call. Shelby and Jeremy listened to his side of the call intently, each fuming for different reasons.

"Hey. I've got them."

"Yeah, she's dead. They'll need the wagon."

"Call the Lieutenant first, then Dallas P.D. I'll need at least two units. You know the drill."

"No. No one's running," he said as he winked at Shelby this time.

"Talk soon." Preston pushed the red button before replacing the phone in his pocket. Now, he could return to his captive audience.

"Now we just hang out for a bit, get to know each other. Who wants to go first?"

They each stared at him with their own brand of hostility.

"Wow, tough crowd. Okay, I'll go first. I'm Randy Preston. I'm a Sagittarius. I enjoy long walks on the beach, a cold beer on a Friday night, and making sure assholes like you, Shelby, get locked up for as long as possible. Do you guys see how it works now? Awesome, Jeremy, your ne…," his last word cut off as a man's scream came from the lobby of the funeral home.

"Shelby! Shelby, come here!!" Steve screamed.

She looked up confused, but only saw Det. Preston blocking the room's exit with his body.

"Hold right there, lady." He warned her.

"SHELBY!!" Steve continued to scream.

The young man in the suit lifted the curtain, face even whiter than it had been just thirty minutes before. "I think it's best for everyone to come to the front, please." He said in a barely audible whisper.

Det. Preston, sensing something was wrong by the kid's face, stormed past him but only made it halfway to the entryway before stopping. Rushing after him, Shelby ran into the back of him, not seeing past him for a few moments.

"Shelby…" Steve called to get her attention. He stood just inside the double doors with Maja in his arms. Her hair was slick and matted, which she could only assume was a mixture of blood and brain matter, still wrapped in her jacket. A small piece of glass fell from one of the folds of her coat in front of him. She saw all these things instantly, but she couldn't seem to comprehend her daughter's eyes. They were open… and alert. How? Then she saw Ansel just beyond the door outside, his image projected like a lit ghost through the glass.

"We need to call an ambulance," the boy said, breaking the silence.

"No," Ansel said sternly while walking through the open door. "Let's take her to the back room. Shelby, lead the way. You know where it is."

She turned to lead them without questioning her old friend.

"Hold on here a sec. I saw that girl not twenty minutes ago. She was dead. I saw her God damn brain and even checked for a pulse. Who is this girl? Where'd you get her?"

"We don't have time to explain it to you, Officer," Ansel answered briskly as he walked right past him on the way to the embalming room. "Steve, bring her in here now."

Steve followed closely, placing her on the bright white embalming table.

Maja's eyes were open and alert, but also frightened. Shelby reached for her hand, rubbing it between her hands.

"She's freezing!" Shelby yelled in Ansel's direction.

Ansel was already rummaging through a cabinet in the corner. "Peter, where is the warming blanket?"

"It's in basement storage."

"Go get it, now," Ansel commanded. Peter left the room on a mission.

In the meantime, Ansel removed a stack of small lap blankets from the bottom of the cabinet and distributed them to each person gathered around the table. They weren't much, just what they gave the women during wintertime burials to cover their skirts while they lowered the casket, but they would have to do temporarily.

"Spread them out one at a time over her body," Ansel counseled them.

Jeremy went first, dumbfounded. He barely had time to comprehend what had just happened. With shaking hands, Steve placed his next and then tried to smooth it out before kissing Maja's ice-cold cheek. Shelby and Ansel spread theirs next, followed by Randy. No one spoke as they stared down at her body.

"Was she really dead?" Det. Randy Preston asked in earnest. Jeremy wondered if there was a real human being somewhere inside of him after all.

Before anyone could answer, Ansel fielded the question. "Yes, Officer, she was dead. Before long, I will be too, and thank God there won't be anyone left to bring me back. Maja is the twenty-fifth soul I have been able to bring back to life. She'll be the last. I knew I was waiting for something or someone. I didn't know who until right now."

"Oh, Fuck! You guys are going to have to get out of here. The Dallas guys will be here in a few minutes. I'll have to come up with something. First, Shelby, I have to ask you a question," Det. Preston said frantically. He had paled almost as much as the boy, and he was shaking.

Shelby nodded her assent.

"Is this what happened to you? You were dead, and he brought you back from the grave? Don't fuck with me, or I'll make sure you're sorry."

"Yes. I wasn't running. I loved my family, Detective Preston, but I wasn't allowed to go back to my old life. I would have had all sorts of experiments done on me, and I couldn't hurt Maja like that," she tried to explain.

"Okay. Go. Jeremy, text me later. But, for now, GO. I've got this." Randy Preston knew he was throwing the promotion right out the window, but that wasn't his concern at the moment. Until you witness a miracle, a man doesn't always know what's possible.

When he was about eight years old, his grandmother told him a story. She was tucking him into bed on one of the many nights his mother was out drinking, and that day, he had been particularly defiant. He'd thrown a tantrum, refused to eat his dinner, and threw his glass on the ground when she told him he would have to stay at the table. What he didn't know then was that he wasn't angry with his grandmother. He was angry with his mom. But as she tucked him in that night, the day's badness seemed to be forgotten. After she read him a short book and ran her fingers through his hair, she told him a story she had been keeping until the time was right.

"When you were about three years old, your Dad was shipped off to Lebanon to help with the peacekeeping efforts between Syria and Israel. We were all scared, but he told us not to worry because they were going to prevent war, not to start one. We got letters from him for almost a year explaining where he was and what they were doing, always ending each letter asking for an update on how you were doing. Your mother and I wrote back to him and sent pictures of you, so he'd know how you were. When we saw things getting bad on the news, he still told us not to worry." She paused for a few moments, considering how to proceed. "The night your dad died; I was watching a recording of one of my stories on the TV when I felt a pain in my chest that I couldn't explain. I thought for an instant that my ticker had given out, but then the pain was gone as fast as it came. When I opened my eyes, your Dad was in the room with me—standing right in front of me, just as clear as you are now. He didn't speak, but he smiled at me. He wanted me to know that he was okay, and he wanted me to look after you. When we heard about the bombing of the U.S. Marines in Beirut the next day, over three hundred dead, I knew he was one of them. I never told a soul about what happened, Randy, not even your Mom. But, I'm telling you now so you know your Dad's looking down on you."

He was never hateful to his grandmother again after she told him her secret. She could have told him that story to keep him in line, but he always chose to believe his grandmother had been telling the truth. Souls were out there. Could they come back into a body? Why not? And that bullet Merle shot in the dark behind Roosevelt Row, how'd he even hit the guy? Tonight… after what he had just witnessed, he chose to believe in miracles.

"Let's go!" Jeremy called from the loading door at the back of the funeral home, holding the warming blanket that Peter just handed him. Maja was back in Steve's arms, and Ansel was leading the way across the street to his house. The wind attempted to blow them back, but they persevered. So far, so good; the coast was clear. With any luck, there wouldn't be any neighbors looking out the window in the next five minutes at two o'clock in the morning. Shelby drove the BMW toward Ansel's house, turning around the back alley and pulling into the driveway. She waited another two minutes before the garage door began to lift. They were all safely inside.

Ansel wasn't worried about Peter. Peter would fall in line

with whatever he asked him to do. He knew because Peter was number twenty-four. The poor kid's entire family died in a car accident about five years ago. He's been grooming him ever since. Right after Peter showed Shelby and Jeremy to the bereavement room, Ansel received his call. When they were on the phone discussing the situation, Officer Preston interrupted them by barging in and demanding to see the people who had just come in. Ansel didn't need much of a description to know it was Shelby who had come back to him. After quickly dressing, he walked as fast as his old legs would allow toward his workplace of almost eighty years. He could see the BMW haphazardly parked out front with the front door and trunk open. As he approached the vehicle, his hands began to feel a familiar vibration and burning deep from within.

Steve saw him approaching from his seat in the back of the car. Mr. Bishop looked like a man under a spell, and Steve didn't want to break it. He crawled out of the backseat and walked toward the open truck, avoiding looking directly at what was inside. By the time he walked around to the back of the SUV, Ansel's hands were already on her, one on her face and one on her neck. When he removed them, nothing had changed.

Anticipating Steve's question, Ansel explained, "Just wait. It may take a few minutes."

Her body began twitching just as he turned back around to

check on her.

"I've seen this type of thing before. I know she will be okay, but she won't be able to communicate for a while. Her head injury is severe. It may be days."

Steve's eyes watered as he witnessed the impossible. His baby girl is alive! He thought as he scooped her into his arms to bring her to her mother. Everything Shelby had told them was true. He was too elated to think about what all of that meant. Ansel waited outside to see mother and daughter reuniting, not wanting to take anything away from their special moment. He wanted to observe, just once, the joy of what it was like to bring a family back together. Whatever happened after this wouldn't be up to him anymore. No more rules were needed. There would never be a twenty-six.

Chapter Thirty

They were gathered around the small twin bed that Shelby had slept in for almost a month. This time, Maja lay sleeping under the warming blanket with several comforters on top of her. Ansel requested that someone put a trash bag under her head to save the pillow and sheets. He recognized that it would only get worse before it got better, a detail he would spare them for now.

"Now listen, everything I am about to tell you is important," Ansel explained. "Her injuries are severe but not the worst I've seen. She will be fine, but it will take longer than it did with you, Shelby. She will need a safe place to heal for at least a month, probably longer. Taking her to a hospital is no good. She would never have survived the injuries she sustained, and her healing would be unprecedented. She needs to hide out. You are welcome to stay here if you wish, although we don't exactly know what's going to happen across the street. It may or may not be safe. How long was she dead?"

Consulting his watch, Jeremy calculated, "About seventeen hours."

"That makes sense. That's why she came back so quickly. For another few days, she won't be able to speak or stay awake for periods longer than a few minutes. When she does wake up, she may remember the crash, or she may have no recollection at all. It's critical to explain exactly what happened and give her the time and space to accept it. I already gave her an injection of morphine and midazolam, but she'll need a few more before the pain starts to subside. Syringes and vials are in the here." He said, pointing to the mini-fridge next to the bed.

"What about infection or the missing bone?" Jeremy asked, fascinated.

"You won't have to worry about either, trust me." Ansel was holding onto the footboard of the bed, clearly exhausted.

"Ansel, why are you explaining all of this as if you're not going to be here?" Shelby asked, worry written on her forehead.

"I don't think I have to explain it to you, of all people, Shelby. You know why."

Shelby walked from the head of her daughter's bed to where he stood, putting her arm around his frail figure. "Come, let's go sit in the living room for a while." She locked eyes with her men, motioning for them to follow her. Steve risked a look out the front window on his way through the kitchen to the living room. A police car was already pulling out of the parking lot. Only the white Impala and one other cruiser remained. Peter's bike was safely parked in the carport on the side. He couldn't bring himself to drive and probably never would after the accident that had put an end to his family.

"Police are leaving across the street," Steve told the group, taking a seat in the middle of the couch next to Shelby and Ansel. Shelby's arm was underneath, and around Ansel's, fingers intertwined with his. She placed her head lightly on his bony shoulder.

"I guess there's not much to see anymore," Jeremy said wryly as he settled in on the corner of Ansel's L-shaped couch.

They were quiet for a while. The day had worn on each of them, and this was their chance to take a breath and realize what had happened. Relief was all Shelby felt, her mission was successful, and her daughter was alive. It wasn't the time to be considering the future. It was a time to rest and be grateful. She simply wanted to be close to the man who gave her and her daughter their second chance at life. This miracle of a man. Shelby was the first to speak, breaking the silence.

"Ansel, tell us a story. Tell us about something from the war or maybe even before that." Her eyes were full of tears for her old friend. She could feel under her head that his breath had begun to slow, and the fear of losing him became very real. He cleared his throat a little before starting.

"Oh, gosh. Let me see. I was born in 1921, so there's quite a bit I could tell you before the war. Ah, I got it!" he exclaimed, his expression brightening.

"When I was young, about fifteen or so, I went to work at the lumber yard up in Melissa. Good work for 1935. The depression was on back then, and any work was considered good work. We were lucky to have it because my father had passed the year before, and there were three kids at home under ten. Worked 7:00 AM to 6:00 PM six days a week, enough so my mother didn't have to clean houses or mend clothes. The Yard Supervisor was a mean old guy, fifty or so, but with massive arms and dark leathery skin from years working outdoors. He pushed us kids like pack mules, never letting up. My body hurt every night when I went to sleep and screamed at me every morning when I woke up, but I didn't quit. I told myself it was because my sister and brother depended on me, or Mother wouldn't have to go to work, but the real reason was something else entirely. Her name was Lois, and she was the young wife of the guy who drove our bodies into the ground. She couldn't have been more than twenty-five, and she was the most beautiful woman I had ever seen. Blonde hair tied up in a blue bandana every day when she would come by with her husband's lunch. I watched her walk up the hill from their trailer a half mile down the road at 11:15 AM every single day I worked there. I checked my watch and patted down my hair when I knew she was coming."

"Excuse me, sir, would you mind getting me a glass of water?" Ansel asked, looking at Jeremy on the other end of the sofa.

"Yes, sir. I'm Jeremy, Shelby's boyfriend. I'll be right

back." He jumped up from the couch, intentionally avoiding Shelby's expression as he walked to the kitchen.

Jeremy returned with a full glass of ice water and handed it to Ansel. He only took two sips before setting it down on the coffee table and letting Shelby place her head back on his shoulder.

"Anyway… I watched her go up and down that hill a hundred times or more. Somewhere along the way, she must have seen me staring. She started unbuttoning her blouse one button more, fixing it before she got to the top and leaving her hair down free, stopping in front of me to put it back up. I was in love with her by my second month on the job, and the other boys saw it, too. I would get ribbed, called "lover boy," and all that. But I didn't care.

By the time it started getting cold, she got a little more daring and asked me to come into the workhouse to help her with something. I followed her in there, where she pushed me up against the wall and kissed me. When she took hold of my hand and put it under her dress, I ran out of there as fast as I could. I never told, and I never looked at her again. I kept my head down and focused on my work. But of all the regrets I've had in my life, not letting her use my hand under that dress is the biggest of them."

The four of them sat in silence for a minute until Steve began laughing first, then Shelby, and finally Jeremy joined in. Ansel let his smile beam around the room, glad he had some company tonight.

"Tell me about you, young man." Ansel directed his statement at Jeremy.

"Well, not much to tell, really. I live in Arizona, work in the energy sector, and met Shelby about six months ago. That's how I ended up here."

"She's a keeper, I can tell you that," Ansel said. He could see Steve was still sore about his wife's new man but respected him for handling it as well as he was.

Shelby had yet to move from her position next to him, worried that if she did, something terrible would happen. Jeremy was waiting for the appropriate time to ask for a few minutes alone to apologize but understood that might take a while. He was ashamed of himself for not believing her, especially since that was exactly why she didn't tell him in the first place. Worst of all, he wasn't sure she could ever forgive him for involving Det. Preston. In one night, he ended up being the most pompous, smart-ass, power-hungry cop he'd ever met, one that would give you the shirt off his back. He would have to find out what the end-game was with him before too long. When Shelby finally decided to get up and use the bathroom, she heard a light knock at the front door. Careful to look out the window first she saw it was Peter and let him in.

"Hey, come in."

"Thank you," he said, shivering a little due to the cold winter wind.

"Come in and sit down. Tell us what happened. But hold that thought for three minutes while I go and pee." As Jeremy watched her speed walk to the bathroom door, he realized he hadn't seen her that happy in weeks. This is who she was, free from the lies and unintentional deceptions that had surrounded her.

"Okay, I'm back! What happened?"

"Well, the police were confused about why they were called out there and got quite angry with Detective Preston when the girl's body wasn't there."

"What did the detective say?"

"He told them he was wrong, and that the girl was fine. He told them he had made a mistake, and so did the cops in Phoenix because no one had actually seen her. He said that once he got eyes on everyone, he told them to go home, and they would deal with leaving the scene of an accident situation later."

"Holy shit! Who would have thought?" Jeremy laughed.

"Not me, by the way. He came up when I was out in the car. He threatened to handcuff me to the door handle," Steve said.

"He was practically dancing when he told me that I was going to jail. I had no idea that a guy like that could see reason, let alone save our asses. My ass, to be exact," Shelby added.

“The cops left after they questioned us for a while. Detective Preston told me to tell you that it’s best for him to go back home tonight so he could explain the situation in person and get some of the heat off right away,” Peter explained. “Now that the girl is back in Texas, it’s easier to claim she’s okay and with her parents.”

“I guess that makes sense. Someone is going to want to get a look at her soon, though. I would think,” Steve suggested.

“I think so, too. Until she’s up and talking, we can’t risk anyone seeing her,” Shelby said.

“I also need to deal with Morgan. She will want to know where Maja and I are. Lots of loose ends to think about here.”

“I think it's too late to solve the world's problems in a single evening. We all need a serious rest before we can figure out where all the landmines are, just because Det. Preston is our hero tonight, that doesn’t mean he will be tomorrow. We need to keep Maja off the radar and Shelby out of prison. I am fine sleeping on the floor, so don’t worry about me. I can grab a blanket or even find a hotel. What do you guys think?” Jeremy asked.

Peter, who was ready to drop after a long day and night’s worth of work, told the group he was finally going home.

“I think it's best if I stay here. The house isn’t big, but after Ansel goes to bed, there is at least room for two on the sofa. You’re right, though. We will have to tackle all this tomorrow. Ansel, how long will Maja be out?" She turned back to the living room and noticed Ansel had already fallen asleep.

Shelby lowered her voice, "Can you guys help him to his bedroom?"

Steve and Jeremy walked over to the couch, where Steve placed a hand on Ansel's shoulder to gently wake him. Ansel's head fell on top of Steve's hand, limp.

"Ansel? Wake up," Steve whispered. Behind him, Shelby placed her hand on Steve's back.

Her words, "He's gone," were barely audible through stifled crying.

Peter rushed over from across the room. "Move over, please," he said as politely as he could manage, considering his obvious distress.

"Jesus. Okay…," he sighed, the exhaustion evident in his every word and motion. "I'll need to call Dr. Evans to come over. We've been expecting this for some time now, and he's given me specific instructions. You guys will need to wait in the back with Maja once he gets here, but it should only take a minute for him to call time of death, and then I'll take him away."

"We'll help you, Peter," Jeremy offered, turning him around

and hugging the boy tightly.

"Thank you," he said, as silent tears were already drying on his chin.

"The house will be yours for as long as you need it. Ansel would have wanted that. I know what it's like to make a recovery, so please understand that I will not be the one to rush you out of here. The house is mine. Ansel signed it over to me a few years ago, but I won't make any plans to move in until Maja is ready."

Shelby took him from Jeremy's embrace and hugged him tightly herself. She kissed his cheek.

"I loved him, too. I'm sure all of his children did. His gift is something that couldn't be understood but also can't be replaced. You, me, and Maja wouldn't be here without him. Not to mention the other twenty-two. I also know what it's like to feel alone in the world. You didn't lose your family tonight. I want you to know that. We can't replace Ansel, but we will be your family. All of us. You won't be alone after this."

Peter shrugged his shoulders, clearly embarrassed by the attention but grateful to have them here with him tonight when he lost the only person who knew the truth about him.

"I promise you won't be. I don't know how old you are, but you've just inherited an uncle or a brother if you'll have me," Steve said shyly.

"I appreciate all of you. Right now, though, I need to take care of Mr. Bishop. I'll call the doctor."

He walked to the kitchen, using the landline and the phone number of the refrigerator to reach Dr. Evans. He answered on the third ring.

"Dr. Evans, this is Peter Bishop. He is gone."

"Okay. I'll be here."

"Yes, he called me to come over when he wasn't feeling well. I was with him."

"Thank you," he said and placed the receiver back in its cradle.

"Twenty minutes. In the meantime, I'll go across the street and get the coach."

Chapter Thirty-One

Randy Preston called his partner on the way back to the airport. Regardless of the time, he was sure Merle would pick up.

"Hey, Change of plans," he said when he heard the phone stop ringing.

"Hold on a second. Let me go into the other room."

"Whoa, you got someone there?"

"Ha, yes. You're not the only one who gets some," Merle joked.

"My "some" is my wife, man, but good for you."

What Preston didn't know is that the piece lying in Merle's bed tonight was a man. The only kind of piece he was interested in. While this didn't make him any less of a detective, he understood that his partner and brother wouldn't see it that way. For a man who was often his idol and mentor, Preston was missing something in him that allowed him to see the world differently. A shortcoming he had forgiven his partner for several years ago, but it still didn't mean he trusted him with his personal life.

"So, what's up? What's changed?" Merle asked.

"Everything. Every Fucking Thing! I know this goes without saying, but what I am about to tell you stays between us. Like

Roosevelt. Understood?"

Preston had his attention. Merle sat in his oversized Lay-Z-boy, phone held tightly to his ear.

"Understood."

"You're going to think I'm crazy, but you and I have been partners long enough to know that I'm no bullshitter. Man… I was so right and so wrong about everything. The woman was Shelby. I confirmed it. Had her and Locke by the short and curlies, just waiting for Dallas P.D. to get on scene. The husband from Dallas was waiting in the car and confirmed they had taken the body of the girl from the accident. Even made sure she was dead before calling you…"

Merle waited for him to continue for several moments before asking, "What happened, Preston?"

"I saw the girl's brains, Merle. When I touched her neck to check for a pulse, she was cold as ice and stiff as a board. Not my first rodeo. The old guy did something to her. I don't know what, but he brought her back to life." Preston stopped, waiting for some response from his partner.

Of all the things Dennis Merle had prepared himself for when he sat down in the Lay-Z-Boy, this was not one of them. Accidentally shot a suspect, sure, but not this.

"Guy at the scene was sure she was dead, too. Why do you think she's alive?" Merle asked cautiously.

"Because I fucking saw it with my own eyes. She was wide awake and breathing, not twenty minutes after I made sure she was dead. But, it's not only her. That's what happened to the woman, too. She didn't fake her own death and run away to Arizona—she WAS dead."

"I don't know what you want me to say here, partner."

"Say you fucking believe me. That's what I want you to say."

"Okay, man. Yes. I've never known you to bullshit."

"The problem is that now I have to come back and figure out a way to explain all of this away. I'm not sending some God damned miracle to jail. We only have one witness, which works in our favor, and also where you come in. I need you to visit his home tomorrow morning and convince him he may not be thinking too clearly about what happened."

"No problem. Word on the street is that the guy was released from the hospital this afternoon."

"I have to convince traffic that the worst of their crimes is leaving the scene of an accident and that I saw the girl alive and well in Texas. I'll call Dallas and have them back off on the fingerprint situation. It's going to piss some people off, but I hope that covers everything. What am I missing?" It was past three in the morning, and his adrenaline was still pumping, but his brain was moving a little slowly.

"What about Locke's case?"

"We'll close it… and destroy the fingerprints. Just to be safe."

Merle continued to be shocked by what he was hearing but agreed. He wouldn't really call this being open-minded and seeing the world differently. He would call this "losing your ever-loving mind." After nine years, he knew better than to be the unwanted voice of reason.

"Sounds good. You okay?"

"No, brother. No, I'm not. I don't know if it's God or the Devil or neither; I just witnessed it tonight. All I know is that I have to do the right thing."

Now Merle confirmed it in his own mind: Preston's cheese had officially slid off his cracker.

It was three days before Maja was able to say her first words and the day of Ansel's funeral. Just like every mother dreams when their child is born, her first word was "Mom."

"Yes, honey, I'm here."

"I'm sorry. I'm so sorry I yelled at you and then got in the car…"

"Stop. Everything is going to be fine now. No one is mad at you."

"I heard everything you said. How you died, and that old man brought you back to life. Just like me. I understand why you couldn't come back to us."

"Thank you, baby. Are you in pain? Do you need anything?" Shelby was standing over her and stroking her cheek.

They purchased a bump cap for her head the day before, covering her healing wounds, but she still had a hole over the size of a quarter yet to repair itself. The skin would take longer. Steve gave her a dose of morphine about six hours ago.

"Hurt's a little, but don't give me a shot. Makes it hard to stay awake."

Shelby looked over at Jeremy.

"Go on. You won't want to miss it. I'll stay with her," he said.

She looked back down at her beautiful daughter and kissed her forehead before leaving the room. When she got to the door, she looked back and said, "I love you, princess."

"Love you too, Mom."

She joined Steve in the living room. He handed her the black hat with a veil he had picked up that morning to hide her face. Now that they were no longer fugitives, they were free to use the BMW to pick up the items they needed to stay there. Steve and Jeremy took turns shopping at Target for clothes, bathroom items, and food. Steve took care of buying Shelby's underwear, a detail Jeremy hadn't missed. Her knee was also healing. It was swollen up to the size of a cantaloupe for a few days, but after icing, it was almost back to its normal size.

"I look ridiculous. No one wears these things anymore. What am I, an old Italian widow?"

"Better to look ridiculous than to get recognized," Steve admonished.

"Ugh, I hate when you're right."

"Always did," he says with a smile.

"Okay, you go first. I'll hang back about five minutes or so and then find a spot in the corner somewhere."

"Deal." He opened the front door and crossed the street, noticing how full the parking lot was already getting.

At this moment, he thought, his wife of five years would hopefully be moving her belongings out of his house. He didn't offer her much of an explanation for Maja and his whereabouts this last week but did give her a check for fifty thousand dollars. The condition was that she asked no questions and a forty-eight-hour window to move all her shit. She didn't cry, and she didn't argue, but quickly placed the check in her pocket before he could change his mind. Knowing her, it was already in the bank. He considered it the fairest deal he had ever made.

Steve called the school yesterday to provide an excuse as to why Maja missed finals and a potential timeline for her return, explaining about a relative's death overseas and not knowing exactly when they would be back. Maja's fantastic grades would most likely keep her on track to avoid repeating the term. He would explain this all to her when she was finally up and around. Morgan not being around would be a big change for her, and he felt guilty for that, but he knew Maja would now be finally getting her real father back in exchange. He felt hopeful for the first time in years.

When he entered the front doors of the funeral home, Peter was at the door to greet him and the other guests. It was standing room only, even more people than Shelby's. By the time she got there, the overflow was out into the parking lot. Peter packed everyone in throughout the hallways, his office space, the bereavement room, and the entryway. He then came on the loudspeaker to tell the group the entire service would be broadcast through the system. For a man with no family, no wife, and no children, he certainly made an impact on people's lives, Shelby thought. She wondered if any others were amongst the crowd, like her and Peter.

The service didn't quite do his life justice. There was no way it could have. When it was over, she didn't bother saying goodbye, she was one of the very last who got to do that. A blessing really. Without a word to Steve or Peter, she walked back across the street, noticing a very old man with a cane watching her intently as she opened the front door of Ansel's house. She lifted her veil, smiled, and gave him a wink. He winked back.

"Grandpa, wait up!" a teenager called to the old man.

She saw two other kids and a grown woman help the old man into a waiting Suburban. He made more of an impact than anyone would ever know, she thought, and smiled again despite the cold.

That night, Maja was able to sit up, and they brought her out to the living room. Shelby cooked a simple dinner of roasted chicken with new potatoes, carrots, and onions. It was the night before Christmas Eve, but the last night they would all be together in the house. They invited Peter to attend, and he arrived just as Shelby set the plates on the table.

"Come in! Holy cow, it's not getting any warmer, is it?"

"No, ma'am, it's not."

"Peter, you have to stop that. All that does is make me feel old. Come inside and take your coat off. We are going to eat and open some presents."

"Presents? Oh shoot, I didn't bring anything. I apologize."

"Don't worry about that," Shelby said, ushering him to the table.

"Come on in, guys, dinners about ready!"

They gathered at the table as she brought out the meal.

"It's not much, not really a full Christmas dinner, but it will have to do."

"Mom, seriously? This looks amazing!"

The men were already busy digging in. Dinner conversation was easy, like the talk of cavalry men around a campfire who had fought and won together, but the tone was bittersweet. Jeremy would be leaving back to Phoenix in the morning, but Shelby was staying for the foreseeable future. They had yet to talk, but they both knew tonight was an inevitability. Shelby had already decided to move back to her own house as soon as she went back to Phoenix. Even though she would like to stay close to Maja, living here was still out of the question. But she wouldn't leave until Maja was perfectly fine and back in school, no matter how long that took.

Shelby recognized that she would never be able to forgive

him for involving Preston, almost creating a barrier between her daughter's life and death, not to mention almost sending her to prison. When she needed him to come through, he hadn't been able to. She'd been alone before, and it sucked, but at least she had Maja back and Steve, too, in a way. A missing piece of her soul had been restored, enough to keep her happy for the rest of her second life, she reasoned.

After dinner, they all gathered in the small living room to open a few Christmas gifts. Maja opened her first. It was a yellow gold necklace in the shape of a heart; in the middle were three different colored stones representing her father, mother and herself. Steve helped her put it on, hardly able to keep herself from touching it. Peter went next, opening a beautiful platinum Cartier watch. Shelby directed him to turn it over, where he saw the word inscribed on the back: Family. Shelby opened hers, a picture of Maja standing next to her car in a sterling silver frame, reminding her simultaneously of her love for her daughter but also how close she came to losing her. Shelby picked up Steve a sweater. It was dark grey and warm. He told her he loved it. Jeremy was the only one left without a gift, but he claimed he didn't mind.

Once the presents were done Steve offered to clean up, wanting to give Jeremy and Shelby a little space. Peter took Maja back to the living room and explained his experience through the recovery process. Shelby watched her nod and smile, so very grateful.

Jeremy walked down the hallway and into Ansel's room. Shelby followed him, closing the door behind them. No one had used his bed, even with the limited space, since he passed. Some things were just sacrilegious, Shelby considered.

"I want you back," Jeremy declared without hesitation.

Shelby sighed and went in to hug him, his hand supporting the back of her head and running his fingers down her hair.

"I love you so much, more than any man. That will never change."

He pulled away, holding her hands but gazing down at her with his brow furrowed.

"But?"

"I appreciate everything you have done these last few days. You've been amazing with Maja and Steve. I'll always be glad you were here, and I will make sure Maja never forgets it."

"Is this the part where you tell me: it's me, not you?"

"No, it's the part where I tell you it's both of us. I couldn't trust you, and you didn't trust me. It's gone both ways, and it's far too late to fix it."

"You mean you don't want to put in the work to fix it?"

"That's not fair, Jeremy. I mean, the kind of trust that we have broken cannot be fixed. I lied to you for months about who I really was, and technically can never be again. I am still Scarlet Winchell. I have to be."

"None of that matters now. I understand what you've been through and why you couldn't tell me."

"Now that it slapped you in the face, I get it."

"No offense, Shelby, but no man on God's green Earth would have believed you before seeing it. The guy who saw it with his own eyes didn't even believe you!" Jeremy said, raising his voice. "And what you are trying to avoid saying is that I threw you under the bus with Det. Preston. Right?"

"Yes! That I cannot forgive. You had my daughter's life in your hands…"

"If I showed you the text message, you might think a little differently. He already knew about everything. He knew you were alive and that it was you at the accident. Everything. He was on to us, and I had no idea who he was going to turn into once he got here. I swear. I did give him the name of the funeral home because I thought he would be able to help." Jeremy put his hands on her cheeks, tilting her head up to look at him. "It gets worse, too. I know who broke into the house, Shelby. I figured it out the night they came, and I didn't tell you because I didn't want you to get involved."

"I know, Jeremy. I'm not an idiot. I read it all over your face any time we talked about it. I figured there was a good reason you were keeping it from me, and it wasn't important enough to lose you over."

"Jesus, Shelby. I want you in my life. We had---we have---a rare and precious thing that happened between us. So, you want to throw it all away because of unrealistic expectations that no man could live up to? It doesn't make sense! You were given a second chance that no one in this world gets, and when you are about to have everything, you have ever wanted, you're going to turn your back? You have your child back, and what you said was the love of your life right in front of you. Don't do this because you're too stubborn to see reason!"

"You think insulting me is going to help?" Shelby said with a faint smile on her lips.

"You never fail to surprise me. Come here." She allowed him to pull her in close to him, not wanting to give up her anger so quickly, but the overwhelming need to be held by him was more powerful. Just feeling his warmth and smelling his skin was enough for the moment.

"You're right," her words muffled as she pressed her face against his chest. "I do have everything I could ever want. I just need to accept, but it's hard. You know what I mean?"

"You mean like finally finding everything you could ever want and then worrying that at any moment it could be taken away?"

"Um, yeah. I get your point."

"I love you, Shelby… Scarlet, whatever. Just give us a chance. I'll be waiting for you as long as it takes. Maja's the priority, I get that."

Other than his one complete and total betrayal, he really is pretty incredible, Shelby thought wryly.

Chapter Thirty-Two

Jeremy attempted to slip out in the morning with as little fanfare as possible, but Steve and Maja were already up by the time he got out of the bathroom. He had booked the 7:30 AM direct out of Love Field, eager to return to his life but reluctant at the same time. His world and everything in it had changed since the last time he was home, just five days ago, but instead of being frightened of the changes, he was ready to embrace them. He had even picked up a few new friends along the way.

"Hey!" Maja called from the sofa. She was wearing her bump-cap with her hair underneath, making her look more like a little girl than the young woman she was.

"Hey, back at ya!" He said, sitting down next to her.

"Thank you. I don't remember much other than yesterday, really, but my Mom said you were a big help."

"I'm glad to know you, Maja, and something tells me that this isn't the last time we'll see each other."

"I know. My Mom and Dad said you are part of the family now," Maja said matter of factly.

Jeremy was startled by hearing this, turning to Steve, who was listening in the kitchen.

"Thank you. That means a lot to me. He kissed her forehead

and said see you soon, not goodbye.

Steve met him at the front door, a strange smile on his face.

"Well, man, I never thought I would say this, but… I'll miss you. I thought that you sleeping with my wife would put a damper on our relationship and all. But you're a good guy. Thank you for everything."

They embraced for a single second, Jeremy patting his back as men do when they are embarrassed to show emotion.

"I'll miss you guys too, but I'm sure it won't be too long."

"Oh, and thanks for the car too. It's nice you're letting Shelby keep it to get around."

"How else am I going to make sure she comes back?" He said with a wink. "I'll see you soon."

Jeremy waited on the front porch, not bothering to sit on the cold cement, as he waited for his Uber. After everyone was asleep, he took Shelby back to Ansel's room. He had said his goodbyes to Shelby last night, at first, to kiss her, but the rekindling of their relationship was too much, and they ended up making love. For the first time, they embraced each other in perfect honesty, reveling in the freedom it gave them. It didn't last long, but they both felt the power and renewed passion between them. He loved her, and there was no going back now.

"I will come back, and we can start over," she told him. Jeremy stood watching the cars drive by hoping, knowing in his heart that Shelby was the best thing that ever happened to him, that was his miracle.

"You're making me nervous!" Steve playfully yelled from the passenger seat of Maya's used Volvo S40. He had taken her to get her official license that morning, and he was letting her take her birthday drive home before her celebratory dinner. The Volvo was more than Maja had hoped for after the insurance company refused to pick up the tab on her Honda. Her mother had insisted she pitch in for the fines and damages caused by the accident and gave her Dad an undisclosed amount for her new car, as well.

Her Mom and she stayed at the old man's house for three months before they declared her fit to leave. Her hair was growing back, but they ended up having to cut the rest kinda short to mask where her skull had been missing and then repaired. After the first month, they brought her work from school to catch up on, which eased her boredom significantly, but they didn't get her a new phone until just a few weeks before they left the house. She posted on Insta for all her friends to re-send her their numbers, and texts started flooding in.

We thought you were dead!

Where have you been????

You alive?

Even at fifteen, she comprehended the repercussions of telling anyone about what they had been through. But, honestly, she thinks, it was kinda cool to have a secret.

She invited four of her friends for a sleepover at the house tonight, where they would watch scary movies and eat all the junk food they wanted before going back to school on Monday for three days of finals. Then, she and Dad were flying to Phoenix for Christmas. Mom apologized but said it was easier to show her face in public, especially because they'd be going back a few months later for the wedding. Maja didn't care. At least they were flying and not driving, she thought. Peter was flying out early tomorrow morning. He had a service tonight that he couldn't miss, or otherwise, they would've traveled together. He came to the house for dinner at least once a week, and he always called to check on her every few days. It was like having a big brother for the first time, a bonus of her second life.

This would be her first time back in Phoenix, and she would have to see the exact spot where she died, down the road from Mom and Jeremy's house, but it didn't bother her as much as her Mom thought it might. Unlike her Mom, there was nothing she had to give up. She felt like the luckiest girl in the world.

"Watch that stop sign!" Steve called out again.

"Dad, you're driving me crazy. You do realize I drove over a thousand miles by myself without crashing, right?"

"I wouldn't really say that "without crashing" part is true."

"That doesn't count."

"Why doesn't that count again?"

"Because I was mad."

"Okay, so keep you out of the car when you're mad. Got it!"

"Dad!"

Steve laughed and beamed at his only child. Life hadn't been this good in years. Dating wasn't something on his radar, but someday, maybe, he would consider it. This time, with different intentions than when he got mixed up with Morgan. His half a decade of shame.

Maja rolled up to the stop sign, making a complete stop. But, as she was counting from one on her way to three, they heard a loud booming sound to their right, beyond the houses. Maja didn't lift her foot from the brake but waited for her father to give her an indication of what to do next. When a dark cloud of smoke began billowing up from beyond the neighborhood, she gave her Dad a worried look.

"Hop out, hon. Now."

Maja threw the car in park, unclipped her seat belt, and opened the door, giving over control to her father willingly. Steve did the same and pulled the seat back before getting in and immediately turning right toward the direction of the smoke. They began hearing screams from just beyond the houses before Steve found his way out and toward what they both feared was an explosion. The smoke and fire were coming from a restaurant directly across the intersection. From their viewpoint, Steve could see the northwest corner of the building almost gone and black smoke billowing out from the gaping hole in the wall. There had obviously been some kitchen fire or gas leak that ignited and caused a small explosion. Bystanders from the businesses nearby were standing around screaming about the people still inside the building.

It was cold, but there was no rain that would have helped to tame the flames, and the fire trucks had yet to arrive.

"Dad, we have to help them!" Maja screamed.

"No, hon, we don't know if there will be more explosions or what caused it. I can't risk taking you over there…"

Before he could finish, she was out of the car and racing across the street. Cars were stopped in both directions, gawking at the blaze, but no one other than Maja attempted to get out of their vehicles.

Steve slammed the car in park as Maja had done moments

before, jumping out of the car after her.

A small group of restaurant workers, cooks, and wash staff, from the looks of them, were huddled around something lying on the ground outside of the front entrance. They had drug out a woman and her child who had been sitting in a back booth of the restaurant enjoying their lunch just prior to the explosion. The woman had lost part of her leg from the knee down, and most of her hair was gone or singed black by fire. The three or four-year-old child next to her was intact but with a significant head wound. The child's eyes rolled around briefly as Maja ran up to the group, and then her eyes closed. Seconds later, she was dead.

Maja screamed, holding up her hands as they began to burn and tingle.

Thank you for following me on the journey that Second Lives created for Shelby and Catherine; I hope you enjoyed it. As my favorite author would say… If you have come this far, maybe you are willing to come a little further. I am already underway exploring the lives of two more of the original twenty-three. If you would like more information about upcoming projects and the next book in the series, please join my newsletter and follow me on the socials of your choice.

https://www.facebook.com/people/Carrie-Mack/61562172512787/

https://www.instagram.com/carriemackauthor/

https://x.com/CarrieMackBooks

About The Author

Carrie Mack is a full-time educator and historian, living in Denver, CO, who loves to craft fantastical tales of character-driven adventurous romance, ones where the women always get what they want! After raising four exceptional children, she uses her free time to write or travel. Her favorite is doing both at the same time. You can visit her at http://carriemackbooks.com, she would love to hear from you.

Made in the USA
Coppell, TX
06 January 2025